Betsy's body still burned where his hands had been, as if he had left a fiery imprint.

And warm tingles were spreading to the rest of her body. She'd never experienced anything like it. Men had touched her before, when helping her alight from a carriage or during the measures of a dance. But none of their hands had felt as if they'd seared their way through every single layer of clothing she wore.

"P-please don't." She found herself begging him. In regard to what he'd said, rather than what he'd done. "If you were to turn up at the house, I would be sure to give away the fact that I already knew you, by blushing, or being unable to meet your eye or something of the sort. And Mother, who is a veritable bloodhound when it comes to that sort of thing, would be bound to sniff out the truth, somehow."

"Then, to spare your blushes," he said, giving her that mischievous smile once more, "I shall wait to present myself to your father until Sunday."

"Thank you," she breathed.

"I shall be counting the days," he said.

"I...I..." She would be too, she realized.

Author Note

Many of you who read *A Scandal at Midnight* wrote to me to ask what was going to happen with Ben's property and if I had any plans to write about any more of Daisy's brothers.

Well, you'll be pleased to hear that in this story, *How to Catch a Viscount*, I return to the world of The Patterdale Siblings by sending James, Daisy's oldest, haughtiest brother, to Bramley Park to see if he can sort out the mess that Ben has inherited. Because at the end of *A Scandal at Midnight*, Ben goes charging off to Belgium to rejoin his regiment the moment he hears that Bonaparte has escaped from Elba.

And after this, I plan to write a story featuring Gem, Daisy's brother who instigated the prank that forced her and Ben together in the first place.

I didn't set out to write a trilogy, but I should have known that giving the heroine of a book five boisterous brothers would inspire several more ideas!

I hope you enjoy this venture into the world of The Patterdale Siblings and will look out for the other connected books.

Oh, and while I'm here, I'd just like to apologize to the inhabitants of Tunbridge Wells for the negative thoughts that my heroine, Betsy Fairfax, has of the place, though in the end she realizes she is mistaken—about a lot of things!

ANNIE BURROWS

———

How to Catch a Viscount

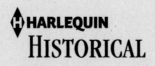

HARLEQUIN®
HISTORICAL™

Recycling programs
for this product may
not exist in your area.

ISBN-13: 978-1-335-40785-6

How to Catch a Viscount

Copyright © 2022 by Annie Burrows

For questions and comments about the quality of this book,
please contact us at CustomerService@Harlequin.com.

Harlequin Enterprises ULC
22 Adelaide St. West, 41st Floor
Toronto, Ontario M5H 4E3, Canada
www.Harlequin.com

Printed in U.S.A.

Annie Burrows has been writing Regency romances for Harlequin since 2007. Her books have charmed readers worldwide, having been translated into nineteen different languages, and some have gone on to win the coveted Reviewers' Choice Award from CataRomance. For more information, or to contact her, please visit annie-burrows.co.uk, or find her on Facebook at Facebook.com/annieburrowsuk.

Books by Annie Burrows

Harlequin Historical

The Captain's Christmas Bride
In Bed with the Duke
Once Upon a Regency Christmas
"Cinderella's Perfect Christmas"
A Duke in Need of a Wife
A Marquess, a Miss and a Mystery
The Scandal of the Season
From Cinderella to Countess
His Accidental Countess

The Patterdale Siblings

A Scandal at Midnight
How to Catch a Viscount

Brides for Bachelors

The Major Meets His Match
The Marquess Tames His Bride
The Captain Claims His Lady

Regency Bachelors

Gift-Wrapped Governess
"Governess to Christmas Bride"
Lord Havelock's List
The Debutante's Daring Proposal

Visit the Author Profile page
at Harlequin.com for more titles.

Chapter One

James Patterdale, eldest son of the Earl of Darwen, and Viscount Dundas in his own right, paused at the crossroads, wondering which way to go.

He glanced along the road to his left, then the one to the right. In one sense he didn't suppose it would matter which way he rode next. Wherever he went on Lord Bramhall's estate he was sure to find the same sort of thing. He'd spent just the one, rather uncomfortable night in the big house, which was virtually derelict, and so far today, during his ride through the nearest village, he'd noted roofs in need of rethatching and shops that looked as if they were barely getting by. The only place that looked as if it was still flourishing was the hostelry, which didn't bode well for the state of the locals' sobriety.

Everywhere else he looked, there were signs of neglect. In the park, tree branches that had come down during storms lay where they'd fallen, blocking paths. On the farmland, weeds flourished in fields which should have produced profitable crops, considering the richness of the soil. And round the neglected house, meadows brightly dotted with wild-flowers had taken over where, at a guess, the lawns had once been.

Perfect! This was exactly the project he'd needed. His only dilemma was, where to begin?

He wasn't a bookish sort of chap and had always detested poetry in particular, but as he sat astride his mount, debating which way to ride next, he got a sort of notion that he'd just stumbled across a metaphor for his own life.

Because, although he was healthy and rich, he'd been feeling, of late, that he was being neither pro-ductive nor meaningful. Just like Lord Bramhall's estate, which should have been highly profitable.

Socks shifted beneath him, as if picking up on his tension. James reached down and patted her neck.

'I know, I know, you want to be going somewhere and doing something, don't you? Well, so do I. That's why I came here.'

He'd told everyone that he had to leave the house party because his recently married sister, Daisy, needed him to sort out the mess her husband, Ben, was in. Namely, this estate. It wasn't Ben's fault the place was in such poor heart. Ben had only just in-herited and although he'd started making plans, he'd abandoned them when Bonaparte somehow managed to escape from Elba. He'd thought it more impor-tant to return to his regiment. The letter Daisy had written to him couldn't have come at a better moment. Because James had been at breaking point, with his family.

Everyone always spent the entire summer at Wattlesham Priory, along with as many friends as they could pack into the rambling house. While everyone else seemed to be having a wonderful time, he'd been watching their antics with increasing irritation. It was fine for his younger brothers, who were enjoying the traditional pastimes of fighting mock battles all over the grounds, or playing pranks on each other. But James was twenty-four years old now. And he'd long since outgrown the joy of rigging buckets over doorways to catch the careless unawares, or rigging tripwires in the shrubbery for the pleasure of watching his victim falling face down in a puddle.

His four younger brothers had been making things worse by accusing him of being no fun any more and saying that just because he was the eldest he had no right to be so toplofty. They had then redoubled their efforts to bring him back down to their level. He'd managed to dodge those attempts, on the whole. But he hadn't been able to avoid his father, who had berated him for putting a damper on everyone else's enjoyment.

'You should be encouraging the younger ones in their horseplay,' he'd complained, rather peevishly, James had thought. 'Boys of that age *need* to find a healthy form of release for their high spirits.'

Which had been just about the last straw. 'By the time Father had been twenty-four,' he informed

Socks, resentfully, since lately his horse had been the only creature he'd felt he could talk to, 'he'd been the Earl for almost a decade. There had been nobody breathing down *his* neck, telling him how to behave, or expecting him to live up to impossibly high standards, while refusing to let him have any real work to do. What was more, he'd been married and had already fathered both me and Daisy. Nobody had stood in *his* way, preventing him from growing up.

'Hell's teeth, Socks,' said James, his brows shooting up. 'That's two epiphanies in the space of as many minutes.' Because he'd just seen that was what his father was doing. He was keeping James in an extended state of boyhood, preventing him from growing up by refusing to allow him to take on any responsibilities. He only wished he'd perceived that before. It might have enabled him to have a more constructive, reasoning sort of conversation with Father, rather than growing increasingly resentful at the feeling he was banging his head against a brick wall and grinding his back teeth away with the effort of keeping his frustrations unvoiced.

'Thank goodness Daisy wrote to me when she did,' he informed Socks, who snorted and shook her head as though she understood completely how it was. That was the thing about a horse—that connection they shared with whoever was riding them. 'Yes, because her letter gave me a jolly good excuse to leave, before either Father threw me out, or I stormed out. Before words were spoken that could have led to a complete breach between us.'

Socks flung her head up and down, making the tack jingle.

'Yes, exactly so. Chafing at the bit. That was what I'd been doing. Wanting to…to prove myself, I suppose. It's all very well for chaps like Ben. They can march off to war and come back covered in glory. But can you imagine the chaos I'd cause if I joined some regiment, knowing as little as I do about tactics and stuff? I'd be at best a liability and at worst throw away not only my own life but also that of any unfortunate subordinates under my command. And for what? To show that I'm a man now, not a boy?'

He snorted. And then so did Socks, as though totally agreeing with everything he'd just said.

'But I could make a real difference here,' he mused, gazing about him. Because he did know about land management. Father might not let him take part in any of the decision making that went on, but he encouraged him to watch and learn, so that he'd be ready to take up the reins when it was his turn. Although that could well be another forty years or so, considering how young Father had been when he started filling his nursery.

'Must be something in the air of this place,' James mused. 'It's all suddenly obvious to me. Daisy's letter was just what I needed. A golden opportunity to *do* something *and* show Father that I'm ready. Because she had total faith in my ability to sort everything out for her while Ben is off trouncing Bonaparte. And what's more, Father couldn't argue with my desire to help my sister, could he? Not after telling me, my whole life, that it is my duty to set an example to the younger sibs. Hah!'

Socks shifted sideways, then pawed at the ground as though impatient to move on.

'Exactly,' he said, reaching down to pat her neck. 'Past time we stopped sitting about contemplating how we got here. Let's abandon the road altogether and head across country. See what we can find up there, shall we?' He pointed Socks's nose uphill. 'I wouldn't be a bit surprised to learn that, on a day as fine as this, we might be able to see the Welsh mountains.'

That was the one thing about Ben's estates he couldn't fault. The views. Whichever way he looked, there were stunning vistas over rugged hill country, with rocky valleys that had vigorous streams foaming along their floors. The soil covering those hills wasn't the thin, stark sort you got in some parts of the world, which would only produce gorse and bracken. The hills here were a rich, lush green. Which ought, he thought irritably, to be put to use, not be left lying fallow.

He put Socks at the steepest hill he could see, one which had a massive oak tree growing at its summit. He'd noted that oak tree several times already today and reckoned that it was probably something of a landmark in these parts. And that from underneath its spreading branches, he'd be able to get a really clear view of most of Lord Bramhall's holdings, as well as the foothills of the Welsh mountains.

* * *

It wasn't until he was within a few yards of the tree that he noted somebody huddled between the gnarled roots and an outcropping of rock to which the tree appeared to be clinging with gigantic wooden fingers.

A trespasser. It had to be. There was no reason for anyone to be up here otherwise.

James had swung out of the saddle, looped Socks's reins over his arm and begun striding over to where the person crouched, before recalling Lord Bramhall's warnings about the mood of a certain proportion of the tenants. One farmer, at least, had threatened his brother-in-law with a gun over an issue the previous Earl had instigated.

But it was too late to take precautions now. The person had heard him approaching and had lifted their head. Her head. For it was a woman. And she had been crying, to judge from the blotchy state of her complexion and the puffiness of her eyes.

James almost wished she *had* been a trespasser, toting a gun. That, he thought he could have dealt with. He might not have been a soldier, but he didn't lack physical courage, or at least he didn't think so. A chap couldn't grow up in a house full of brothers without learning a thing or two about standing his ground.

A weeping woman, however, was not something he felt equipped to tackle. He wasn't much in the petticoat line, for a number of reasons. First and foremost was Father's insistence that as eldest, he set a standard for his younger brothers. Particularly over what Father termed 'loose women'. It had made him think twice about every temptation and opportunity that had come his way, from that quarter. And society ladies, the ones he did know more about, never wept in public.

It would be cowardly to retreat, however, and so James simply stood there, looking at the woman, wondering what he ought to say. He rejected his first impulse, which was to turn and walk away, because he probably ought to offer her assistance, if he could. She was clearly in distress and it would not be the act of a gentleman to abandon a female in distress. So he'd have to make a push to say something.

'Who are you?' she said, rather crossly, before he could come up with an appropriate salutation. 'And what are you doing here? Don't you know that this is private land?'

'Yes, and it isn't yours,' he found himself retorting, his fleeting feeling that he ought to offer her assistance evaporating far more quickly than it had formed. For one thing, he'd never met anyone who didn't know exactly who he was and what he was worth. For another, he resented the fact that she was cross with him when all he'd done was approach her with a view to seeing if there was anything he could do to help her.

Well, *eventually* he'd considered that, once he'd seen she was crying, *and* had nobly resisted the impulse to turn tail and leave her to it. Which reminded him why he'd approached her in the first place.

'You are the one trespassing,' he said. 'At least, you are if you don't work for Lord and Lady Bramhall...' It didn't seem likely. When he'd arrived last night, he'd found only three servants left in the house. That was all there was, according to them. And this girl had not been one of them. So...

'*Work* for them?' The girl's tone, and face, expressed disgust that he could have suspected she was guilty of such a heinous crime.

He rapidly scoured his mind for any set of circumstances that could account for her attitude that implied she had every right to be here.

'You are friends with them, then?' Her accent was certainly refined enough for her to pass muster in any society drawing room. Nor did she act the way a member of the servant classes would. No, she behaved rather more like his sister would, if he'd ever, God forbid, caught her crying in some out-of-the-way spot. Which was with resentment, tinged with a hefty dollop of haughtiness.

The woman gave a bitter laugh. 'Friends? Not likely. In fact, you could almost say—' She shut her mouth firmly and frowned as though annoyed with herself for having almost admitted to something better left unsaid.

Then she tossed her head. 'What business is it of yours, anyway? You have no right to question me!'

James felt a smile creeping across his face. Along with a sense of something he hadn't felt for a very, very long time. A dissipation of the boredom and frustration that had been dogging him, as questions began to tumble into his mind. Who was this girl? What had she done that made her feel she could not describe herself as friends with Lord and Lady Bramhall, even though she felt she had the right to sit under their oak tree, to indulge in a fit of weeping?

'I beg your pardon,' he said without feeling the slightest bit apologetic. 'But I have come to Bramley Park to look after the place while Lord and Lady Bramhall are away.'

That was what Lord Bramhall had asked of him, anyway. Ben's letter, unlike Daisy's rather disjointed outpourings, had contained a list of all the projects he'd set in train, along with the progress he'd made, and had expressed the hope that he'd oversee them if it wasn't too much of an imposition in spite of what Daisy had assumed. He'd also absolved him of the task if he had anything better to do, knowing that Daisy could be rather impulsive.

Well, he *had* nothing better to do with his time, had he, thanks to Father's dogged refusal to give him any real responsibilities. And as Daisy had pointed out in her letter, a challenge such as he would find on Ben's neglected estates would do him good.

The girl scrambled to her feet. 'So they didn't just run off and turn their backs on everyone, then, in spite of—' She shut her mouth firmly again and then gave a little shudder. 'That is such a relief. You have no idea…not that anyone could. At least I would hope not.' She gave him a considering look. 'I mean, of course,' she said, lifting her chin, 'that it is going to be a great relief to everyone in these parts, to learn that Lord Bramhall has arranged to have a steward managing his holdings in his absence.'

What he should have done, he supposed, was inform her that far from being a steward, he was a viscount. The brother of Lady Bramhall.

Only, it was a long time since he'd been in the habit of explaining himself to anyone.

And believing he was a steward had stopped her crying, hadn't it? The thought had given her comfort. So why upset her all over again, by telling her she was mistaken?

Besides, it was rather a novel sensation to have somebody behaving so…freely with him. A freedom that would vanish the moment she learned his rank.

'I'm so glad you've come,' she added, while he considered the effects a full and frank confession would have on the situation. 'It means…well, that Ben didn't leave in such a hurry that all the things he planned to do with his estate will come to nought. I really thought I'd…'

Ben? She was so close to his brother-in-law that she felt free to call him Ben?

James frowned. What might that mean for the state of his sister's marriage to the lad? It hadn't come about after a regular courtship, but had been forced on them, in haste, after some of his younger brothers had propelled them into a particularly scandalous situation, as the result of a drunken prank. If he were to admit, now, to being the brother of Lady Bramhall, any chance that this girl might admit to what was clearly making her feel guilty, and what might even explain why she was sitting in this lonely spot, crying her eyes out, would vanish. And he'd rather like to know, just in case it had any bearing on his sister's welfare.

Oh, who was he fooling? He just wanted to find out all he could about this girl. He'd never encountered one who'd piqued his interest in just this way before. Not someone who had no idea who he was and who therefore could not be setting some kind of trap for him. Which they all did, the moment they knew who he was. They fluttered and giggled and sidled up to him, talking with affected lisps, with childish language, if they were the sort who wanted to marry his title. Or leaned forward to give him a view down their bodices if they were the sort who merely wanted a rich protector. Speaking of which, now that she was standing up he could see that, although she wasn't particularly tall, she had curves in all the right places. Her features had a pleasing cast to them, too. He suspected that if her eyes weren't so puffy and her complexion so blotchy, and her dark hair so windswept, she'd probably look rather pretty.

But there was rather more to it than that. He was, frankly, rather impressed by the fact that she appeared to be upset at the thought she might have done something that would harm others. Most women he'd encountered, other than his mother and his sister, didn't seem to have any qualms about behaving as badly as they wished, nor what effect their actions would have on others.

He had, in fact, stumbled across the first female he'd ever met who he felt would be worth taking some effort to get to know.

Chapter Two

'What,' said the ruggedly handsome stranger with a rather mischievous, yet somehow coaxing smile, 'did you think you'd done?'

Betsy might have been at very low ebb, but she hadn't lost all sense of self-preservation. So far nobody but she and Ben, and his wife, knew what she'd done. And since they'd left before they'd had time to spread any malicious gossip about her, it looked as though that was the way it was going to stay. As long as she didn't succumb to the temptation to unburden herself on the first sympathetic and tolerably presentable man whose chest looked broad enough to support her should she fling herself, weeping, on to it.

So she tossed her head. 'I am not telling you. You could be anybody.'

'I could be,' he agreed, his smile spreading wider. Which made him look more mischievous than ever. And somehow, like the sort of person who would completely understand why she'd done what she'd done.

'Even if I did behave, well, rashly, and even though it might have contributed to...' What was she doing? She couldn't trust a total stranger with her secret. There wasn't a single soul in the world she could trust with that secret. 'That is, at least now you are here I can see that it has not caused any lasting damage to the folk around here, which is a weight off my conscience.' Ah. Perhaps that was why she'd experienced that insane feeling of wanting to confide in him. His very presence here was a sign that she hadn't done any real harm. He was a cipher. A symbol of hope for the future.

Apart from that she knew nothing about him. And just because he had a mischievous smile and a handsome face, a sympathetic look in his eyes and a very broad chest, that did *not* mean he was trustworthy. Mother had warned her often enough about not trusting first impressions—especially in regard to men.

'Shall I,' he said gently, as though he was afraid if he spoke too roughly she might start weeping again at any moment, 'see you safely home?'

'There is no need,' she said, briskly. 'I know my way about far better than you, having lived in this area most of my life.'

'Well, yes, I'm sure that is true,' he said apologetically. 'But I don't like the feeling that I have run you off the land where you clearly came for some privacy. Nor that I've sent you home when you are still so upset.'

'Pish,' she said, even though her mother would have punished her for uttering it had she been able to hear such a vulgar word escape her mouth. 'I no longer feel like crying, not now I know you have come to take up the work Ben started. And it wasn't as if I was ever in the state where I was considering throwing myself into the millpond over him,' she added bitterly, 'even if that is what *some* people may think.' Mother, to be precise. But the fact that Ben had married someone else had hurt Mother far more than it had ever hurt Betsy. 'For one thing, I am not so poor-spirited that I would *ever* consider flinging myself into a millpond over a man—' especially not one she hardly knew '—and for another, there is no millpond within walking distance.'

The steward gave a short bark of laughter. 'That would make it very hard to drown yourself, I agree,' he said. 'By the time you reached the pond you might well have changed your mind, even if you had set out with that intention.'

She narrowed her eyes and gave him the benefit of her most disdainful glare. 'Just when I thought you were a gentleman, and kind, you prove you are nothing of the sort by making fun of me.'

'Not a bit of it,' he said, laying his hand on his heart. 'Because you are not the sort of girl who would do anything so hen-witted as set out for a millpond several miles distant, to drown yourself—you just said so. If I was making fun of anyone, it would be the type of female who *would* do something so silly.'

'Hmmph.'

'Besides, I have offered to escort you home,

haven't I, when normally the sight of a female in tears would send me running in the opposite direction?'

'You have a lot of experience of weeping women, do you?'

'Very little, I am happy to say. As I said, normally I would take steps to avoid such a person.'

'So why are you making an exception for me?'

He tilted his head to one side. 'Blessed if I know. It might be, perhaps, because…' He petered out, looking a bit confused. Then he cleared his throat. 'I say, would you mind telling me your name?'

'I'm not sure that would be wise.'

'Why not? We are bound to cross paths with each other since I am going to be living at Bramley Park for the foreseeable future. I know that introducing ourselves may not be the completely correct thing to do, but our meeting has been a touch out of the ordinary, hasn't it?'

She supposed he was correct, up to a point. 'It is not that I mind us introducing ourselves to each other, informally, it is just that…well, I would rather nobody knew that we had met like this, on our own.'

'Why? It is not as if we have done anything wrong.'

'But there is nobody to vouch for that, is there? No chaperon. And my mother is so desperate to see me married she might take it into her head to find you eligible and accuse you of compromising me, and marching us both up the aisle.'

His look of alarm at the prospect of being marched up the aisle was far from flattering. Which was so annoying she couldn't resist the impulse to take immediate revenge. 'Or, indeed, I might.'

'You might what?'

'Decide to set my cap at you.'

'Why,' he said, with a scowl, 'would you do that?'

'Tunbridge Wells,' she said, with a shudder.

'Er...is that a euphemism for something in these parts? Or...?'

'It is exactly what it says. Tunbridge Wells. The town. To be specific, I have recently discovered that there is no telling what desperate measures a girl might take in order to avoid the dreadful fate of being sent there to act as a companion to a spinster aunt.' Measures which had led her to commit the deed of which she was so dreadfully ashamed. Measures that made her go into a cold sweat, whenever she thought of the look on *Lady* Bramhall's face when she'd walked in and seen Betsy with *Lord* Bramhall. Measures that robbed her of sleep, or, when it did come, filled it with lurid nightmares.

'An awful fate,' he conceded, though he still looked a bit wary of her. 'That is, I have never actually been to Tunbridge Wells...'

'Don't bother. I hear it is the dullest place on earth. If Great-Aunt Cornelia had even lived at Bath, it might not be so bad. I mean, they have balls and concerts there, don't they? And although I hear most of the residents are elderly, they must have relatives who visit them from time to time, mustn't they? So that at least I might have the chance to make some friends. But this morning, I came to the realisation that there is no escaping Tunbridge Wells, not now. In spite of all I did, or at least tried to do…'

She felt her shoulders drooping and therefore straightened up and fixed a smile to her face, adopting the posture and the demeanour a lady should always display when in public. Which would, hopefully, convince him she was recovered from her despondent mood so that he'd let her walk home on her own. 'It was good to meet you, um…'

'Dundas,' he said and then flinched, as though he couldn't believe he'd told her his name when so far she'd refused to tell him hers.

'And mine is Fairfax,' she confessed. 'Although if you ever let on that you know my name, before we are properly introduced, I shall…' She faltered. There wasn't much she could do, by way of a threat. And Mr Dundas knew it, the beast, to judge from the grin he was giving her.

'I am quaking at the prospect of what you shall do,' he said. 'However, I suspect that the mere threat of you withdrawing your good opinion of me will be enough.'

She peered at him suspiciously. That had sounded remarkably as though he was flirting with her, which naturally buoyed her spirits and made her wish to respond accordingly. 'What makes you think,' she said, challengingly, 'I have a good opinion of you now?'

'Because you are talking to me as though I was your…brother. You are not giving yourself airs to try to make yourself seem more interesting than you already are. There is nothing calculating about your manner. Which leads me to deduce that, for some reason, you are being yourself with me. You did not hide your indignation at being found crying, nor were you crying to try to draw attention to yourself, or you couldn't have been so tart-tongued. I mean—' He took off his hat and thrust his fingers through his hair. 'I am not putting this very well,' he said ruefully, 'am I?'

'On the contrary, I think you are putting it exceedingly well,' she said, turning from him and setting off down the hill. Which was the height of bad manners. But then, what did it matter? His attempt to flirt with her, if that was what it had been, had been short-lived. 'You think I am a vixen. A tart-tongued, ill-mannered shrew!'

'But not a calculating one,' he pointed out, looping his horse's reins over his arm, she noted as she glanced over her shoulder, and setting out after her.

'Why are you following me? I told you I don't need you to see me home.'

'For the pleasure of your company?'

'Hah! What pleasure can you possibly take in the company of a tart-tongued shrew?'

'You'd be surprised.'

'I certainly would!'

'It isn't easy to explain,' he said, catching up with her in a few long, lazy-looking strides, which she resented, since she'd felt as if she'd been hurrying as fast as she could safely go down the tussocky hillside. 'It is perhaps that I have never met anyone who has ever been so…open with me. So honest.'

'You can blame that on the fact that I was so cross with myself,' she said. 'And so ashamed of myself for something I did that was, well, if we are talking about being honest, it was downright spiteful.' She stopped and looked up at him. 'I don't know why I keep on telling you things I have never told, and would never tell, anyone else. Sometimes I don't know what comes over me,' she said, feeling perplexed.

'You have an impulsive nature, perhaps?'

'No. I don't think that is it. Most of the time I am, or at least I have been, very, very careful about the way I behave. My mother drilled so many manners, and the like, into me that I was like a performing… puppet,' she said with disgust.

'Perhaps it was liberating to just say whatever you felt like,' he suggested thoughtfully.

'Liberating.' She pondered his choice of word for a moment or two. Yes, it had been liberating to sit and cry as noisily as she wished. To sit on the ground, heedless of her dress, and let all her pent-up feelings have free rein. Perhaps that was what had led her to be so frank with this stranger. She'd already let down her guard. And everything she'd been holding back for so long had been so close to the surface it had all come pouring out. Well, not all of it. Not the bit about talking herself into kissing a man, only to have a woman walk in and catch her doing it…a woman who, it turned out, was that man's wife! When nobody, least of all she, had suspected he was married.

But even so, she'd admitted a good deal more than might have been wise.

'I wish I were a man,' she said resentfully. 'You don't have to take care of every move you make in public, of every word you say, in order to preserve your reputation. And if you want something you just jolly well go off and take it.'

They reached the bottom of the hill and she paused on the edge of the brook. It would be no use chatting while she crossed it. There were plenty of stones she could use to make her way across, but she would need to pay close attention to where she placed her feet for the next few minutes.

'Just because I'm a man doesn't mean I can have everything I want, or *do* anything I want,' he said, with more than a hint of resentment.

She left off her search for a series of handy stones she might use to cross the foaming brook and glanced up at him. At his bitter expression, first, then at his muddy, well-worn riding clothes and the scuffed and wrinkled boots, and felt a strong pang of sympathy.

'No, I don't suppose it can be much fun having to run someone else's estates, for a pittance, while they get the majority of the rent money. And go swanning off to France when the notion takes them.'

She saw a muscle working in his jaw. 'That is not… I mean, you make it sound as though Lord Bramhall has just gone abroad on a pleasure trip, whereas he has actually gone to fight for his country. And I…' He sighed, and looked off into the distance. 'I have to confess I envy him the opportunity to do that. He is doing something that will become a part of history, isn't he, going off to fight Bonaparte and his armies? While I...' He frowned down at his boots. 'What you said about it not being *fun*, working here, is correct. But I don't resent it in the way you might imagine. In fact, I suspect I will enjoy the challenge of putting into effect the improvements Lord and Lady Bramhall have informed me they wish to attempt, in their absence.'

'Good for you,' she said. Because he sounded like a man who chose to see the positive side of things, rather than harping on about what he couldn't do and making himself peevish.

He smiled at her and held out his hand.

There was no impropriety in taking a man's hand, so that he might steady her as she crossed a brook using precariously wobbly stepping stones, was there? Well, even if there was, she didn't care. She didn't want to slip into the water and get the hem of her skirt wet, or possibly even turn her ankle, either of which would mean giving an account of where she'd been and what she'd been doing.

So she took it and smiled back.

He urged his mare, who had taken the opportunity of dipping her head to drink while they were standing talking, into motion. And, while Betsy sprang from one stone to the next, he and the horse simply waded through the water, with a good deal of splashing.

'I do admire the way you put it,' she admitted, as

she finally stepped on to the far bank. 'Very tactful. Very respectful.'

'Put what?'

'What you said about the challenges of putting Ben's—that is, Lord Bramhall's plans into effect. I mean...' she added, finding her cheeks heating when she found he was still holding her hand. Or she was still holding his. 'Apart from the fact that his ideas are somewhat radical,' she said, tugging her hand free, 'he wasn't brought up to the role.'

'You seem to know an awful lot about Lord Bramhall's plans,' he said, looking none too pleased.

'Everyone in these parts knows a lot about his plans,' she said, shaking her head at the implication that she and Ben might have been close. 'For one thing, him inheriting against all the odds was the talk of the neighbourhood. And...' She paused and glanced up at his sombre countenance. 'Um, how much do you know about your employers?'

He glanced away. Cleared his throat. 'I know that he spent most of his adult years in the army and has recently come home to find his father has left his estate in a terrible mess.'

'There, you see,' she said and couldn't help smiling, 'that was a masterfully tactful way of putting it. You should have been a diplomat, not a steward.'

He rubbed at his nose with one thumb, looking a bit awkward. And rather vulnerable. All of a sudden, her heart went out to him.

'Look here, if you really want to succeed in your work here, it would probably help if you knew a bit more about the state of affairs. And the truth is that the fourth Earl became very eccentric in his latter days. Both his older sons died within a few months of each other, which may have tipped him over the edge. But anyway, after they'd gone, he went about deliberately wreaking as much havoc as he could before going to meet his Maker. Mostly to make things difficult for poor Ben, I dare say, but his spite spilled over to affect everyone else in the area as well. He put up rents to such ridiculous levels that some people couldn't afford to stay on their farms and he turned off all the servants in the big house, bar the cook.'

'Ah. I did wonder why there were so few servants in the house. And why the place looked so…well, as if the bailiffs had been in.'

'As bad as that? I have only seen inside one room since he passed, but—' She bit her tongue. For, to tell the truth, she hadn't taken much notice of anything in the room except for the fact that Ben had been in it. Alone.

'Well, the point is,' she continued, swiftly marshalling her thoughts into order once more, 'he didn't actually manage to wreak as much damage as he might have done, because of his increasingly irrational behaviour. For instance, when some of the farmers protested at the rent increase and refused to pay, and he threatened to evict them, he couldn't actually do so, because he'd fired his steward.'

'Hah!' Mr Dundas let out a bark of laughter. 'He wouldn't have had anyone to go and collect those rents, either, would he, once he'd fired his steward? So the farmers would probably have claimed that, since nobody had come to collect the rents, they were not in breach of their tenancy agreements.'

'Well, I wouldn't know about that. But certainly the more belligerent ones among them neither paid their rent, nor took any notice of his threats of eviction.'

'I can see that I will have to handle them with great tact, then,' he said, his face sobering, 'when I start doing my rounds.'

'Well, since we've already established that tact is one of your talents, I expect you will have hardly any trouble getting them all eating out of your hand.'

He grinned down at her. 'You are good for my self-esteem, young lady.'

She felt her cheeks heating and, for the next few moments, studied her feet as they walked up the hill, rather than glance up at him too often.

'Might I ask,' he said presently, 'how you know so much about the farmers and their views of rents and evictions, and the like? Is your father, perchance, of their number?'

His insulting assumption made her promptly take back every single complimentary thing she'd thought about him. 'Do I look,' she cried, with great indignation, 'like a farmer's daughter?'

He glanced down at her in such a way that she became aware that in spite of the precautions she'd taken crossing the brook, her skirts had become rather damp and muddy, and that twigs and leaves had stuck in that mud after the time she'd spent sitting on the ground. She wouldn't be a bit surprised if the back of her jacket was covered with moss, either, from where she'd leaned against the trunk of the oak tree.

'I will have you know,' she said, 'that my father is just about the most senior-ranking man in these parts, now that Ben has gone away. And we pay rent to nobody. We own Darby Manor outright, and the land on which it stands. Acres and acres of it!'

'I beg your pardon,' he said, although he didn't look all that apologetic to her. On the contrary, he looked as though he was struggling to keep a straight face. 'The truth is that I know very little about ladies' fashion. I was misled, perhaps, by…' He paused, to glance at her muddy skirts once more, before continuing, 'The, ah, vast amount you knew about the farmers and their struggles with the rent, and so forth.'

'The reason I know so much about what local people feel is because they all come to my father with their complaints and grievances, which they all talk about for hours on end, at the top of their voices. Particularly if they come to him after any time spent at the Grapes.'

'The Grapes? That is, I take it, the name of the local tavern?'

'It is what people about here call it, yes.'

'I wondered. There was no name painted on the sign.'

'I see,' she said, revising her opinion of him yet

again. 'It was the first place you went to look at, was it? Well, it sounds as though you will fit in very well!'

He chuckled. 'I rode past the place earlier as I was exploring the area. I didn't deliberately seek it out. As a matter of fact, I was a little disturbed to see how very prosperous it looked, in contrast to many of the other shops and buildings about here.'

'Indeed?' She lifted her chin and gave him her haughtiest look.

'Why would I lie,' he retorted, 'about that?'

'I have no idea. No idea what you might take it into your head to do.'

'Well, before long, you will learn that I have no taste for frequenting taverns. You may search, but you won't find me in the Grapes.'

'Why would I search for you? What are you implying?'

He pulled his lips in, making him look as though he was biting back a scathing retort. Which, for some reason, rather disappointed her.

She was in the mood for a fight, that was what it was. And there was nobody else she could fight with. Or just let down her guard with. She'd been enjoying just saying whatever came into her head, without weighing it all up and considering the consequences, she realised. It had been liberating.

But they had reached the crest of the hill, which was crowned with a perfectly maintained drystone wall.

'You and I must part here,' she informed him.

'No. I mean, I am sure I can get Socks, that is, my mare, across this wall.'

'That is not it. This is the boundary to my father's land. Once I am on the other side of it, I will be, more or less, home.'

His face fell. Then brightened. 'You know, if your father really is as knowledgeable about the feelings of the folk in these parts, and so influential, I really ought to visit him and make myself known to him.'

'No! I mean, not today, anyway. Or at least, not with me. Not like this! Please!'

He tilted his head to one side. 'You really don't want anyone to know we have been alone out here, do you?'

'No!' Her reputation was in a precarious enough state as it was. 'You are bound to meet him at church on Sunday. Can you not wait until then? And meet him in a perfectly natural fashion? Everyone is bound to want to know who you are, and once Father learns why you have come here, he is bound to want to further your acquaintance, since the state of the Earl's holdings has been vexing him for years.'

'If that is the case, could I not simply call on him and pay my respects?'

She turned her back on him and began to scramble over the wall. Even though she could manage perfectly well, and had done on many occasions, he seemed to think he needed to place his hands at her waist to steady her, lest she take a tumble.

It was all she could do to turn and face him once she was safely on the other side. Her body still burned where his hands had been, as if he had left a fiery imprint. And warm tingles were spreading to the rest of her body. She'd never experienced anything like it. Men had touched her before, when helping her alight from a carriage, or during the measures of a dance. But none of their hands had felt as if they'd seared their way through every single layer of clothing she wore.

'P-please don't,' she found herself begging him. In regard to what he'd said, rather than what he'd done. 'If you were to turn up at the house, I would be sure to give away the fact that I already knew you, by blushing, or being unable to meet your eye, or something of the sort. And Mother, who is a veritable bloodhound when it comes to that sort of thing, would be bound to sniff out the truth, somehow.'

'Then, to spare your blushes,' he said, giving her that mischievous smile once more, 'I shall wait to present myself to your father until Sunday.'

'Thank you,' she breathed.

'I shall be counting the days,' he said.

'I... I...' She would be, too, she realised. Not that she could tell him so. Or even let him guess she might be thinking such a thing.

Her head in a whirl, her body tingling and her heart pounding, Betsy turned away from him, and pelted down the hillside.

Chapter Three

James stood watching her flounce down the hillside, black curls flying, skirts swishing, wondering if he'd ever met anyone so vibrant. So open. So
mercurial. Her mood changed from one moment
to the next, so that he'd never been sure what was
likely to come out of her mouth next. She was like
a breath of fresh air in comparison with the people
he normally met.

She'd certainly blown away the creeping sense of
ennui that had dogged him for the past year or so, no
matter how hard he'd fought it. It never did him any
good reminding himself that he was a lucky dog not
to have to work for a living. He just couldn't shake
off the feeling that he was frittering away his days
in idleness.

Part of that was probably his own fault. He could
easily take the remedy that so many of his peers did
as a matter of course. He could simply spend his

youth and his wealth on pursuits such as drinking and gambling, and whoring.

Only, he had no taste for that sort of idleness. He'd never, for example, been able to derive any lasting satisfaction from attending the kind of house parties where scantily clad women draped themselves over the wealthiest-looking male guests, promising them all sorts of pleasure on payment of a fee. Lots of chaps accused him of being too fastidious. That was no doubt due to the fact that Father had made it clear to him what happened to people, men and women alike, who indulged in what he termed vice. He'd never be able to forget the lecture about how the disease of syphilis could sweep through a whole family, as a result of one man's selfish, licentious behaviour. Or the deformed faces of the poor little children who'd been born to mothers who'd suffered from the pox. And, since Father also reminded him, as often as he could, that it was his duty to produce the next heir, the next *healthy* heir, so that the Patterdale line would not only survive, but thrive, it didn't half put a damper on his natural appetites at the most inopportune moments. Instead of wanting to take any of those scantily clad women to bed, he often felt as if he ought to be warning them to cease plying such a dangerous trade and to take up some safer, more wholesome way of life instead.

He'd had to stop attending that kind of party.

He'd had to cut back on the amount of alcohol he consumed, too, because he found that drinking overmuch was a sure-fire way to rouse his urges to the extent he feared he might throw caution to the wind. The last thing he wanted was to wake up, after a night of debauchery, to discover he'd dipped his wick where, when sober, he would never, ever have dreamed of venturing. He would never be able to look his father, or mother, in the face if he'd let them down so badly.

So, what with one thing and another, his circle of friends had shrunk considerably. He couldn't blame them. Who wanted to spend time with a fellow who was starting to behave like an early Christian martyr? If he was sick of himself, it stood to reason that others would grow sick of him, too.

The answer to all his frustrations, Father would say, had James ever confided in him, would be to marry young and slake his natural appetites in the marriage bed. Indeed, during Daisy's Season earlier this year, both he and Mother had urged James to start looking about him for a wife.

But as he'd dutifully looked over the debutantes vying for his attention, he'd asked himself if marriage shouldn't be about more than that. More than slaking an urge, or keeping himself healthy, or dutifully producing the next little Earl to succeed to his title. Shouldn't it be about finding a…rapport with someone? Feeling as if they understood you? Or at least liked you for who you were, not what you could bring to her family in terms of status or wealth?

Which was, perhaps, why he'd enjoyed the little interlude with Miss Fairfax so much. *She* didn't know he had a reputation for being a stick-in-the-mud. She didn't know he was a viscount, either. He'd given her his title, when she'd asked him for his name, because that was the correct way to introduce himself. Only, she hadn't realised that he was *Lord* Dundas. She'd assumed he was just *Mr* Dundas. He really ought to have told her of her mistaken assumption straight away. Only, it would have sounded pompous, wouldn't it, to have corrected her? Especially when she was already so upset?

And then again, she wouldn't have spoken to him as though he was her equal, either, after that, would she? She might have started behaving the way other women did, when they knew he was the heir to a prosperous and venerable title. Either fluttering and simpering, or, if they believed he was as toplofty as people said, behaving as though everyone else in the room was beneath their notice and everything they did was a great bore.

The last thing that Miss Fairfax was, was boring. She might be tart-tongued and hot-tempered, but she definitely wasn't boring. She wasn't toplofty, either, even though she had been annoyed when he'd asked her if she was a farmer's daughter.

The memory of the way she'd flared up when *he'd* made an incorrect assumption about *her* origins made him grin as he watched her disappearing into a stand of beech trees. He'd told Miss Fairfax that he would be counting the days until Sunday, implying that it would be for the pleasure of seeing her again. And there was more than a grain of truth in it. He would enjoy seeing if he could make her blush, for one thing. Or goad her into making an unguarded response in the hallowed precincts of the churchyard.

But there was more to it than that. His grin faded. Miss Fairfax had not been crying for no reason. She'd done something of which she was ashamed. Something which, he suspected, involved Lord Bramhall, or Ben as she kept on calling him.

He eyed the stone wall over which she'd so recently scrambled. The wall that divided her father's land from Bramley Park. Which made her a neighbour of Ben's. Which meant that, growing up, she and Ben might have played together. Or had some sort of intimacy. The sort that so often sprang up between highest-ranking children in such a district. They might have attended dancing lessons together, perhaps. They'd certainly have seen each other in church every week. Which meant that there might be nothing more in the way she spoke of him with such familiarity than a habit of long standing.

But he had a suspicion there was more to it than that. And if she was sitting weeping over Ben, the man who had so recently married James's sister, then it was probably his duty to look into the matter, in case it spelled trouble for Daisy.

And Miss Fairfax wasn't going to confide in him if she knew that he was Lady Bramhall's brother, was she?

So, on the whole, he was glad that he hadn't made his identity crystal clear. Glad, too, that both Ben and Daisy had written to him, asking him to come and sort out the mess Ben had inherited. There would be plenty of work to occupy him in the coming weeks. Problems to solve. Ruffled feathers to soothe, from what Miss Fairfax had just told him about the tenants. Just the kind of challenge he would enjoy getting his teeth into.

And the mystery of why Miss Fairfax had been crying to solve.

He tugged on Socks's reins and began leading her back down the hill, in what he hoped was the general direction of the house. His stomach suddenly reminded him that he'd set out without having any breakfast. His eyes told him that the sun was so high in the sky now it must be getting near the time for a midday meal of some sort. He couldn't believe he'd been riding about all over the district, all morning. Still, the time he'd spent exploring, and especially the time he'd spent with Miss Fairfax, had been most instructive. He hadn't learned much from the hastily penned letters Lord and Lady Bramhall had, separately, sent him. But now he felt as if he had a much clearer idea of what he had to deal with. And what was more, he also had a feeling that it would be a worthwhile endeavour, not just the excuse he'd seized on to escape the irksome conditions at Wattlesham Priory during the summer house party.

He was looking forward to meeting Miss Fairfax's father. In fact, he rather wished he hadn't promised Miss Fairfax to stay away from him until Sunday, because he sounded like the very person he ought to consult. He would be glad of any tips as to how he ought to proceed.

* * *

Between his occasional recognition of landmarks and Socks's instinct to find her stable, James had made it back to the house without further incident.

His groom, Briggs, took Socks's reins from him in the stable yard, where he'd been lounging against a wall, chewing on a straw as though he had nothing better to do. James went across the yard and entered the house by way of a back door that led into a sort of mud room. There, he sat down on a bench and tugged off the boots which had, he suspected, led Miss Fairfax to assume he must be a working man. Certainly, precious few titled men he knew would be seen abroad in boots that fit so badly he could pull them off without the aid of a valet. But then, they weren't his own.

He shook his head as he recalled the way the Tartar of a cook-cum-housekeeper had scolded him, the night before, when he'd arrived and asked to be shown to his room.

'If you go trailing mud through the house from them boots,' she'd said, ungrammatically, *'you'll be cleaning it up yourself. I got enough to do a-getting of meals on the table, and growing the vegetables to put on that table, and keeping the kitchen in order.'*

That was the first glimmering he'd had that Daisy's warning, about the lack of staff, had not been an exaggeration. Daisy's husband had inherited a house that had two wings aside from the main block, with only three servants to manage the place. Although, from what he'd seen so far, they hadn't managed very much of it. The Tartar did keep the kitchen in order and did keep everyone fed. But she claimed to be able to keep only one bedroom fit for habitation, and, further, that if it didn't suit him, he'd have to bed down in the stables with Wilmot.

Wilmot, James had noticed, with faint surprise, looked vaguely familiar, though he still hadn't placed him. He would, though, in due course, he reflected, as he set aside the boots he'd found in a pile of odd footwear in this mud room and thrust his feet into the morocco slippers he'd left by the bench before going out that morning.

He found his way back to the room he'd been allotted the night before, after taking only one or two wrong turnings, and only as he walked in did he wonder if he ought to have fetched his own can of hot water from the kitchen on the way up. Because, he'd just recalled, there was no way of summoning a servant from that room to fetch whatever he might want.

Perhaps it wasn't so surprising that his younger, pampered sister had thought going abroad preferable to staying in this appallingly run house.

But to his immense relief, when he opened the door to his room he saw his own valet, Bishop, setting out a towel and a fresh set of clothes for his use. There was a can of water with steam still drifting from it upon the floor by a shaving stand, which hadn't been there when last he'd looked.

'The Lord bless you.' James sighed, wondering how on earth the man had both known he would be wanting a wash and also managing to produce the means for him to take it, before he himself had found his way up here.

Bishop quirked one eyebrow. 'The Lord bless you, too,' he said piously, 'my lord.'

James turned his back so that the man could help him out of his riding jacket. And to hide the expression of irritation the man's piety had probably brought to his face. Bishop couldn't help the way he was. And James had nobody to blame but himself for hiring him. 'You have been busy this morning, I see,' he observed, striving to see the benefits of having hired a man with such a strong work ethic. 'Where on earth did you discover that shaving stand?' And what had he done with the dainty little dressing table, so clearly designed for a woman's use, that had been there before?

'I took the liberty of searching out items more appropriate for your use, my lord,' said Bishop. 'And rearranging things in a way that I hope will be to your satisfaction.'

'Indeed they are. You did, I mean,' he finished on a grimace. He really must stop correcting his grammar, whenever he expressed himself so clumsily. Bishop was not his tutor. Just because his valet happened to hold very strict religious principles and raised them at every opportunity, it didn't mean he would even blink at the odd slip of the tongue, coming from his own employer. Or at least he ought not.

'That is,' he said, slipping into the habit he'd fallen into, of late, of explaining himself to this man, 'it wasn't until I set foot in this room, last night, that I fully comprehended what the Tartar who rules the kitchen had meant about me not finding the room suitable.' It was clearly a room last occupied by a female. To be specific, his sister. Which had led him to the further deduction that if this was the only bedroom in the house fit for use, then it meant that his sister, and her husband, must have used it.

He hadn't thought it would matter too much, until he'd got into bed. And had promptly started being plagued by images of what his sister and her husband, as newlyweds, must have done when they'd been occupying it.

Which had led to a most uncomfortable night, during which he'd slept only fitfully, so that this morning he'd got out of bed far earlier than he normally would, using the excuse that he was eager to go out and explore. He had taken the precaution of pulling on boots he could remove himself, by the back door, without having to summon Bishop. Well, he couldn't have summoned Bishop, could he? None of the bell pulls worked, the Kitchen Tartar had gleefully informed him. He suspected that either she or her skinny little assistant were responsible for that. No matter how eccentric the late Earl had been, he couldn't have been so reckless that he'd have removed the means to summon servants.

But anyway, Bishop had effected a subtle transformation in here. It no longer resembled a feminine boudoir, into which a man would venture for only one purpose. It looked like the bedchamber of a bachelor.

'You have worked a miraculous transformation,' said James, pulling off his shirt and going over to the shaving stand, determined to give the man credit where it was due.

'I hardly think so, my lord,' said Bishop repressively, as he poured warm water into a basin. 'Miracles being the work of God and God alone.'

As the valet pinched his lips together, James suddenly saw several things, in rapid succession. The first was that no matter how worthy or hardworking Bishop might be, James was definitely beginning to regret hiring him. A valet had no right to adopt an attitude of constant disapproval for his master. To begin with James had thought it would be an improvement to have a valet with such a highly developed moral code that he wouldn't have to worry about him stealing his cufflinks, or that he'd stumble in to shave him one morning with hands shaking from a hangover, as his predecessor had done, and because he'd seemed the type to support his master's abstemious behaviour. But now he could see that the man's determination to avoid sin in all its forms, as he put it, since his conversion to Methodism, might become a bit of a drawback. Because he could no more tell a lie, or uphold one that someone else had told, than he could dance a jig naked on the high road by moonlight.

Not that James had told a lie, precisely, he thought, as he dipped his hands into the basin, so that he could splash his face with water. He'd just allowed Miss Fairfax to remain unenlightened about the truth.

But if he wished her to remain in that unenlightened state, which he rather thought he did, it meant that from now on, he'd have to start telling people he was *Mr* Dundas, rather than Lord Dundas, and would have to get the staff here, who knew his true identity, to back him up.

His groom would have no trouble in pulling the wool over the locals' eyes. He was a young scamp, who'd think it a lark.

He could probably persuade the other three to indulge him, on payment of sufficient cash.

But Bishop was incorruptible.

He wiped his face with the towel Bishop handed him as he strolled back to the bed, on which the man had laid out a fresh set of clothes, wondering how on earth to solve the problem of Bishop. He couldn't just dismiss the man. He had no grounds. It would be most unfair to turn him off just because he was about to indulge in a bit of behaviour that the man would frown on.

'I hope you approve, my lord, of the raiment I have set out. It did not seem appropriate to dress you in the type of attire you would normally don to take meals in an establishment such as the Priory. Not when you are going to have to sit down in the kitchen,' Bishop said, his whole being quivering with affront, 'with menials.'

It was something of a surprise to hear Bishop, a man who professed to hold strict Christian principles, take exception to his master having to sit at the same table as a valet, a groom and a scullery maid. What about all men being equal in the sight of God?

'This is not,' Bishop continued, 'at all what I am used to. Nor what I hoped for when I entered service with Your Lordship.'

James felt a grin tugging at his mouth, for Bishop had just handed him the solution he needed, on a plate.

'And I gather,' said James, putting his hands on his hips as he studied the clean breeches, shirt, waistcoat and jacket lying on the counterpane, 'you had to sleep in the stables last night?'

Since James had taken the only room deemed fit for habitation in the main house, apart, he assumed, from whatever place the Tartar and her assistant slept in, all the male staff had had to bed down out there.

Bishop breathed in through his nostrils so hard they all but met in the middle. 'I know that our Lord was born in one and that I ought not to complain. But He was a baby at the time, and was probably totally comfortable in a manger. And I have to confess, my lord, that hay is not at all conducive to the comfort of one's back, at my age.'

'I am heartily sorry to hear that,' said James untruthfully. 'It seems hardly worth changing at all,' he observed as he dropped his stained breeches to the floor, 'when I am going to eat in a steamy kitchen. And then this afternoon, you know, I shall probably have to go straight back out to visit more of the tenants.' He'd planned to spend the afternoon in the study, one of the only other rooms in the house that looked as though it had been kept up, going through the accounts, the rent books and so forth. But he could easily go out again, if doing so would help solve the problem of Bishop.

'In fact, I am hardly going to need you at all over the next few weeks,' he said as he picked up the shirt and dropped it over his head. 'And as I can see you are uncomfortable here and that this sort of adventure is not at all what you were hoping for when you gained your position with me,' he added, 'I think this would be the perfect time for you to take a holiday.'

'A holiday?' Bishop uttered the word with as much disapproval as if James had suggested he visit a brothel. 'I have never,' he declared indignantly, 'in all my career, taken leave from my duties. Why, I have only ever taken the liberty of visiting my family when I was between jobs.'

The mention of Bishop's large, and scattered, family, gave James another idea. 'Yes, I know, and that is very commendable, but didn't you mention that brother of yours has a wife who's been ailing ever since the birth of that longed-for son?' Bishop had not been working for him for long, but he'd already learned rather a lot about his numerous siblings and their woes, probably because James had encouraged him to talk about them whenever it looked as though he was about to wax lyrical about one of his favourite sermons.

'I...well, yes, my lord, my sister-in-law is very low, at present,' he said, stooping to pick up the discarded breeches as James stepped into fresh ones, 'but I don't see...'

'Well, why don't you toddle off to visit him and see what you can do to help out? I mean, you are not just good at keeping my clothes in order, are you?' James waved his hand round the room. 'You managed to make this place comfortable, in the space of a morning. So I am sure you could work m— I mean, wonders, with your brother's affairs.'

'Far be it from me to…'

'Only for a couple of weeks, mind,' he said, forcing some sternness into his voice as he tucked his tails into the waistband. 'I am not sure I could manage without you for much longer.' He was perfectly sure he could. Not when it wasn't going to matter what he wore for most of the time. 'Especially,' he pointed out, 'since it is hardly going to matter what I wear to visit farmers and wade round half-flooded fields.'

'But…'

'In fact, why don't you take the curricle?' It wouldn't do to have such a smart, expensive vehicle standing in the stables, where anyone could stumble across it, if he was going to carry off the fiction of being a hardworking, lowly paid steward. And this would be a marvellous way of disposing of both it and the strait-laced valet. 'You could take your sister-in-law out for drives. To take the air by the seaside, perhaps. They are not very far from Brighton, I seem to recall?'

He held out his arms, so that Bishop could slot him into his waistcoat.

'My lord, that is most generous of you, but…'

'Then that is settled,' said James, hearing the note of capitulation in the man's voice. 'Too late for you to set out today, I dare say, which means you will have to spend another night in the stables, I am afraid,' he said, ruthlessly reminding the fellow that conditions at Bramley Park were far from ideal, 'but you should be able to leave tomorrow.'

'Yes, my lord. Thank you, my lord.'

James grinned to himself. That was one hurdle neatly cleared. Without distressing Bishop, or even letting on that he'd become a problem.

Hanged if Miss Fairfax hadn't been right about him. He might have made it in the diplomatic service, after all!

Chapter Four

James glared at the backs of Wilmot, Sally and Briggs, who were walking ahead of him across the meadow, which had once, according to Sally, who'd heard it from her grandmother, been the most beautiful stretch of lawn in the county. He would have glared with equal resentment at the Tartar, if she hadn't said she was staying behind to prepare a lunch for the rest of them for when they returned from church. Apparently, she preferred evensong.

He supposed he could just about accept the reasons why Wilmot and Sally had taken the stand they had. They worked for Lord Bramhall. They had no obligation to support him in his bid to conceal his identity.

But Briggs was his man. Where was *his* loyalty?

'If you're paying them to keep quiet about who you really are,' he'd said, when James had told the others, the moment his valet had driven off in his elegant curricle, that for private reasons, he would

prefer nobody about here knew he was Lady Bramhall's brother, *'then it's not fair not to pay me, too.'*

'I could turn you off without a character,' James had pointed out. Which had only made the rogue's grin spread wider.

'You could, o' course,' said Briggs. 'Only, what would stop me from complaining about my employer, *Lord Dundas*, all over the neighbourhood?'

So here he was, his pockets considerably lighter, following the others to the church, where he hoped he was going to meet Miss Fairfax again. And her father, of course.

Would it be worth it? Worth all the subterfuge and bribery, and inconvenience?

Probably not. In fact, he couldn't think what had come over him. He wasn't given to flights of fancy. Or thinking he'd like to see what it would be like to live as a plain mister. He knew he was better off as a viscount than a man who had to make his own living.

Only...hadn't he been conscious of a growing resentment, that, as the eldest, he couldn't just go off and pursue a career, the way his younger brothers would? That his duty was, primarily, as a place-holder? Someone whose main function in life was to produce the next generation of Earls to run the vast estates the family owned? A feat which he was reluctant to perform, he reflected bitterly, since he could not stomach the prospect of making an alliance with either a ninny or a snob.

He removed his hat, to push his fingers through his hair. Perhaps it wasn't so surprising he'd given in to the temptation to see what it would be like to be plain Mr Dundas. Now that he considered it, he'd been growing heartily sick of Lord Dundas for some time. The apparently prudish, aloof, stick-in-the-mud who appeared too toplofty to condone the games his younger brothers played, games he'd enjoyed himself at their age.

The trouble was, he didn't approve of the way plain Mr Dundas was behaving so far, either.

He sighed. Church would perhaps be a good place for him to sit and contemplate his next move. Perhaps it would be best to make a clean breast of it. He could explain to Miss Fairfax, if she should remonstrate with him about the apparent deception, that…

Only, there his mind sank into a morass of half-thoughts. There was no excuse that would appease a girl of her temperament.

But if he didn't confess, he'd have to keep on shelling out to these rogues of servants. He'd even had to pay Wilmot extra, that morning, for a shave, even though James had, eventually, worked out why he'd looked familiar. The man had been Lord Bramhall's body servant, from his army days. And had acted as his valet.

'*Yes, my lord, I do have experience valeting,*' Wilmot had said when James had asked him if he'd help him smarten up for church. '*But I ain't your valet. If you want a shave, you can either go to a barber, or pay me what you would for the service in such a place.*'

Once a week, James vowed, as he watched the two

men helping the skinny little scullery maid over a
tumbled section of stone wall, which he was certain
she could have stepped across completely unaided.
He would only pay Wilmot once a week for a really
good shave. The rest of the week he would either do
without, or have a go at shaving himself. How hard
could it be?

Damn, but this was getting complicated.

But not boring, he reflected as he came to the
tumbledown wall himself. No, certainly not boring.

Unlike the sermon, which, combined with the
heat in the stuffy little church, sent several of the
older parishioners into a doze. Their snores rose in
volume the longer the sermon went on. Combined
with the cooing of the pigeons somewhere up on the
roof, James very nearly dozed off himself. The only
thing that kept him awake was the knowledge that
Miss Fairfax was sitting three pews in front of him,
on the other side of the aisle. She was sitting in between a bulky older man and a slender older lady.
He assumed they were her mother and father. But
since she hadn't turned round, he hadn't been able
to greet her, or them.

It didn't stop him watching her as she stood up
and sat down, or knelt at all the appropriate places,
though. And admiring her trim figure, or the gloss-
iness of the one or two curls that peeped out from
beneath the confines of a bonnet that was the exact
same shade of greeny-brown as her spencer.

But at last, the vicar descended from the pulpit,

the congregation yawned and woke up, and everyone shuffled to the door, where, he suspected, if the people here were like the rest of the human race, they'd all gather in the churchyard to gossip.

His assumption proved to be correct. Not only did people gather to gossip, but they were also lingering to take a look at him. Not because he was anyone in particular, he suspected, but simply because he was a stranger.

It wasn't long before the stocky, older man who'd been sitting with Miss Fairfax came bustling over, his hand extended. James saw at a glance where Miss Fairfax got her diminutive stature from. It wasn't often that James met men who had to look up to him, in a literal sense.

'Good morning,' said the man, grasping his hand and pumping it up and down. 'Colonel Fairfax, at your service. You came with the party from Bramley Park, I perceive. Welcome to Bramley Bythorne. Come to take over the running of the place in His Lordship's absence, have you? You have the look of something more than a groom, or a footman,' he concluded, running a shrewd gaze over James.

Now was the time to put things right. To tell the man that, no, actually, he was Lady Bramhall's oldest brother. That he was a viscount in his own right, and heir to the earldom of Darwen.

Only, Miss Fairfax had just stepped up to her father's side. And a ray of sunlight was falling across her face. Now those eyes were no longer puffy from weeping and the blotches had dissolved from her

cheeks, he saw that his first impression had been
correct. She was extremely pretty. Not in the languid, deliberate way of so many of the debutantes
thrust at him in London, or in the vulgar, showy way
of the girls who attended country house parties to
amuse the male guests, but in an unaffected, vibrant,
breathtaking way.

At least, he felt a curious sensation of breathless-
ness. And when he tried to speak, all that came out
of his mouth was a sort of gasping grunt. The sort of
grunt he'd make should someone land a lucky punch
to his stomach.

'Meet the wife,' said Colonel Fairfax, making
James aware that the older woman who'd been sit-
ting next to Miss Fairfax had stepped up to the
Colonel's side.

Mrs Fairfax looked him up and down, making him
aware, with the slight lifting of one brow, and the
pinching of her lips, that apart from being an inartic-
ulate fool, his coat did not fit as well as it might have
considering this was a Sunday, that he hadn't tied his
neckcloth with any great degree of success and that
his shoes could have done with a bit more polish. He'd
claimed he could do without Bishop, but only two
days after the man had left him his sartorial elegance
was slipping away like butter from a toasted crumpet.

Yet, perversely, her disdain made him feel like
grinning as he bowed from the waist because she
was the first mother of a marriageable daughter who
hadn't gone into raptures the moment she'd gained
an introduction.

'And this is my daughter,' Colonel Fairfax continued, as Miss Fairfax dipped a curtsy, smiled and blushed.

She really was stunningly lovely, in her Sunday best. Her gown wasn't all-over frills, but fell neatly to her feet. The bonnet framed her face perfectly, leaving just a few dusky curls peeping out, tantalisingly, and her spencer hugged her bosom in a becoming manner. He supposed she'd set out to look neat and orderly, and modest. Certainly, if she appeared at the Chapel Royal in such a get-up, he reckoned most of the matrons present would say so. The younger women, those whose idea of attracting a man involved wreathing themselves in frills and flounces, might well look askance at her plain attire. But he didn't think he'd ever seen a woman who looked more attractive.

He wished he could tell her so, without sounding like a fathead. If only he had more practice at paying pretty women compliments, he could have come up with one of those phrases he'd heard others employ. Such as, that he'd never thought he'd find such a rose blossoming among the thorns, which would be rather apt, actually, since this village was Bramley By*thorne*, or...

Hang it! He'd always thought such phrases ridiculous when uttered by men he'd previously thought intelligent.

But how on earth did a man pay a pretty woman a genuinely felt compliment, without sounding like a mountebank?

Mrs Fairfax cleared her throat, making James suddenly aware that he'd been standing, gazing at Miss Fairfax for several moments, with his mouth open.

'I…er…' he said, deciding it really was time he said something. No matter what. 'I am charmed to make your acquaintance,' he blurted.

Miss Fairfax shot him a look of gratitude, then lowered her eyes demurely and began fiddling with the strings of her reticule in a perfectly innocent manner, yet all of a sudden he was imagining what those fingers would feel like, making those same fluttery little movements over his flesh.

At which point, all the blood in his body converged in the worst possible place. Thankfully, he'd removed his hat before making his bow to Mrs Fairfax and he was holding it over the offending part of his anatomy already, otherwise he'd have disgraced himself.

'You must come and dine with us,' said Colonel Fairfax, jerking James's attention away from his lovely daughter.

Mrs Fairfax shot her husband a look of exasperation. Which thankfully awoke James's sense of humour to the extent his brain began to tick over again.

'I should be glad to,' said James, miraculously regaining the power of lucid speech. 'As I believe you are the man to speak to about local affairs?'

'Well, I don't know about that,' said the Colonel, puffing up with pleasure at the compliment. 'But I've lived hereabouts for a good few years. And I've always known how many beans make five.'

'Then, if you have the time, I should like to consult with you.'

'Of course! You need not say it. You have the devil of a mess to sort out on Bramhall's estates. Beg your pardon, my dear,' he said to his wife, who'd prodded him with her parasol the moment he uttered the profanity. 'Comes of being a military man,' he announced to the churchyard at large.

'But anyhow,' the Colonel continued, 'you don't want to jump in with both feet only to find yourself in the mire. Don't want to tread on the wrong toes and so forth. Much better to consult with me before you go off half-cocked. So we'll expect you tomorrow evening. At four?'

'Thank you, Colonel,' said James, bowing once more as the Fairfax party turned and began to make their way across the churchyard.

James stood watching them go, admiring the rear view of Miss Fairfax as she swished away. So he saw the exact moment she glanced over her shoulder and mouthed the words 'thank you' at him. Though he already knew she was grateful he hadn't revealed the fact they'd already met. She'd made him aware of it the very moment he'd said he was pleased to make her acquaintance. She hadn't needed to mouth the words as well. But he was glad she had. Glad to know that he'd pleased her.

Which astonished him. And would astonish those who knew him well, if they'd witnessed his sudden lack of aplomb. Why, if any of his brothers ever found out that he was putting himself out to please a woman, there'd be no end to their teasing.

And he'd deserve it. First of all he'd lost the power of speech, then experienced what he could only describe as an erotic fantasy, and now he was standing rooted to the spot, gazing after a female. And it wasn't the first time, either. He'd done exactly the same that first morning. He'd watched until she'd disappeared into those trees, on her father's land, hadn't he? As though he couldn't drag his eyes away from her.

Was this what was known as a *coup de foudre*? No, no, surely not. That was supposed to happen on the first meeting, wasn't it? And he hadn't been struck dumb the first time he'd seen her. On the contrary, he'd never found it so easy to speak to a female. In fact, he couldn't remember the last time he'd just chatted with anyone, male or female, in the way he'd done with her. Most of the conversations he'd had of late had been heavily larded with sighs and complaints of boredom. And interspersed with criticism of the present company. Or mockery of the ludicrous fashions the more flamboyant of their set were trying out.

And he hadn't felt anything remotely amorous, in her regard, not then. He'd been intrigued by her, yes. Amused, too. And more than a touch troubled about what she might have done that had made her sound so guilty whenever she mentioned Lord Bramhall.

But now he was shaking hands with various people without registering who they were. Nodding and responding to them without engaging his brain at all.

And when the crowd eventually began to thin, and he set out on the return journey to Bramley Park, the vision of Miss Fairfax's lovely face kept on swimming into his mind, so that he had scarcely any idea of where he was going. If it hadn't been for the servants walking along in front of him, he doubted he'd have been able to find his way home.

Was this love? Surely not. He couldn't be in love with Miss Fairfax. He scarcely knew her.

But time, he reminded himself practically, would remedy that. Over the next few weeks he would take every chance he could to meet with her. Speak to her. Get to know her better. Because if nothing else, she was like a breath of fresh air. And he wanted to breathe her again. There was nothing wrong with that, was there? But as to love…

He frowned. Because before he would admit to anyone, himself included, that he was in love with her, or in danger of being so, he was going to have to get her to tell him what, exactly, she had been crying about, that morning he first met her.

Chapter Five

'I wondered,' said Mother, looking at Betsy through narrowed eyes, as they set off for home, 'why you took so much trouble with your appearance this morning. I take it that you heard that there was a newcomer to the parish. A young, unmarried man, but,' she added sternly, 'I sincerely hope you are not thinking of setting your cap at *him*.'

'Of course I am not,' said Betsy vehemently. Because it was the truth. She might have taken a teeny bit more trouble with her appearance this morning, when getting dressed for church, but it was not because she had any intention of setting her cap at Mr Dundas. It was more a question of pride. Last time he'd seen her, she'd been wearing a dress that was such a mess, due to her flinging herself to the ground, that he'd mistaken her for a farmer's daughter and had practically accused her of trespassing. Which had, technically, been true, but if there was anything more annoying than being caught out in a misdeed it was knowing that the person doing the reprimanding was completely justified. Which had made her lose what little hold she'd had on her temper, so that she'd been unforgivably rude. And then a good deal more blunt with him and revealing in what she'd said than had been prudent. Then, when she'd reached home, she'd taken one swift glance in the mirror and seen exactly why he might have thought what he had. Not only was her dress a mess, not only had she not behaved the slightest bit the way a properly brought-up young lady should, but her face had been in an ugly, blotchy, dirty state as well. Which she should have known. She wasn't one of those women who could cry without ruining their looks. Her nose ran and her eyes puffed up. And at some point she must have wiped her tears away with a hand that wasn't all that clean, to judge from the smuts and smears all over her face.

So, naturally, she'd decided to take the opportunity to show him that she *was* a properly brought-up young lady, rather than the rag-mannered hoyden he'd encountered on the hill.

'Good,' said Mother, her steps lengthening into what someone who was much braver than Betsy might have described as an unladylike stride. 'Because he is entirely unsuitable. He has to *work* for a living. And need I remind you that, though your father may only be the third son of a grandson of a viscount, *my* father was the second son of the Duke of Mainwaring.'

No, Mother had no need to remind her. She'd been

repeating the same thing on a regular basis ever since Betsy could remember.

'You need not point out that *I* made that mistake,' said Mother, with bitterness. 'That I married beneath me. That I was carried away on a tide of romantic nonsense—' and probably, Betsy had often thought, a good deal too much champagne '—heightened by the moonlight,' Mother continued, oblivious to her daughter's private speculation, 'and the way your father's scarlet coat fitted his broad shoulders.'

It was very, very hard to imagine Papa had ever been a dashing young officer, looking romantic in a scarlet uniform. She couldn't recall, for one thing, a time when his hair hadn't been white, and his chest was now all but indistinguishable from his waist. But it must have been the case. Because she couldn't see why else Mother, who was so conscious of her social superiority, could possibly have married him. She never had a good word to say about him. Or to him, for that matter.

'I don't want you throwing yourself away on a nobody, the way I did.' Which was something she'd told Betsy, also on a regular basis, ever since her fourteenth birthday. And which wasn't, strictly speaking, true. Papa might not be a lord, but he was definitely not a nobody. He came from a good family, if not such an exalted one as Mother's. But, which Betsy considered far more important, he gained the respect of just about everyone he met, because of his intelligence and his character. People respected and trusted him. What more could a woman want from a husband?

'And what is more,' Mother was continuing, 'it is your duty to marry well, so that you may restore our fortunes.'

Betsy knew it was her duty to marry well. That was the duty of every decent and well-brought-up young lady. But she was starting to resent Mother's insistence that it was her duty to restore the family fortunes. Betsy wasn't the one who'd gambled them away, was she? No, that had been Mother. However, since pointing this out would accomplish nothing, would, indeed, only earn her a severe scolding, she sensibly held her tongue.

'When *you* select a husband,' Mother continued, gripping her reticule so tightly it looked as if she was strangling an eel, 'you must keep a cool head. You must consider the suitability of the man, not what he looks like, or how charmingly he pays you compliments, or, God forbid, the way he sets off a uniform.' None of which applied to Mr Dundas, so why was Mother saying this again, just now? He wasn't in uniform. He'd certainly never paid her any compliments. And most women would not call him handsome, she didn't suppose. At least, he didn't resemble all those foppish eligible men she'd met during her Season who were generally described as being handsome.

Though she did find his rugged, manly looks very attractive, she had to admit.

'You are pretty enough,' Mother was saying, 'and well connected enough to be choosy.'

Hah! And look what good being choosy, during her one and only London Season, had been. Here she was, unwed, with no dowry left to speak of and with the threat of Great-Aunt Cornelia perpetually hanging over her like some kind of geriatric, acid-tongued sword of Damocles.

Mother prodded her with one bony, gloved finger. So Betsy dutifully said 'Yes, Mother', in as meek a tone as she could, although she was still nursing a deep sense of injustice on that score. For, while Betsy had been dutifully turning down the most flattering proposals from men who would have made perfectly reasonable husbands, Mother had spent the Season hobnobbing with her ducal relations, on the pretext, she still kept on insisting, of procuring invitations to the kind of events where Betsy could meet men worthy of her lineage.

The trouble with those ducal relations, however, was that none of them thought twice about playing cards for ridiculously large amounts of money. When Mother had been unable to settle the debts herself and had to apply to Papa, he had, well, exploded. There was no other word to describe it. There had been shouting and slamming doors, and weeping all over the house. Even in front of the servants. And then they'd all quit London, with Papa vowing never to take either of them there ever again.

Which was patently unfair, since Betsy had not put a foot wrong.

Mother sighed as they turned off the main street and on to the lane which led to their front gates.

'There, well, enough said. You are a good girl, I don't deny it. You have done your best, under the most trying of circumstances.'

Yes, she had. She'd done as Mother had told her, time and time again. But what good had it done? She was single and so poor, now, that it looked as though, in spite of Mother's plots and schemes, she would have no alternative but to go to work as a companion to an elderly relative so cantankerous that she had to hire new companions as often as most ladies sent their smalls to the laundry. Because Papa was talking about selling this house, and going to live somewhere cheaper. Where he'd be a nobody, instead of the most respected man in the neighbourhood. Oh, and if there had been anything she could have done to avert such a disastrous fate befalling the dear man, when none of it was his fault, she would have done it. *Had* done it.

But all to no effect.

'If only I'd married a man with real money,' Mother was saying bitterly as she pushed open the double gates to the front drive. 'Or a title. Someone who couldn't sell his house, because it would be entailed,' she said, looking up at the ivy-clad frontage of the only home Betsy could remember.

Papa, who had lingered in the churchyard, chatting to his cronies, chose this moment to catch up with them.

'Perhaps I wish I'd married a woman who could think of anyone but herself,' he barked, making his presence known. And the fact that he'd overheard the last bit of Mother's complaint. 'A woman who would think twice before frittering away her daughter's dowry!'

'I was doing it *for* Betsy,' Mother protested, whirling round to face her husband.

As Papa began to launch into his usual response to Mother's excuses, Betsy sidled away from the pair. Neither of them noticed her leave. These days, they never seemed to notice whether she was there or not, so intent were they on their never-ending quarrel. Which was what had made it so easy for her to slip away and spend the whole morning up on the hill, under the oak tree, the day she'd met Mr Dundas. The only time her parents stopped shouting at each other was when there were other people present, when they spoke to each other through clenched-teeth smiles in the hopes of concealing the fact that they were now existing in a state of perpetual warfare.

Which was why she was glad someone was coming to dinner tomorrow. They might be able to get through the entire meal without anyone throwing dishes or cutlery at anyone else. It wasn't because it was Mr Dundas, necessarily. Anyone would have done just as well to act as a damper.

Anyone, she repeated, as she ran upstairs to put her bonnet and spencer away.

An opinion she revised the next morning at breakfast, when Papa brazenly revealed that while he'd been lingering in the churchyard, he'd invited not only the vicar and his wife, but a couple of men who served on the parish council and even Mr Humboldt, who held the office of parish constable, as well as running the smithy.

'Never,' said Mother, setting down her teacup with such precision that Betsy could tell she'd been on the verge of flinging it, 'have I had such a set of nobodies sitting down at a table over which I am expected to preside.'

Betsy, who could see the way it was likely to go, grabbed two slices of toast and began buttering them swiftly.

'I promised the lad to introduce him to men who'd put him in the way of finding out about local affairs,' said Papa, buttering his own slice of bread with defiant strokes of his knife.

Betsy seized the opportunity to reach for the pot of marmalade while nobody else was interested in it.

'Yes, but when arranging a dinner party,' said Mother, 'one ought to consider the seating arrangements. There are entirely too many men.'

'You wish me to include their wives?' Papa asked her, raising his eyes from his plate, a challenging gleam in his eye.

Mother glared at him, breathing in and out deeply, her lips twitching as she chose, and discarded, several pithy words, from the looks of it. It was one thing having a bunch of parish councillors at her table, when the topic was local affairs, but if she included their wives, then she'd have to entertain them in the drawing room, after, while the men carried on discussing their business.

'It would be better,' Mother said tartly, as Betsy smeared the marmalade over both her slices of buttered toast, 'to just have them attend you in your study, the way you usually do. Then I wouldn't have to be bothered with them at all.'

'Perhaps it is past time you were a bit more bothered about what you term ordinary people,' said Papa. 'Perhaps I should have just invited their wives without consulting you.' He leaned back in his chair with a rather reckless air, as Betsy crammed as much of the first slice of toast as she could into her mouth. 'Would be just like the kind of dinners over which I used to preside, when I was a bachelor. In the army. Those women, with whom you wouldn't deign to rub shoulders, used to be very jolly.'

'I notice,' said Mother with a sniff, 'that you don't refer to them as ladies.'

'Because they weren't ladies. And had no pretensions to being anything other than what they were. And they were a damned sight better company than you turned out to be.'

'Perhaps you should have married one of them, then,' said Mother, gripping the handle of her teacup with a dangerous glint in her eye.

Betsy grabbed her second slice of toast even though she was still chewing her first, got up and left the table. It was clearly going to be one of those days when she'd need to keep well out of the way, or risk getting dragged in to bolster one parent against the other. A thing she could never, ever bring herself to do.

Normally, on a day when hostilities between her parents raged unchecked, and bystanders risked getting caught in the crossfire, Betsy would go out for a walk, most often making for the oak tree, which had become a favourite spot to sit and look down on the village of Bramley Bythorne. But she didn't think that would be a good idea today. Because if Mr Dundas happened to be riding in that direction and happened to see her sitting there, he might think she was hoping to meet him again. And she *wasn't*. And even if she was, she was going to see him tonight, wasn't she? And what sort of girl hung about under trees in the hopes of seeing a man they *knew* they were going to see that night?

Girls with no pride.

Or girls who were too stupid to have learned any lessons from mistakes they'd made before.

Since she fell into neither category, she decided to stay within her own grounds, rather than venturing out into areas where she risked coming across Mr Dundas, even if it wasn't under that oak tree.

It had made it much harder to dodge Mother and Papa, so what with one thing and another, Betsy was rather wrung out by the time the first guest, Mr Slocombe, arrived.

Mother, though, appeared to have worked herself up into one of her moods of cold fury, because her reception of the man was so chillingly polite that he swiftly backed away, looking as though he'd just been run through with a sharpened icicle.

Betsy, who'd always rather liked the man who ran the grocery, as well as sitting on the parish council, tried to put her own nerves aside, stepping in front of him before he blundered into any of the furniture.

'How lovely to see you, Mr Slocombe,' she said, taking another step so that she was physically between the poor man and her furious mother. 'Would you care for a jug of ale?'

He swallowed, looking as though a jug of ale was exactly what he needed.

'Do step over to the sideboard,' Betsy continued, waving in the direction of the refreshments that had somehow been arranged, in spite of all Mother's refusal to take any part in the planning of what she considered to be a calculated insult on Papa's part.

She was probably correct in that assumption, Betsy reflected, as one by one, the humble locals appeared, and started clustering round Papa. It was as though he was, nowadays, doing all he could to rub Mother's nose in his own fairly humble origins by consorting with men he kept on saying were worth ten of any society fribble or monied, conceited aristocrat.

And delivering a deliberate insult now, by inviting them into his house to dine and obliging her to act as hostess.

Mother only unbent, and that very slightly, when the Reverend Knowles with his wife, the only female invited to attend, arrived, but only as far as to take the arm of Mrs Knowles, steer her to a sofa set by the window overlooking the garden and lean in to launch into what looked like the kind of conversation Betsy had no wish to overhear.

Mr Dundas was the last to arrive and the only person who appeared totally unmoved by the gorgon-like stare with which Mother had frozen so many others. Far from avoiding her, and joining the cluster of men who were huddled round Papa like so many sheep taking shelter beneath the nearest oak when a thunderstorm was raging, he strode nonchalantly across to her sofa, made a bow that wouldn't have looked out of place in a society drawing room and thanked her for receiving him into her home.

So, he was as brave as his rugged looks suggested. But not a braggart, for he didn't swagger over to join the rest of the men, who were looking at him in varying states of awe. He just acted as if he'd done nothing out of the ordinary.

'Good evening, Miss Fairfax,' he said, as he came to where she was standing, pouring out jugs of ale for Papa's guests. 'You, ah, have a lovely home,' he said, accepting a tankard from her hand.

'Thank you. I think so,' she said, touched with sadness by the thought that very soon, if nothing happened to prevent it, they would all be leaving it.

'And acres of land around it,' he added, with a teasing smile. 'Just as you told me.'

'Shh,' she hissed. 'How could I have done any such thing, when we are only supposed to have met on Sunday, in the churchyard?'

'Ah, yes. I must have heard it from somewhere else. My memory,' he said, shaking his head sadly. 'It happens to us all, with advancing age.'

'You cannot be more than thirty,' she said.

He clapped his hand to his heart. 'Do I look so old to you? I vow I am not a day over twenty-four. But perhaps that seems old to you, when you can hardly be more than eighteen.'

She tossed her head as though offended, although what woman could really be offended when a man claimed to believe she was much younger than she really was? 'I had my come-out when I was eighteen. I will have you know I am all of twenty years old.'

'As old as that? And unmarried still? I find that hard to believe. What is wrong with the men in this locality?'

'There is nothing wrong with the men in this lo-cality.' No, that did not sound right! 'That is to say, I am extremely choosy—' She broke off, her cheeks growing hot, because since the humiliating encounter with Ben, she could no longer claim that was true.

'What are you saying,' said Papa, choosing that moment to come over and greet his guest of honour, 'to put my Betsy to the blush?'

'I...er...um,' said Mr Dundas, his own cheeks turning an interesting shade of red.

'Well, you had better not do it again. My wife is looking daggers at you. Don't want to fall foul of *her*,' he said with a shudder. 'Come and meet some of the best fellows I could round up at such short notice. Excuse us, my dear,' he said to Betsy, giving her what looked suspiciously like a slight wink as he turned Mr Dundas round, took him by the elbow and led him over to the flock of parish councillors. He'd winked? When it had looked as though she and Mr Dundas had been flirting? Why…that must mean… Papa *approved* of him.

Or did it? Perhaps he was just being conspiratorial, because she'd done something in public of which Mother *dis*approved?

When it was time to go in for dinner, Papa bade Mr Dundas sit next to him, at the head of the table, while Mother and Mrs Knowles sat at the foot.

'Betsy, come and sit with us,' said Mother, indicating a chair on her left. 'There is no point in you sitting anywhere else, because you won't be able to join in with the conversation.'

'It will be all turnips and drainage, and Speenhamland, I shouldn't wonder,' said Mrs Knowles with a titter.

And, since Mother had made it clear she had no intention of acting as hostess over such a motley collection of diners, let alone trying to steer the conversation into what she would deem acceptable topics for the dining table, and Papa was in the mood to demonstrate that he was in charge of the room, the party and his wife, the prophecy made by Mrs Knowles came true.

Mr Slocombe put forth his view on the benefit of growing turnips, timidly, darting nervous glances in Mother's direction. But Mr Humboldt puffed out his chest, as though determined to show that nobody was going to prevent him from saying exactly what he thought about landlords who turned good, hardworking men out of their homes on the slightest pretext.

'What,' asked Mr Dundas, as though he was really interested, 'do you mean by that?'

'Well, you must have seen that many properties stand empty and in a state of disrepair,' said Papa. 'And it is entirely due to the fact that the late Lord Bramhall drove as many men as he could from the area with his infamous policies.'

'I think you will find,' put in Mr Warner, a sidesman, who'd clearly gained courage from Mr Humboldt's act of bravado, 'that the rot started in the time of his father, who enclosed much of the common land, thereby obliging many of the labouring men to seek work in the towns.'

'Yes,' snorted the Reverend Knowles. 'And then when they grew too old to be fit to work in those factories any longer they came slinking back to claim aid from the parish where they were born. Disgraceful state of affairs.'

From that point on, the discussion about what exactly was wrong in the state of Bramley Bythorne grew more animated by the minute. Mr Dundas interposed a few questions which, although Betsy didn't understand why it should be so, caused Papa to look at him with growing respect and the other men to nod and say he'd made a good point.

To his credit, the compliments didn't appear to go to his head. He accepted them, then just carried on listening to the others as they exchanged various warmly held, and totally contrary, views with increasing vehemence. His reticence was not because he was shy, she didn't think. After all, Mother had not terrified him into fleeing to the consolation of the refreshment table, the way she'd terrified Mr Slocombe. Nor was he bombastic, which she had to own Papa was growing, as he attempted to make the others fall in with his position. Nor was he sanctimonious, like the vicar, who was starting to annoy everyone by referring every problem to some text in the Bible that sounded completely irrelevant.

He was the only person there who seemed completely at ease. Who appeared content with his position and felt no need to swagger and shout to try to make himself out to be more important or influential than he was.

Mother, suddenly, got to her feet. The conversation, which was growing rather animated, ceased abruptly.

'The atmosphere prevailing around this table is not suitable for ladies,' she said icily. 'We shall therefore withdraw.'

So Betsy, too, had to take her leave.

Only this time, because she hadn't had the forethought to eat as swiftly as was compatible with decent table manners, she hadn't anywhere near finished with her meal.

Chapter Six

'I cannot believe,' said Mother, walking to one of the chairs pulled up in front of the fireplace, 'that he would invite such a parcel of men to my house and expect me to act as hostess to them.' She sat down and twitched her shawl round her shoulders. It was growing chilly as evening drew in. And, of course, there was no question of lighting a fire. Not with Papa so determined to make household economies to offset the vast amount Mother had squandered.

'He's becoming quite the radical,' Mrs Knowles tittered as she went to take the chair on the other side of the hearth.

Betsy went straight to the sofa tucked just behind the door. She'd discovered recently that it was one of the least draughty spots in the room, and therefore the least uncomfortable in which to sit of an evening. Where once the fireplace had been the prime spot, Betsy would not now choose to sit there even if Mother didn't still consider it as her right. Cold, damp air seemed to whistle down the unheated chimney whenever the wind got up and trickled down it at all other times.

'No,' said Mother bitterly. 'He's just doing whatever he can to spite me. He—' She stopped short of admitting Mrs Knowles completely into her confidence. Because, Betsy supposed, if the vicar's wife knew that the current state of affairs had come about because of Mother's gambling, she risked forfeiting her sympathy. Instead, she put on a martyred air. 'But enough of me. What do you make of young Mr Dundas?'

Betsy's ears pricked up. She'd expected the two older ladies to fall into their usual habit of sharing whatever titbits of gossip they'd heard since last meeting, before advancing to the more pleasurable pastime of picking various people's reputations to shreds. Only once had she been tempted to join in and that was when they'd been discussing Lady Bramhall. To her shame, she'd said one or two rather spiteful things about the girl who'd married Ben. But that had been on the day she'd had to report back to Mother that he was married when she was still churning with a mixture of guilt, horror and mortification at what she'd done.

She'd wanted to lash out at someone, even though it was herself she'd been angry with, and since Lady Bramhall had been the one to catch her in the very act, naturally a lot of her emotion had spewed out in a torrent of insults aimed at the woman who'd ruined Mother's scheme. A scheme she should *never* had agreed to take part in. But, in that frame of mind, she'd told Mother that Ben's wife was like a bean-pole, she was so tall and skinny, and had a lot of yellow hair. Whereas, in fact, Lady Bramhall was stunningly beautiful. And rich, as they later discovered. And seemed every inch a lady. She could have easily ruined Betsy's reputation by telling everyone she'd discovered her hanging off her husband's neck, attempting to get him to kiss her, but she hadn't taken any of the opportunities she'd had to say as much as a single disparaging word.

She would never, she had vowed when Ben and his wife had left the area, ever, let jealousy and spite make her say nasty things about another female, ever again. Or attempt to kiss a man who did not want to kiss her back.

Mother, she reflected, eyeing her parent rue-fully, had made it sound as though what she would be doing would be no more than a lark. A lark carried out by a rather daring, bold, dashing kind of girl who was prepared to do whatever she could to save her family from penury. She'd agreed to walk over to Bramley Park and see Ben, imagining herself as a heroine in a story, boldly seizing the future by the scruff of the neck and pushing it in the direction that would be best for all.

Best for Papa, who wouldn't need to find her a dowry if she could get Ben to fall in love with her. Best for Mama, who would no longer face Papa's wrath for losing that dowry. Best for the people of Bramley Bythorne because, if she didn't have to go to Tunbridge Wells to work for a horrid-sounding lady, she'd be able to stay in the area helping to put right all the wrongs that had brought such hardship to so many people. And, yes, she had to admit, best for herself, because Ben was her last chance at making a good match if she was never going to be able to return to London for another Season.

And as for Ben, well, she might not love him, but she'd vowed she would be the best wife any man had ever had. She'd support him and help him and never, ever moan about the fact she could have married better, or fling any of his irritating habits in his face, because he was bound to have plenty…

But the moment Ben had gone rigid with distaste, all her castles in the air had come tumbling down. She'd suddenly wondered how she would have felt if the situation had been reversed. If some man she hardly knew had come into *her* house by a back way and kissed *her* without the slightest provocation.

And she'd felt sick. Sick with shame.

'He seems very gentlemanly,' Mrs Knowles said tentatively, pulling Betsy's attention back to what was going on in this very room, rather than an episode she wished she could erase from her memory, yet which kept on rising to the forefront of her mind at the slightest provocation.

Mother sniffed. 'Seems,' she sneered. 'Men can *seem* to be all sorts of things, but always end up being a huge disappointment. Oh, not your husband, of course. As a man of the cloth…'

Mrs Knowles sighed. 'I fear that even he…' She

fumbled in her reticule for a handkerchief. 'I mean, not that I have any real cause to complain, it is just that when we married, I had such high hopes of advancement. The bishop said…' She shook her head. 'But we are still here, in a rural parish with a dwindling congregation…'

At this point Betsy did stop listening. The two ladies had endless complaints about their husbands, which often turned into a sort of competition about who had the most to put up with from their unsatisfying spouse. It was amazing that Mother should be so determined to marry Betsy off, when she clearly held such negative views of her own husband and, it often seemed, men in general. But then, what else could a woman do to earn her keep? If she couldn't find a husband she'd either have to stay with her parents for ever, or take up some genteel yet deadly dull form of employment such as that of paid companion to a wealthy and cantankerous old lady.

Anyway, if they'd known any more about Mr Dundas than she already did, then they would be talking about him. The fact that they'd returned to their usual topic of their unsatisfactory spouses meant they didn't.

So she picked up her work bag, which she'd left on the little table by the sofa earlier, and took out the bit of canvas she'd been embroidering for some weeks. The hassocks in the church were all very worn and there were not many ladies in the area who had either the time, or the skills, to effect repairs. And it felt like a suitable penance to perform. A way to atone for her dreadful behaviour with Ben, since stitching the finished designs on to the stiff hessian backs took a good deal of effort.

She had calculated, over the evenings spent trying to shut out either Mother and Papa's arguments, or vapid and unpleasant gossiping such as Mother and Mrs Knowles were indulging in now, that it would take her approximately seventy-two years to repair and re-cover every single kneeler in the church. She had worked this out in her head by tallying the number of hours she had so far spent on the ones she'd completed and multiplying it by the number of kneelers in the church.

Would she feel absolved of her sin by then? Or would nothing ever wash away the stain of having deliberately attempted to compromise a man into marriage, only to discover that man already was married? Perhaps dwindling into a shrivelled spinster with calloused fingers, a stooped back and failing eyesight would be a just punishment for what she'd done.

Only, if Papa never did manage to turn his fortunes round and had to sell this house, and they all really did have to move away from here, she'd have to go to Tunbridge Wells. Papa had explained how, with one less mouth to feed, he might still be able to keep a couple of indoor servants so that Mother would still be able to hold her head up in public. And then the punishment would take a different form. Which perhaps would be more fitting for her, since it had been her dread of exile to the place which had, finally, driven her to make that doomed attempt to make Ben fall in love with her. She could admit it now. In fact, she'd started to face the truth about her motives the day that Mr Dundas had found her sitting under the oak tree. That was what had made her cry so bitterly.

But after a day like today Betsy couldn't help wondering if going to Tunbridge Wells would be such a bad thing, after all. Could it possibly be any worse than things as they were in Bramley Bythorne nowadays? Perhaps Great-Aunt Cornelia was not as bad as everyone said...

Which was the big stumbling block, wasn't it? She didn't know Great-Aunt Cornelia, except by reputation. At least she knew Mother, and Papa, and all the people living here. She recognised the signs that meant it would be wise to duck and take cover and where to go to avoid the most unpleasant of scenes. That oak tree on Ben's land had been one of her favourites, until the risk of running into Mr Dundas up there had put it out of bounds. For, up there, looking down at the rotting roofs of the villagers and the cold grey slate of her own home, she felt above it all. Or as though she could rise above it all, all the petty squabbles and myriad miseries of village life. Somehow.

The sound of booted feet in the passageway, then the front door opening, caused conversation by the fireplace to pause.

'It sounds as if they are leaving,' said Mrs Knowles.

'Good. Because if he'd dared to invite any of that...rabble, into my drawing room...' Mother petered out, but the way she sat up straighter, rearranging the folds of her shawl, made her look as if she was preparing to go into battle.

Betsy braced herself as the door to the drawing room opened. Naturally, the Reverend Knowles would come in to collect his wife and might take a cup of tea before he left. Mother wouldn't mind that. But she shuddered to think what would happen, over the next few days, if Papa dared to flout his wife's notions of who was a suitable guest for their drawing room.

When Mr Dundas came in, right behind the vicar, Betsy wasn't sure what Mother would make of him. Neither, to judge from her face, was Mother herself. If it had been any of the parish councillors, Mother would have been so frosty that they would know they had intruded where they had no business to go, but Mother was not yet certain of Mr Dundas's standing. He seemed to be a gentleman and, surely, if he had the job of a steward to a great estate, even if it was an estate that had seen better days, he must be both well educated and also have connections to some of the noble houses.

Mr Dundas certainly entered the room with every appearance of ease, as though joining ladies after dinner was something he did on a regular basis. Instead of cowering, or cringing, the way any of the parish councillors would have done if Papa had tried to coax them into this feminine sanctuary, he merely bowed to Mother before glancing round and then making straight for her sofa.

'You have most skilful fingers,' he remarked, then shifted from one foot to another. 'That is, the embroidery is very fine,' he said, indicating the work on her lap. 'I mean to say, um, are you a keen needlewoman?'

So he wasn't as confident as he appeared. He certainly hadn't been so clumsy, conversationally, when she'd met him outside, without witnesses. She darted a look in Mother's direction and saw she was looking daggers at Mr Dundas, which made her instantly wish to put him at ease. 'It gives me something to do in the evenings,' she said.

'Miss Fairfax,' put in Mrs Knowles in her most penetrating voice, as though to remind him that he could say nothing that everyone else would not overhear, 'is mending some of the hassocks from our little church.'

'Hassocks,' said Mr Dundas, eyeing her work, with what looked suspiciously like a twinkle in his eye. 'Ah, very, er…virtuous.'

Betsy looked at him sharply. What did he mean by that? What was he insinuating?

'My Betsy is a good girl,' said Papa gruffly, suddenly joining the fray. 'Don't say so often enough m'dear,' he added. 'The design on the hassock she is currently mending takes symbols from my regimental colours.'

Betsy looked up at him in surprise. She'd had no idea that he'd taken any notice of what she was embroidering. That he took much notice of her at all, come to that.

'Takes an interest in the progress of the current

conflict, too,' he added. 'Pores over the papers, when we get 'em, to see how Wellington is faring against Bonaparte. Proud to have a military man as your father, eh, what?'

Oh, so that was it. He wasn't praising her, particularly, just using her as yet another weapon in the ongoing war with Mother. Trying to make out that she was on *his* side.

Betsy tried not to shift in her seat, which would betray her feelings of discomfort. Not only because she'd been dragged into the current conflict, unwittingly, but also because the only reason she kept on asking about the progress of the allied forces was because she was worried about Ben. She couldn't help feeling that it had been her behaviour that had prompted him to return to his regiment. She had made such a nuisance of herself that she felt as if she'd more or less hounded him and his wife out of the area.

'After you ladies left us,' said Mr Dundas, 'we discussed the role that Lord Bramhall might be playing over there.'

Betsy's head flew up. Oh, if only she had been able to hear what they'd said. Did one of them know what he was doing and how he was faring? Did Mr Dundas? After all, Ben was bound to correspond with him, regularly, to send orders and receive reports.

'Then it is just as well,' said Mother with a disapproving sniff, 'that we left the table when we did. Military matters are not a suitable topic for females.'

'It wasn't exactly military matters we discussed, ma'am,' said Mr Dundas, turning from his apparently fascinated examination of Betsy's needlework, 'but more how Lord Bramhall's decision to return to his regiment may affect people here.'

'Yes, young Dundas here was hot in defence of his employer,' said Papa with a chuckle. 'Very commendable of you to do so,' he said, addressing Mr Dundas. 'But also very timely to hear that Bramhall intends to undo some of the evils his father did, even though he doesn't care to stay in the neighbourhood and carry out the work himself.'

'I don't think it is a case of not caring to stay in the neighbourhood,' said Mr Dundas. 'He has been in the army for so long that he must have felt that he would be more use returning to his regiment with a campaign of this importance getting under way. Lots of other young men, who have had no experience, have joined up, after all, when they heard Bonaparte had escaped and gone on the rampage again.'

That was interesting. Perhaps her behaviour hadn't been the spur for Ben to leave, after all. Perhaps she didn't need to feel so guilty all the time…

'War talk,' said Mother disapprovingly. 'Need I remind you, young man, of my opinion that such talk should not be brought in here?'

Mr Dundas, to Betsy's surprise, grinned broadly. 'Beg pardon, ma'am,' he said, looking not the slightest bit repentant. 'And thank you for reminding me of my manners.'

'Hmmph,' said Mother, with a toss of her head.

'But what,' said Betsy hastily, hoping to draw Mother's fire, 'sort of things does he want you to do? I mean, his father was so eccentric that it must be hard to know where to start.'

'Betsy!' Mother turned from Mr Dundas. 'Really! It is not your place to ask such questions. Nor to cast aspersions on the character of the fourth Earl!'

'Pah,' said Papa. 'The fourth Earl was more than eccentric if you ask me. Downright unhinged in his latter years.'

Oh, dear. Betsy might have succeeded in drawing Mother's attention from Mr Dundas, but now Papa was all fired up again.

'At least the fifth Earl,' said the vicar, 'seems as though he will be an improvement. I mean, at least he has installed a steward...' he waved his hand at Mr Dundas '...to oversee things. Which, if he intends to be an absentee landlord, shows that at least he has a conscience.'

All those *at leasts*, Betsy fumed. It was just as if the vicar was trying to emphasise the fact that Ben had done as little as possible while he'd been here.

'Yes, but what we would all like to know,' said Mrs Knowles, clasping her hands together, as though in prayer, 'is what, exactly, he intends to *do*.'

'He's going to set the cat among the pigeons, that's what he is going to do,' said Papa, with a shake of his head.

'I am sure he does not mean to,' put in Mr Dundas. Then he turned to her. 'Lord Bramhall wrote that, since many of the properties in the village are in a state of poor repair, he wanted to bring in workers to repair them. And offer them homes in those properties, once they are fit for habitation, in the hopes that those men and their families would stay in the area and help to rebuild its prosperity.'

'Oh,' said Betsy. 'That sounds like a marvellous idea.'

'Not entirely,' said Papa. 'To start with, Dundas here informs us that these incomers are to come from a pool of former soldiers, wounded soldiers, who cannot get work elsewhere. So what good are they likely to be in the long term? I grant you,' he said, holding up one hand to silence Mr Dundas when he took a breath to argue, 'that his motives were good. But who is going to fund those men should they all fall too sick to do any work? Eh? They'll go on the parish and we'll all be worse off than we were before.'

'Ah, no, surely,' said Mr Dundas, 'if they are employed by Lord Bramhall, then he will be responsible for their wages while they can work and their pensions when they no longer can.'

'But where,' put in the vicar, 'are they to live, while those cottages are being repaired? Will we have tents in the fields? Like some sort of—well, whatever they call an army encampment on the move?'

Mr Dundas looked so troubled by this double-sided attack that Betsy leaped to his defence.

'Surely they could stay at Bramley Park itself? I mean, that huge house is virtually empty and...'

'Don't be so ridiculous, Betsy,' said Mother. 'Installing a lot of rough soldiers in a house that fine? The very idea.'

'No,' said Mr Dundas, rubbing his finger over his nose. 'Actually, Miss Fairfax has come up with a very good idea. No disrespect, Mrs Fairfax, but although the house might once have been very fine, at the moment it resembles nothing as much as a great barn.'

'There must be servants' quarters up in the attics,' said Mrs Knowles. 'I am sure they could house a few families, for a short while. And it's not as if Lord and Lady Bramhall will be in residence, to be incommoded by such people, even if they do turn out to be ruffians.'

'The attics,' repeated Mr Dundas. 'I don't know… I mean, I just assumed we could do something in the stables, or the barns…'

'What you need,' said Mother, 'is to have someone with experience of hiring and housing servants, to come and have a look at those attics of yours, to see what wants doing to make them fit for purpose.'

Everyone turned to stare at Mother in surprise. She'd changed tack as rapidly as a mouse when evading the barn cat. But it was only a moment before Betsy saw what had happened. She wanted to get inside Bramley Park and have a good look round. And this sudden interest in the welfare of servants had provided her with a marvellous excuse for doing so.

'Would you,' said Mr Dundas, falling neatly into Mother's trap, 'care to advise me?'

'I suppose,' said Mother graciously, 'I could.'

'I could help, too,' said Mrs Knowles, clearly as keen to take advantage of Mr Dundas's naivety as Mother.

'Thank you, ladies,' said Mr Dundas, with all appearance of total gratitude. 'Lady Bramhall appears to have made a start, tidying up a few of the rooms, but those are for entertaining, not housing staff. And, frankly, I dare not ask Mrs Green to do more than she is already doing. May I hope to receive a visit from you in the next few days?'

'We will come,' said Mother, decisively, 'tomorrow.'

Chapter Seven

James walked slowly back to Bramley Park, his mind whirling. He'd never minded not being handsome, before coming here. But now he rather regretted having a face and build that made him look as though he ought to be driving cows to market for a living. Which was entirely down to Miss Fairfax. Miss Fairfax, who had looked stunning in her Sunday best, but who tonight, in that evening gown, had looked like… He paused in the act of scrambling over the low stone wall that divided the village lane from the start of the Bramhall property… No, it wasn't an exaggeration to compare her to a goddess. A goddess of domesticity, sitting there, stitching away, her head bent, exposing the nape of her neck, with curls brushing it in a sensuous way that made his fingers itch to do the same.

And then he'd watched those slender fingers of hers and experienced the same fleeting fantasy about what they could do to his body. Which was such

an inappropriate thing to be thinking about in a respectable drawing room that for a while there he'd
become almost unable to form coherent sentences.
He'd just repeated whatever she'd said, like some
sort of mooncalf.

Hassocks, indeed! He ran his fingers through his
hair, dislodging his hat, then slapping it back down
firmly on his head again as he trudged on.

His one consolation was that partly because of the
amount of time he'd spent in society ballrooms earlier in the year, supporting Daisy through her Season,
and dutifully looking at the debutantes available, he'd
acquired a little address. He hadn't ended up blushing and stammering, the way his poor friend Cooper
always did when addressed by any female under the
age of forty with a reasonable face and figure. And
Miss Fairfax was more than reasonable in the face
and figure department. She was so pretty that she
must have had beaus swarming round her like bees
during her Season, which led him to wonder why
she was still unmarried.

There was only one flaw in her that he could detect: her complexion was not fashionably pale. But
then, she didn't appear to guard it, the way London
beauties did. His sister, for one, never went anywhere
without a parasol to shield her from the ageing effects of the sun. Nor would she have been caught
dead weeping so copiously it made her face blotchy.
Or weeping in public at all. If Daisy ever did weep,
he would warrant she'd do it in private, then apply
a liberal layer of face powder so that nobody would

guess she'd experienced anything so vulgar as an emotion.

But Miss Fairfax—ah, she was so open in her expression that he could practically read each emotion she experienced as it flitted through her mind. Which was another reason he felt cast down, he supposed. Because he hadn't been able to help noticing how her whole being went on the alert every time anyone mentioned Ben, or anything to do with him. Even her so-called interest in the progress of Wellington and the allies stemmed, he would swear, from her knowledge that Ben was somewhere with those troops.

Perversely, the only thing that had been able to jolt him out of that swirling spiral of what he suspected was jealousy, and awareness of Miss Fairfax, had been her mother's acid tongue. Lord, but he'd wanted to laugh when she'd reprimanded him for his lack of manners. It was, he had to say, a novel experience, after being courted and fêted so assiduously by ladies with daughters of a marriageable age. Not that he'd noticed their true intent, at first, during Daisy's Season, it had been so subtle. In fact, he'd been pleased that Daisy seemed to be making so many friends so quickly. It had only been after a week or so that he'd noticed that the girls were always far more friendly with Daisy whenever he was about to witness what they were doing. And that some of them spent far more time fawning over him than they did talking to her.

He'd always tried to be polite to them all, when he'd still hoped they might be Daisy's friends, even if he hadn't been able to think of them as potential wives for one reason or another. But once they'd shown their true colours, he'd wanted nothing further to do with any of them. His first tactic had been to simply ignore them. But that had only made them redouble their efforts to be fascinating. He'd then, though it went against the grain to be rude, begun to drop hints that he just wasn't interested in them. Which hadn't worked, either. So he'd become increasingly blunt, not to say offensive. But no matter how rudely he'd rebuffed the more determined among them, they still flocked round him, saying they found his lack of manners thrillingly attractive. They twittered about his square, uncompromising jaw being a sign of strength of character. That his manly, muscular figure made them feel all frail and feminine in comparison.

Lord, but he still felt queasy, remembering some of the nonsense they'd spouted if ever any of them had managed to corner him in a secluded spot, about gods of Olympus and the Lord knew what. He knew, thanks to his real friends, decent chaps he'd grown up with, that he had the kind of face that wouldn't look out of place on a professional boxer and shoulders that meant he could do the work of a coal heaver with ease.

Which meant that all their flattery sluiced off him like so much water off a duck's back.

But Mrs Fairfax, who had no idea who he was, or what he was worth, had given him a sharp set-down, which he'd probably deserved.

Her daughter, however, he reflected, his tentative, reminiscent smile slipping away, hadn't. She shouldn't have told Miss Fairfax off like that, in public. Her face had turned red with the humiliation he was sure she must have felt. The poor darling.

A darling who appeared to have her heart set on another man. A squirming sensation in his stomach made him wonder about the quality and provenance of the cheese that Colonel Fairfax had served with the port. That was far more likely to be the cause of such an uncomfortable physical sensation than the prospect of having to fight for the regard of a woman whose heart apparently belonged to another.

What if he were to tell her that she'd made a mistake about his identity? That he was, actually, not only a viscount in his own right, but also the heir to an earldom. And had plenty of money. Her mother would certainly change her attitude. But would Miss Fairfax? Did she care about such things?

And if she did, would he be happy to win her on those terms?

He scuffed his boots through the long grass, silvery in the light of the full moon that made walking across the fields to get home feasible, sending up clouds of seeds and dust. What did he want from Miss Fairfax, that was the question? Her regard, he answered himself almost at once, that was what. And not because of his title, or his wealth, or his prospects. If he had to resort to such methods to take her mind off Ben, then he'd feel like a cheat.

So he'd have to set himself to... Well, how did a man make a woman fall for him?

And was he so sure he wanted to make her fall for him, really? To fall *in love* with him? He would be a villain to set out to do so if he didn't mean to marry her, in the end. And did he want to marry her?

He paused as he emerged from the last stand of trees and saw the house, Bramley Park, squatting amid the overgrown remnants of its orchards and gardens.

Ben's property.

It felt as if the cloud of confusion and jealousy and self-questioning swirled round him even more menacingly, the way the air changed just before a storm struck.

And, with the same force as though he'd been slapped in the face by an icy squall of rain, he re-alised that he needed to make up his mind exactly what he did want from Miss Fairfax before telling her who and what he was. It was all very well admitting that whenever he was in her presence, he found her so bewitching that his wits went wandering. But what did he know about her, when it came down to it? Apart from the fact she seemed overly concerned with Ben. He'd only met her a matter of days ago. And she'd warned him, herself, that her mother was a serious matchmaker. It was better not to give Mrs Fairfax any chance to shove her oar in and push him into something for which he might not be ready, until he was absolutely sure what he wanted.

Still, he mused, there was plenty of work for him to do within that house, and around the estates, to keep him here for several weeks. Surely, during that time, he'd be able to get to know Miss Fairfax better? And, hopefully, come to a sensible decision about what part, if any, he wanted her to play in his life. He could already tell that she'd slot into the role of viscountess with ease. She had pride in herself, and her family, knowing her own worth, which meant she wouldn't feel overwhelmed by the elevation in status. But not so much pride that she would look down her nose at the people he'd have to oversee. She'd demonstrated that clearly in the way she'd set out to put those poor parish councillors at ease, when her mother had all but frozen them out. His tenants would love her, if she treated them with as much consideration.

Yes, he vowed as he set off on the last leg of his journey, that was what he'd do. Get to know her. Find out all he could about what sort of woman she was, beneath the beauty.

And while he was doing so, he'd jolly well find out what there was between her and Ben. Because if he did decide to marry her and bring her into his family, then there would be occasions when they'd all be together. And he didn't want to end up watching her jealously, as she flirted with his sister's husband. Or suspiciously, for signs that she might be hankering after some other man. That was not the sort of marriage he wanted, if it came to marriage. Of that much, at least, he was absolutely certain.

The next day seemed to crawl past as he waited for visitors from Darby Manor. In the end he de-

cided there was nothing for it but to go out on to
the overgrown lawn with a scythe so that he looked
as though he was working rather than just loitering
about watching the lane.

Wielding a scythe, James soon discovered, wasn't
as easy as the workers on his father's farms made
it look. By the time he heard the rumble of carriage
wheels turning into the property, from the lane to
the village, he was extremely relieved to be able to
lay the deadly instrument to one side. The patch of
grass he'd managed to reduce in length was pitifully
small and in the process of cutting it he'd all but ruined the boots he'd borrowed from the mud room.
Though at least the leather had protected his legs,
there was that.

The carriage slowed down as it approached him,
and the face of Mrs Knowles appeared at its window.
His heart sped up as, behind her, he could make out
the silhouettes of two more bonneted females. Which
meant, he hoped, that not only Mrs Fairfax, but also
Miss Fairfax, had come.

'Good morning, Mr Dundas,' trilled Mrs Knowles.
'I do hope we haven't arrived at an inconvenient
time?'

'Not at all,' he said with complete sincerity, reaching into his pocket for a handkerchief to mop his
brow. He would not have believed, before this morning, that so much effort could be expended for such
meagre results. 'If you carry on up to the hall, I shall
meet you there.' And he'd better sluice himself off
at the pump, he decided as he collected his jacket,

which he'd tossed aside the moment he'd discovered that nobody could safely wield a sharp implement in the vicinity of his own legs while wearing such a restricting garment.

By the time he'd reached the house and made himself presentable, the party from Darby Manor were all sitting in the front parlour, sipping tea from a set that had arrived only a few days ago, with a note from Daisy saying that she'd picked it up for a song at a market in Brussels. Though he would warrant the cost of shipping it back would rather have ruined her attempt at economy.

Still, he was jolly glad to see Miss Fairfax sipping her tea from a pretty china cup, rather than having to wrap her dainty fingers round any of the odd assortment of tankards that were in daily use in the kitchen. He would have to make a point of thanking Mrs Green for unpacking the set, washing it and using it to serve these ladies. And try to find some way to stop thinking lewd thoughts every time he caught sight of Miss Fairfax's bare fingers.

'I am sorry to have kept you waiting,' he said, going to the tea tray and lifting the pot.

'Not at all,' said Mrs Knowles, with what looked like glee. 'We had a most delightful chat with Mrs Green, who brought us in here, and I have to say, we were very surprised to see how pleasant and orderly it is. We were expecting—' she said, before shutting her mouth rapidly after Mrs Fairfax jabbed her elbow into her side.

He couldn't help grinning. 'I dare say you were

expecting the whole house to be in a state of disrepair.'

'Well, the rumours have been that—' This time Mrs Knowles pulled herself up short without any interference from Mrs Fairfax.

'The rumours probably did not exaggerate all that much,' he said, taking his cup of tea to a straight-backed chair opposite the sofa upon which all three ladies were sitting. Miss Fairfax kept her eyes on her cup, as though searching for something floating in it. 'However, before she left,' he continued, wondering why she couldn't meet his eye today, 'Lady Bramhall did begin to try to undo the, ah, neglect of many years.'

'I see,' said Mrs Fairfax, glancing round the room. 'You did tell us that she attempted to make one room fit for receiving visitors. It is a great pity,' she continued with a disdainful sniff, 'that she did not think to instal more furniture before she ran off to the Continent.'

At her mother's criticism of their absent hostess, Miss Fairfax flinched and lowered her head even further, which gave him a pretty good notion of what was bothering her.

'The scullery maid,' he said, in an effort to defend his sister from the accusation of dereliction of her duty, as well as to distract and amuse Miss Fairfax, rather than to impart any information to her mother, 'told me, practically the moment I arrived, that the old Earl liked nothing better than dragging his furniture outside to make bonfires. And what you are now sitting on is the best of what Lady Bramhall managed to salvage. Which, apparently, she found mouldering in the orchard. He also used the books in the library as fuel, rather than coal, on a chilly evening.'

'Gracious,' said Mrs Knowles. 'It is a wonder he didn't burn the place down round his ears.'

Mrs Fairfax, who was clearly of a more practical nature, looked round the room in a fascinated way.

'So you can see,' he said in a manful attempt to keep the conversation going, when all he wanted to talk about was what was troubling Miss Fairfax today, 'why this was one of the only rooms Her Ladyship managed to put to rights before accompanying her husband back to his regiment.'

He took a sip of the tea, which had cooled to the extent that it was more refreshing than he'd expected. 'Perhaps you would like to examine the rest of the furniture she rescued from the orchard, which she had moved to the barns to preserve it against further weathering? You could, perhaps, give me your opinion as to which pieces might work in which rooms?'

Both Mrs Fairfax and Mrs Knowles preened slightly at his hint that he would welcome their advice. Or, more likely, that they'd be able to say that they'd had a hand in the refurbishment of such a grand house. Miss Fairfax, however, looked as though she wished the sofa would swallow her whole, she was so embarrassed by her mother's attitude.

He took another sip of tea to hide his amusement. Only wait until they saw the state of the furniture that looked as though it had spent years outside in all weathers before Daisy had become mistress of Bramley Park.

'Well, if you have finished your tea,' he said, noting that each lady had laid her spoon across her cup, 'I could show you over the place so you can see where we might be able to house the new workers. If you don't mind it being me who conducts the tour. Mrs Green is probably the proper person to do it, but she doesn't like to leave her kitchen.'

Mrs Knowles and Mrs Fairfax shot to their feet. Miss Fairfax stood up with a touch of reluctance, as if, now that it came to it, she regretted coming with them.

'Perhaps we could start in the attics,' he said, 'where you so helpfully suggested the new arrivals might stay while they are making homes fit for themselves in the village.'

'By all means,' said Mrs Fairfax.

Well, that had been less of a struggle than he'd thought. He'd half expected to have to listen to all sorts of reasons why it was imperative they saw every single room, so that they could give him the benefit of their wisdom.

He climbed the stairs ahead of them, pausing on each landing to allow them to catch their breath. Once they reached the attics, he simply waved his arm at the corridor, as an invitation for them to poke about as they wished. Mrs Fairfax and Mrs Knowles lost no time in darting along the corridor, peeping into rooms and exclaiming over everything they found. Which was, from his own investigation,

mainly dust and cobwebs and the occasional tragic
remains of birds that must have fallen down chim-
neys and been unable to find their way out.

Miss Fairfax, however, stayed exactly where she
was. 'I am so sorry,' she said, twisting her gloved
hands together, in a way that betrayed her agitation,
as if the expression on her face was not enough.

'What for?' He sidled closer to her, wishing he
could take the chance of them being alone, or rela-
tively alone, to take her hands in his and give them
a reassuring squeeze.

'For my mother. And Mrs Knowles,' she added
with a sigh. 'Pushing in here on the pretext of being
concerned over the welfare of servants. They just
want to get a look at the place about which everyone
has been gossiping for years.'

'I know,' he told her.

'You do?' Her face tilted up so that she could look
him full in the face. And as she did so, it struck him
that very few people ever had to look up at him, this
way. And very few people smelled as sweet as she
did. Or were anywhere near as pretty, with the sun
making the dust motes that swirled round her glisten,
as though she was standing in a cloud of diamonds.
He'd like to give her real diamonds. Tons of them,
to weave through her hair and thread on to her fingers, and hang round her neck.

'Did you hear me?' She was frowning now, as
though he'd annoyed her.

'Ah, beg pardon, wool gathering,' he said, making
her frown deepen.

'That is to say,' he continued, 'I don't mind your mother and the vicar's wife coming here on any pretext, as long as you come with them. That was why I didn't raise any objections, even though it was totally obvious that it was curiosity that was motivating them, not philanthropy. It gave us a chance to meet again.'

He blinked, stunned to hear himself come out with so many big words when, just a moment before, he'd been struck dumb with her beauty.

But at least her frown had vanished. And when she blushed, it was the kind of blush a maiden produced when she was pleased by a man's flattery. He'd never made anyone blush that way before, not on purpose, though he'd seen plenty of other chaps achieve the same result.

'You know,' she added, glancing along the corridor as her mother emerged from one room and swiftly darted into the next, 'that they will come up with all sorts of reasons to poke about the whole place, now that they've got inside.'

'Good,' he said. 'That will mean you will be here for some time. Hopefully, a very long time.' He took a step nearer. He couldn't help it. She was drawing him to her as surely as water rushed downstream to the sea.

She stepped aside, maintaining a more proper distance, and lowered her head. 'I don't know what you hope to achieve, with my mother being close by.'

'I don't care about achieving anything,' he said, closing the distance between them once more. 'It is enough just to be near you.'

Her blush deepened. She shook her head.

'Mr Dundas,' she breathed, 'you shouldn't say such things.' But she didn't look cross. Not in the slightest.

'Perhaps not,' he admitted, since just last night he'd sworn he'd go slowly and find out all about her before starting to flirt, or court, or whatever it was he seemed to be doing this morning. 'But I just can't help myself.'

And that, in spite of anything his rational, sensible self might decide, was the inescapable truth.

He couldn't help himself.

And right at this moment, he couldn't even remember why he ought to want to.

Chapter Eight

While Betsy was struggling to think of something to say in response to what had sounded surprisingly like a declaration, Mother emerged from the last room at the end of the corridor and came striding in their direction.

'When,' she said, 'did you say you expect these *people* to arrive?' She managed to pronounce the word *people* as though she was actually referring to vermin.

'Not for a week or so, I shouldn't think,' said Mr Dundas, cool as a cucumber. When she was feeling all fluttery inside. Or as though she didn't know exactly where to put her feet. No matter where she stood, she was either too far away from him to be able to feel the heat from his body and smell the scent of a man who had recently been working out of doors in the sunshine, and looking so very masculine without his jacket, and with his sleeves rolled up. Or too near for propriety. 'Although there has been a lot of talk about selecting men with some useful skills and with wives.' Had he slid his eyes at her when he said the word *wives* for any particular reason? 'I am not sure,' he continued, 'how much effort has actually gone into looking for them.'

'Hmmph,' said Mother, in such a way that nobody could miss her view that his answer was most unsatisfactory.

'I had thought,' he continued, 'that I would have time to make these rooms up here habitable with just a coat of whitewash.' Though how he could continue with such a mundane conversation, after sending her own thoughts skittering in all directions, she couldn't think. Unless, of course, it had just been words. Something that just popped into his head to say, which he didn't really mean. Men often said all sorts of complimentary things without having any intention of carrying them through. They would say that they had never seen a woman with eyes as lovely as hers, or anyone with hair as lustrous. Oh, yes, certain men, particularly the ones with rank and fortune, could say all sorts of lovely-sounding things. But they only ever proposed to girls with fortune and rank to match their own.

Although none of them had ever managed to make her feel like this, no matter how ardently they'd flirted. Had she sensed they'd been insincere? So that their false words glanced off her? Or was it that Mr Dundas was the first man she'd ever really considered attractive? As a man. Not as a potential husband. When she'd been in London's ballrooms she'd always taken careful note of a man's fortune and pedigree, and bestowed her smiles and her attention accordingly. But Mr Dundas just made her *feel* things and *say* things, just by being there, without her knowing very much about him at all.

'Then, of course,' Mr Dundas said, 'I'd have to get hold of some mattresses, for, as you can see, mice have been at the ones left behind after the last lot of servants quit the place.'

Mattresses! Now he was talking about mattresses. And mice!

'Normally you would set the female servants to repairing and restuffing what you have,' said Mother, as though explaining an equation to a schoolboy, while making Betsy consider a few phrases she knew, but could never use, about stuffing things in uncomfortable places. 'But as you have no female staff, you will need to buy new.'

Mr Dundas gave a nonchalant shrug, which somehow managed to sweep aside her irritation because she couldn't help admiring the way he never appeared to feel the slightest bit discomposed, no matter how disagreeable or condescending Mother was. 'Well, I have sufficient funds to do what must be done to make the quarters habitable,' he said. 'There must be somewhere for them all to sleep, when they do arrive. That is, if these men bring wives, you cannot expect them to bed down in the stables, can you?'

'The stables?' Betsy mentally slapped herself on the wrist. She'd meant to resist the temptation to give in to idle curiosity. But it was such a shock, to hear him suggest the new staff should sleep out of doors.

She knew they'd been soldiers and so were used to such conditions, but surely…

'Yes,' he said, turning to her with a welcoming sort of smile, just as though he was glad that she was finally joining in the conversation. 'At the moment, Wilmot and Briggs, the only male staff currently working here, are bedding down in the stables.'

'Extraordinary,' breathed Mother through flared nostrils. Betsy was not sure what Mr Dundas was trying to achieve by telling Mother so much, but she was sure that he was trying to achieve something. She had the feeling that she got when someone dangled a piece of yarn before a kitten, jerking it to get their attention, then twitching it away to get it to try to catch it. And the smile he'd just given her, when he'd shocked her into joining in, was just the sort of thing a cat would do when it had tempted a mouse in between its paws.

'Where do the female servants,' said Mother, her eyes alight with curiosity, 'live? I saw two of them, when we came in. The cook and that little scullery maid.'

Mr Dundas cleared his throat. 'I believe they have a room just off the kitchen and, although I have never, naturally, seen inside it, they assure me it is very snug, since it has the benefit of being on the other side of the wall against which the range is situated.'

'No need to move them, then,' said Mother firmly. 'However, it would be useful if I could take a look at the state of some other rooms, in case any of them could be put into use more easily than these...' she waved her hand behind her, to indicate the attic rooms that had been the playground of mice '...so that I can give you the benefit of my advice.'

Betsy's cheeks flamed with embarrassment at Mother's determination to see inside every room of the house that had become a byword in the locality. She hardly dared look at Mr Dundas, sure that he would think Mother the most dreadfully vulgar, pushing woman.

But when she did dart a glance his way, all she saw in his face was a sort of struggle to keep his face straight. As if he was fighting laughter. Which made her cross with him all over again. It was all very well for *her* to think Mother vulgar and pushing, but she found she didn't like anyone else laughing at her. Especially not a man who was entirely too full of himself, with his coaxing smiles and his flattering words, and his ruggedly handsome face and his hard, strong body, and his... Oh, dear. She had meant to stay cross with him, this time, not fall victim to his physical charms.

She girded up her loins, therefore, and managed to remember to stay cross with Mr Dundas all the way down the stairs and during the time it took him to show them round most of the floor that they really had no excuse for looking round at all.

Right until he stopped in front of a door which he said led to his bedroom.

'It wouldn't be proper to show you in there,' he said, darting her a glance that made her go hot all over. 'Besides which,' he added, 'since I am already occupying it, it isn't one of the rooms that could possibly be of use to the new arrivals, is it?'

'But what about this room?' Mother was rattling the handle of a door further along the corridor that was, to her evident frustration, locked. Thankfully, that meant she'd missed the glance he'd darted at Betsy. And, more importantly, her corresponding blush.

'Ah,' said Mr Dundas, strolling along to where Mother was standing. 'Now *that* room was last inhabited by the late Countess, I believe. It is the only room in the house that stays locked. Mrs Green holds the key to that room and I doubt very much that she would let you look inside.'

'Why not?' The moment Betsy had asked the question she wanted to kick herself for giving way to vulgar curiosity yet again. And it was of no comfort to remind herself that if she hadn't asked the question, either Mother or Mrs Knowles would have done. Because she didn't care what he thought of *them*. Or not so very much, anyway.

Oh, Lord. She cared what he thought of her. In fact, she was dangerously close to wanting to impress him. Wasn't that why she'd taken such pains with her appearance on Sunday?

No. Absolutely not! She'd only been trying to counteract the awful impression she'd made at their first meeting.

Hadn't she?

'Apparently,' said Mr Dundas, stepping closer

to the ladies, and lowering his voice, 'the late Earl wrought havoc in there after his Countess died, smashing and tearing all her things, and then forbade anyone to enter again. Even I have not set foot inside.'

Betsy looked at the closed door and comforted herself with the thought that there was nothing more likely to arouse curiosity than a locked door, especially one with a story of such grief and madness attached to it.

'Don't you wish,' she found herself saying, 'to see inside? If I lived here and knew there was a room with a locked door, and such rumours circulating about it, it would drive me mad with curiosity.' And she didn't care if he did think her guilty of displaying vulgar curiosity. Why should she?

Mr Dundas chuckled. 'I have more important things to do than go into a room that is, from all I've heard, in a dreadful mess. My task is to try to restore the land, not the house. It is for Lord and Lady Bramhall to see to, er, family matters, such as the cleaning up of the Countess's room, when they come back.'

'Aren't you in the slightest bit curious to see inside?'

He shook his head. 'What would be the point? I cannot do anything about it. And why would I want to look at a scene of such devastation? It would be...' he frowned as though searching for the right word '...unsettling. And why should I unsettle myself, to no account?'

'How like a man,' said Mother with disgust, realising that no matter what she did, this was one room she wasn't going to see the inside of. But, to be honest, Betsy, too, found his attitude rather surprising. It was as if he was not interested in anything beyond the strictly practical.

Although, she reflected as they went down the stairs to the ground floor, wasn't Papa rather like that, too? Restricting himself to matters that he said he could do something about, rather than spending much time reading about, or discussing, topics that he described as irrelevant. He didn't even like reading books, she recalled when they peeped into a room that had clearly once been a library, but now contained bare shelves and only one armchair with the stuffing leaking from the seams, unless he could learn something from them. Papa said stories were a waste of time. If he ever did borrow a book, it would be about something like crops, or soil, or the history of his own regiment.

'And this,' said Mr Dundas, flinging open the door to yet another room, 'is the study. One of the very few rooms that has been regularly maintained, as far as I can tell. But I don't propose to give it up for a bedroom, since I work in here just about every day.'

Mother and Mrs Knowles walked in, exclaiming over the heaps of paperwork on the desk and wondering how any man could concentrate on work when he had such a splendid view from the windows. But Betsy stayed right where she was, a sick, swirling sensation in her stomach taking her by surprise. She hadn't bargained on feeling like this when returning to the scene of the crime. Well, she'd never planned to return to this room, for the rest of her life, if she could help it. And now she bitterly regretted allowing Mother to persuade her to come to Bramley Park today.

'Is something wrong?' Mr Dundas was looking at her with concern, making her aware that she had wrapped her arms round her middle. She shook her head. There was no way she was going to tell Mr Dundas what had happened the last time she'd come here. How she'd hammered at the windows, which were more like doors with lots of glass panes in, until Ben had let her in. And how she'd disgraced and humiliated herself.

Her eyes flew to Mother, who was opening the windows and stepping outside, remarking how convenient it was to have access to the terrace that ran the entire length of that side of the house.

And something sort of flipped over in Betsy's brain. She'd been so racked with guilt at the way her encounter with Ben had turned out that she'd almost forgotten that it was Mother who had sent her here. Mother who had urged her to do whatever was necessary to get him to see her as a woman. Mother who had wound her up, with tales of Aunt Cornelia, and Father losing his home and his position unless she married well, before sending her off. Mother who'd reminded her it might be her last chance of ever getting a husband with a title, since eligible men were so thin on the ground in these parts.

And Mother who'd said she would *enjoy* having a look round this very house today.

'Are you feeling unwell?' Mr Dundas took her by the elbow, as though offering support. It was all she could do to stop herself from turning to him and leaning her head upon his chest, and blurting it all out.

Only, what would he think of her if he knew? He wouldn't be darting her those admiring, sidelong glances any longer, would he? Or smiling at her ever again. No, he'd probably shun her altogether. A realisation that made her feel ten times worse.

'Do you need,' he said with concern, 'to sit down? Have a glass of water? It is rather hot today and the house has been shut up for so long that it has become unbearably stuffy. I have got used to it, but perhaps I shouldn't have let you run all over the place for such a long time.'

Gently, he led her over to the desk, pulling out the chair by hooking it with one of his feet.

'I d-don't want to sit there!' That was where Ben had been sitting when she'd started rapping on the window.

'You *would* probably be better outside, in the fresh air,' Mr Dundas said at once. And he steered her past the horrid desk, and the dratted chair, until they were outside on the terrace, where he kept hold of her arm until he'd brought her into a shady spot where there was a sort of low trough, which had clearly once been filled with flowers, but which now looked more like a hay-stuffed cushion since it had been taken over by weeds, which in their turn had withered and dried through lack of care.

'Shall I call your mother over?'

No! The last person she wished to speak to was Mother. Not in this particular spot, anyway. Besides, Mother was busy poking about on the lawn, or what had clearly once been a lawn, at the far end of the terrace from where Mr Dundas had brought her.

As she shook her head, Mr Dundas squatted down on the ground before her, and peered up, his brow wrinkled with concern.

'What can I do? Shall I fetch you a drink? Something to eat? Do you feel faint?'

His words produced a rush of gratitude. He wasn't prying. He wasn't telling her what she ought to do. Even when she'd shown reluctance to sit in the chair he hadn't tried to persuade her he knew best. Instead he was asking her what *she* wanted. What she needed. She didn't think anyone had ever done that. All her life, people had been telling her how to behave and even what to think.

At that moment, Mother came bustling over, her brows drawn down in displeasure at the sight of Betsy sitting in the shade, with Mr Dundas crouched at her feet, just as though he was proposing to her. Which he never would do, she reflected with resignation, if he ever found out what she'd done.

No one would. But, oh, how she wished she could marry a man like this. A handsome, kind, considerate man whose body and face she found so appealing.

'What,' said Mother frostily, 'is going on?'

Mr Dundas got to his feet. 'Miss Fairfax appears to be rather unwell. The heat, perhaps?'

Mother clucked her tongue. 'I suppose that means we will have to go home, instead of finishing our examination of the property.'

Mr Dundas stiffened, ever so slightly. 'I would have thought—' he said, as though he was about to say that surely Betsy's welfare should rate higher than her vulgar curiosity. At least, that was what she hoped he might be about to say. He certainly looked as though he had a mind to defend her.

But before he could do such a foolish thing and start an argument with Mother that there was no prospect of him winning, she interrupted.

'I am sure you don't need to cut short the visit on my account, Mother. And actually, I don't think it would be a good idea to get straight into the carriage and set off for home. Perhaps, if I could just go to the kitchen and get a glass of water, and sit somewhere cool for a while…'

'I shall escort you there,' put in Mr Dundas swiftly.

Which suggestion did not please Mother in the slightest.

'Who is to conduct us around the barns and stables you spoke of and show us where the furniture is being stored?'

'If we all walk round the outside of the house,' he said, 'we can reach a spot where I can point out the way to the outhouses, which you can then find easily. I can then escort Miss Fairfax to the kitchen, where we will be chaperoned by Mrs Green and Sally. There will be no impropriety, I assure you.'

Oh, the clever man. He'd given Mother an excuse

to cover up her selfish outburst, making it sound as if her irritation was all about the propriety of allowing him to walk off with her, instead of showing the older ladies round the stables.

Mother chewed on her lip for a moment, as though deciding whether to capitulate or not, but at that moment Mrs Knowles came to the rescue.

'A perfect solution, Mr Dundas,' she said, her eyes alight, because, probably, she'd just realised that they would have much more freedom to poke about wherever they wanted, and say whatever they wanted about what they found, without Mr Dundas there to constrain them.

And so Mother and Mrs Knowles scurried off to the buildings Mr Dundas pointed out to them, while he, keeping her arm tucked in his, carried on strolling along with her in the direction, she supposed, of a back door, which would open into the kitchen.

'Are you sure it won't be too hot in the kitchen for you, with the stove going?'

'It wasn't the heat that overset me,' she blurted out. Well, he'd been so kind. So very much like the ideal sort of man she wished she could meet that it didn't seem right to lie to him. 'It was a m-memory which overset me.'

She thought she felt his arm stiffen under her fingers.

'Would you,' he said, in a casual tone, 'like to tell me about it?'

Ah. Would she? Well, no, at least, certainly not in the kitchen with other people able to hear. And perhaps not ever. So far, nobody knew exactly how badly she'd behaved. Not even Mother. When she'd gone home that day, she'd just said it was too late, that Ben was already married. And that was the way she wanted to keep it.

So she shook her head.

And he didn't press her to tell him anything. But somehow, for the rest of the visit, she felt as though he'd withdrawn from her. Or as though she'd taken a step back and he was permitting it. Or something. She couldn't explain it properly.

She only knew that whereas before there had been a tentative sort of reaching out to each other, she now felt as though they were standing on opposite sides of a sheet of glass, looking at each other, but no longer able to touch. Even if they wanted to.

Chapter Nine

For once, Betsy didn't mind that Mother and Mrs Knowles chattered nineteen to the dozen, without either expecting, or wishing, her to join in, on the drive home. Because her mind was full of Mr Dundas and what he would think of her if he knew why she'd come over so peculiar in the study, and how much she cared what he would think.

What if hearing about what she'd done did give him a disgust of her? Would that matter so very much? A writhing sensation in her tummy told her that, yes, it would. It would matter very much. It hadn't just been natural caution that had kept her silent when he'd asked her what was amiss, seeming so genuinely concerned about her. Even after knowing him for such a short time, she already cared what he thought of her, in spite of trying not to let that happen. Which was foolish beyond measure. The only sensible reason why she might care what he thought of her was if she were to consider him in the light of a prospective husband. And she shouldn't. Because he wasn't eligible. Or at least, not by Mother's criteria.

She glanced at Mother, who was still so deep in conversation with Mrs Knowles that Betsy might as well not have been there.

Mother wanted her to marry a man with a title, or money. Preferably both. But Mother wasn't the one who'd have to spend the rest of her life married to this theoretical person, was she? And it was all very well saying she ought not to repeat Mother's mistakes by marrying beneath her, but surely there must have been something about Papa that made Mother cast aside her natural ambition and marry him in the first place?

Betsy didn't have to reflect very long before coming up with an answer to that conundrum. It could only have been down to the kind of intense physical attraction she felt for Mr Dundas. Something she'd never been able to understand before, having never experienced it.

Though in the case of Mr Dundas it wasn't just physical attraction, was it? She'd only just begun to experience that, when he stood close to her. But at first there had been more of a sort of a…connection with him, which had made her feel as if she could talk to him. Because somehow she'd known he would understand her.

The carriage swayed as their driver steered it from the lane and in between the gateposts of Darby Manor. She couldn't believe they'd arrived so soon.

She wasn't anywhere near making up her mind what to do about Mr Dundas. If anything.

She wasn't any nearer by the time she'd sat through dinner, for once not paying much attention to the state of hostilities still simmering between her parents. Because she was coming to the conclusion that if she ever truly wanted something to come of these fledgling feelings for Mr Dundas, it would be no good keeping a secret from him. She certainly didn't want to end up like Mother and Papa, always at loggerheads because Mother had thought she could get away with behaviour she knew Papa would condemn, and had condemned, and kept on condemning, so that there was never any chance of restoring any sort of harmony in the household.

She escaped up to her room as soon as was possible, where she went through the routine of preparing for bed without involving her mind at all. For it was still taken up with Mr Dundas.

This would not do. As she lay in bed gazing up at the ceiling, watching the shadows creep steadily from the corners until they'd blotted out every last remnant of light, she came to a decision. She would tell him the truth. All of it. Because if there was one thing she knew, it was that secrets always had a nasty habit of getting out, and usually at the worst possible moment.

Hadn't Mother kept on hoping that Papa need never find out about her gambling debts? That her unlucky streak would end and she'd win back all she'd lost, and more, without having to own up to having such huge losses in the first place? And didn't Papa keep saying that if only she'd come to him, herself, and explained that she was in such a muddle, he would have paid up, if not gladly, then at least without the resentment that he still felt at having to hear from her creditors how much she owed.

If she didn't want to end up existing in a relationship like the one her parents had, she needed to learn from their mistakes, not repeat them. Besides, if she attempted to deliberately conceal the worst of her behaviour from Mr Dundas, he was bound to find out from someone else. Not that anyone else knew. Excepting, of course, Ben himself, who was, she must not forget, his employer. It was all very well saying that he was abroad and so could no longer pose a threat to her reputation, but what if she and Mr Dundas became involved and Ben heard about it? He'd be bound to warn Mr Dundas what she'd done and tell the tale in such a way that she'd come out sounding like the very worst sort of woman.

And until the moment he did she'd be worrying about when he would. Or might. Or...well, anyway, she would never be able to stop worrying about the threat of exposure. But if she could tell it all from her viewpoint, explaining what had driven her to take such measures, maybe, just maybe, he would understand.

She groaned and turned her face into the pillow. Of course he wouldn't understand. He'd be too shocked. Too appalled. He'd stop flirting, or at least almost flirting, with her. He'd start avoiding her altogether, probably, instead of claiming he wanted to spend as much time with her as he could.

It would all be over before it had even started.

She rolled on to her back, staring up into the dark, and sniffed back angry tears. Wouldn't it only serve her right? To find a man she'd thought she could truly like, only to have him recoil from her in disgust because of what she'd done.

She sniffed again and dashed away the one tear that had leaked from her eye and started trickling in the direction of her ear, telling herself that if she felt this upset at the prospect of forfeiting his regard after such a short time, then…well, she had to act swiftly. Because the longer she put off making her confession, the harder it would become, not only to make that confession, but to recover from the aftermath.

She'd go back to Bramley Park, tomorrow, first thing. Before she had time to change her mind.

And so, right after breakfast, while Mother attended to her correspondence and Papa went out to the kennels, Betsy put on her stoutest walking shoes and set off for Bramley Park.

She couldn't say that she was looking forward to the encounter with Mr Dundas. But it was better to get it all over with now, than to keep on putting it off. It would be far easier to recover from this growing fascination she was feeling for him now, if it was going to come to an ignominious end, before it took an even stronger hold.

And at least she'd find out what kind of man Mr Dundas was and whether he really, really liked her, or was only amusing himself by flirting with the first young, unmarried female that he'd met in this area. And if that was the sort of man he was, then… then…good riddance!

When she reached Bramley Park she went round to the back of the house, since she knew nobody would want to come to the front door to answer it if she should go and knock there. She'd learned as much yesterday, when Mother had the carriage stop at the front steps and had waited for an age for somebody to let her in the front door. It had only been her mother's determination to satisfy her curiosity to see inside the house that had finally overcome her reluctance to go round to the back just as if, she'd grumbled, she was a tradesperson.

Betsy had to cross the stable yard to reach the kitchen door, from the direction she'd taken from Darby Manor today. And, the moment she entered it, she saw that there was a fight taking place. The two men servants, whose names she couldn't, for the moment, recall, were laying into each other with fists, scowls on their reddened faces and their jaws set pugnaciously. On the back kitchen step, the little scullery maid was watching them, her hands clasped at her breast and her eyes alight with excitement. And lounging against the wall, a little to the left of the door, Mr Dundas was observing the two combatants with a kind of detached interest.

She hurried round the edge of the yard, so as to avoid the flailing fists, and, oh, goodness, was that allowed? Boots?

'Mr Dundas! Why aren't you trying to stop them?'

He turned his head sharply and straightened up as he heard her voice. And smiled, as though he was glad to see her, before his face fell a little.

'This is not the sort of thing you should witness,' he said, as the younger of the two combatants landed such a blow on the older man's stomach that he went staggering back several paces.

'Well, stop them, then! Before someone gets really hurt.'

'I am sorry, but this is a matter for them to settle between themselves. They'd not only resent my interference, but would only take up the issue again the minute my back was turned. At least this way I get to ensure fair play.'

'I suppose that does sound sensible. In a way. But wouldn't it be better to all sit down and sort it out without resorting to violence?'

He chuckled. 'A man cannot sort out this sort of contest by talking. Wilmot had a perfect right to punch Briggs, as far as I'm concerned, when he tried to steal a kiss from Sally. Wilmot's been trying to fix his interest with her for some time now. You see, he came to Bramley Park with Lord Bramhall, as his body servant, but then fell for the girl and stayed on rather than returning to the regiment with his master. So he feels that Briggs, who is something of a ladies' man, is poaching on his territory…'

Betsy felt her temper mounting as Mr Dundas ex-plained what had sparked off the fight with a grin on his face as if it was all a big joke. As if this Sally was a possession, rather than a person with feelings. As if, in short, it was all up to the men!

'But what about,' she pointed out, 'Sally? Doesn't she have a say in all this?'

'Sally?' Mr Dundas turned to her with a look of incredulity, which sent her temper spiking even higher.

'She doesn't *belong* to Wilmot,' Betsy snapped. 'No matter what he may or may not have done in order to fix his interest with her.'

'Well, no, but...'

'But nothing! This is...totally outrageous!' And if nobody else was going to do anything to bring a halt to this shameful outpouring of violence that contin-ued to ebb and flow across the yard, then she'd just have to do it herself. And there, right in front of her, she could see the perfect means to do so. The bucket of water standing next to the still-dripping pump.

So she marched across to the bucket, muttering under her breath about the stupidity of men, picked it up, chose a moment when the two men were grap-pling with each other as though trying to break each other's ribs and threw the entire contents over the pair of them.

They broke apart and turned to her with matching expressions of surprise and resentment.

'That's enough,' said Betsy, slinging the empty bucket away so that it bounced and rolled across the cobbles. 'You cannot fight over a woman as though she is a prize to be won at a fair. It isn't a matter for you to…*settle* with your fists. She has a mind of her own. And the right to choose which of you she wants.'

Both of them turned, dripping, in Sally's direction.

'Well, you've certainly cut through that particular Gordian knot with an impressive turn of speed,' observed Mr Dundas.

But Sally didn't appear to appreciate having the focus turned upon her. For, after looking from one to the other of her suitors, she blushed a deep scarlet, hung her head and darted back into the kitchen.

Betsy drew a deep, exasperated breath. Because it looked just as though the girl had *enjoyed* seeing the two men fighting over her. And, even worse, that she *didn't* prefer one over the other. Because if she had, then the fight need not have happened at all. She could have dropped the older one a hint, couldn't she, that there was no point in staying on after Ben had left? Or, if she hadn't wanted the younger one to kiss her, she could have slapped his face.

'Back to work, you two,' said Mr Dundas, firmly. The two men, who both looked somewhat taken aback by not only Betsy's bucket of water, but by the way Sally had fled from both of them, shambled off in the direction of the stables.

'Well, that certainly seems to have settled that,' said Mr Dundas with a chuckle. 'They will now probably spend the next few days drowning their sorrows and comparing stories about the fickleness of women until they end up fast friends.'

'And is that why you didn't try to stop them? You think that friendship between two men is more important than earning the love of a woman? Or that her indecision means she has no mind of her own?' She pushed aside the niggling little voice reminding her that Sally didn't appear to have appreciated Betsy's intervention. And the realisation that part of the reason she had reacted so badly to seeing men trying to settle it on the girl's behalf was because she was sick of not having any choices over her own life. She'd been the dutiful daughter, relying on her parents to arrange her future by means of a so-called brilliant society match. And then, when they'd made all that impossible, she'd once again obeyed her mother's promptings to go and snare Ben, the only titled man within her reach. Never mind whether she actually liked him, or would have been happy with him.

She was sick of seeing other people treating her like a puppet that had to dance when they pulled the strings, without asking her what she wanted.

At least these two men considered the little scullery maid worth fighting for.

But Mr Dundas seemed to think the whole episode was amusing. Perhaps he was one of those kinds of men who didn't think a woman's feelings mattered. Perhaps he saw nothing wrong with flirting for its own sake. Perhaps he just thought it was an amusing way to pass the time, rather than being so important she could lie awake at night puzzling over what to do.

Perhaps she was just nothing to him, after all.

'Don't you think a woman's feelings are important? That she might even be worth fighting for?'

'Well,' he said, looking a bit taken aback. 'I dare say some women…'

'Some women?' Her temper, which had not been relieved by slinging water over the two combatants as much as she'd expected, climbed a notch higher. 'I had not taken you for the kind of man who doesn't believe women have anything between their ears. I had thought you were different.' For some reason she couldn't fathom, she could feel tears starting to well up.

'So,' she said, drawing herself to her full height, because never had she felt so desperately in need of every single inch she possessed, 'I may as well tell you what sort of woman *I* am. It is why I came here this morning, after all. I am the sort of woman who does the opposite of what started this fight. Yes,' she cried, when he frowned in confusion at what she realised had been a rather perplexing statement. 'I am the sort of woman,' she declared recklessly, 'who snatches kisses off men! Not so long ago, I forced my way into this house and kissed Ben, and got caught kissing him by the very wife I never knew he had. There, what do you make of that?'

His face went white. 'You…kissed Lord Bramhall?'

'I just said so, didn't I? It was in the study,' she flung back at him. 'That was why I felt so ill when we went in there yesterday.'

'You kissed Lord Bramhall,' he said again, as though he couldn't believe it. 'In the study. And my… my Lady Bramhall saw you?'

He looked about as shocked and disgusted as any man could, which told her all she needed to know.

Turning on her heel, she marched off back across the stable yard, her head held high. She refused to look over her shoulder to see what he might be doing. Because to do so would be to show him that she wanted him to come after her. Which he wasn't doing, or she'd be able to hear his boots ringing across the cobbles. Hot, angry tears streamed down her face and soaked into the neckline of her gown, because she refused to dash them from her cheeks, or reach for a handkerchief to blot at them. Because then he'd know she was crying. Crying because she'd shattered whatever chance they might have had of getting closer. Shattered it by losing her temper and flinging the truth at him in the worst possible way, making it sound far worse than it had been. Without explaining any of the extenuating circumstances.

She'd made, in short, a complete mull of it. The first time she'd tried to be open and honest, and take the higher path! Well, she'd never do anything so totty-headed again as long as she lived.

Chapter Ten

James clenched his fists as he watched Miss Fair-fax march off, her head high. If only either Wilmot or Briggs was still hanging about. He could relieve the feelings ripping through him by knocking one of them down. As it was, he had to just stand there, repeating what she'd said, over and over in his mind.

She'd kissed Ben. A married man. And Daisy had seen her doing it. That could be the only reason she'd owned up, because she knew he'd find out, sooner or later.

But why? Why had she kissed Ben, that was what he wanted to know? Was she in love with Ben? If so, then he supposed he could understand her behaviour. Ben had been away for a long time, fighting. He could see why she'd rushed in to welcome him home. And if she'd been appalled to discover he was married, all that would explain why he'd found her, up on the hill, crying her eyes out.

Except…she didn't behave as though she was

broken-hearted, most of the time. Hardly *any* of the time, to be honest. Which meant… He frowned. If she wasn't in love with Ben, had never been in love with Ben, then the only reason she would have kissed him…

His mind flew back to the earlier part of the year, when he'd gone to London to support his sister making her come-out. And the women who'd tried everything to get close to him, even pretending they wanted to be friends with Daisy, only to give themselves away by fawning all over *him* whenever he was in the room.

Was Betsy no better than them? Was she the kind of girl who'd adopt any stratagem to bag herself a title? The kind of girl he couldn't trust for a lifetime, if she could be deceitful about her feelings?

Thank God he hadn't told her *he* had a title, then. Because she might never have shown her true colours.

He told himself that he'd had a narrow escape. That it was a relief. So why, as he went across the yard and mounted Socks, and went about his business, did it feel as if a thick fog was blotting out the sun? Why did his body feel so heavy and his brain so sluggish?

Shock, he told himself as he rode back to the hall at the end of the day for supper. And disappointment, that was all. He'd feel better in the morning, after a good night's sleep.

But the fog and the sluggish feeling were both still there the next morning. So much so that it took a real effort to get out of bed at all, let alone go about such work as he chose to do. And even what little he did manage to do was undertaken more to take his mind off her, and the blow she'd dealt him, than out of concern for Ben's tenants, or to be productive. There was no need, after all, was there? He would inherit vast holdings of his own in due course, whether he proved to be a good landlord or not. It didn't matter what sort of man he was.

Nothing mattered.

By the end of that day his jaws ached because, he realised, he'd been grinding his teeth incessantly. And as he ran his hand over his chin, feeling the stubble it hadn't seemed worth the effort of trying to scrape off, he noticed the others at the table watching him warily.

He'd been curt with them all, the night before, he recalled. And rightly so after that scene in the yard. They probably thought he was still angry with them. Well, what did he care what they thought? As long as they didn't suspect his mood had anything to do with Miss Fairfax. As long as they left him alone.

Which they did.

Over the next few days he took great care to stay well away from anywhere he might risk running into her. Like the hill where the oak tree grew, for example. Though he couldn't avoid seeing it. The blasted tree was visible for miles. Stuck up there with its branches spreading out in smug assurance at its own strength and longevity, so far above humans, with their short little life spans and their petty concerns.

But at least he could avoid seeing her pretty, deceitful, conniving face. And her hair that gleamed like polished ebony when sunlight played on it. And her shapely body with its scent that he'd breathed in on the few times he'd stood close enough to be able to smell it. A scent that was like no other.

But he couldn't avoid Colonel Fairfax. The man was everywhere. Trotting about on his big sorrel gelding and wishing him a good morning and remarking on what fine weather it was. And telling him he was welcome to come and take his pot luck with them at any time.

'Don't let my wife's attitude put you off,' he said, when James had made yet another excuse as to why he wouldn't be going to dine at Darby Manor. 'She's the same with everyone these days.' He sighed and shook his head. 'Prettiest thing you ever saw when she was a girl. Much like my Betsy is now.' He'd darted a sidelong look at James. 'Has a temper, though. Well, we all do, in our family. Say things we don't mean, in the heat of the moment, and then have too much pride to back down.'

So, the man thought he and his daughter had quarrelled, did he? Where had that notion come from? Unless Miss Fairfax was as miserable as he was. It occurred to him, suddenly, that although he'd been careful to avoid going anywhere he might see her, he hadn't seen her anywhere. Just as though she was being as careful to keep out of his way as he was to keep out of hers.

But then Sunday came round. And it occurred to him that the only way to avoid meeting her today would be by not going to church. By skulking at home. His whole being revolted at the prospect of appearing as though he was afraid of confronting her. Which he wasn't! Not at all. What's more, it was about time he jolly well showed her how little he cared about her going round kissing other men. Which he could do by marching into church…no, *strolling* into church, with a smile on his face and a pleasant greeting for everyone.

Even her. Yes, he decided, as he yanked his neckcloth into a knot that would have caused Bishop to fling up his hands in horror, she'd encroached on enough of his week. Time to draw the line.

He was going to bid her good morning in a friendly manner, just as though nothing had ever happened between them. That would show her he didn't care!

But he never got the chance. After dithering about whether to go to church or not, he ended up sliding into a pew that was several rows behind where Colonel Fairfax and his household were already sitting. He then spent the entire service darting looks at the back of her head, or, when she bent that head to pray, at the nape of her neck and the few dark curls that peeped out so saucily from under the edge of her bonnet, while he planned what he'd say and how he would stand as he said it, with one hand on his hip and his gloves in the other. And the exact expression he would have on his face, which would be either a condescending smile, or a look of boredom.

Only for her to dart off down the path and out of the churchyard the moment the vicar intoned the dismissal, without giving him the chance to so much as bid her good morning, leaving him standing in the churchyard watching her flit through the gravestones as though fleeing from some ghoulish apparition.

'Good notion of yours to test a sample of the meadow those lawns have become,' said Colonel Fairfax, following the direction of where James was staring in frustration. After all the effort it had taken him to get there, and all the cudgelling of his brain to work out how the confrontation would go, she'd denied him the chance to prove that she hadn't wounded him. At all.

'Lawns?' James tore his gaze from the back of Miss Fairfax, to try to work out what her father was talking about. He had to. He didn't want to look like an idiot.

'Though you won't get a good crop from it this year. Has been left too long to have much value as fodder. But if you take my advice, you'll get it mown soon anyway. We've had a good spell of weather, so it won't get any better than it already is. And then next year...'

While Colonel Fairfax carried on advising him

about the mowing and drying of hay, James's mind went back to the day he'd spent waving a scythe about to make it look as if he'd been working, so as to conceal his impatience to see Miss Fairfax.

It didn't matter what anyone else thought. He *was* an idiot. The kind of idiot who'd been deceived by a pretty face.

'I'll start mowing this week, then,' he said, mustering the ability, from somewhere, to carry on a conversation in which he had no interest at all. Although, he reflected, it probably *would* do him good to take a swipe at something. And to make Briggs and Wilmot do some actual work, instead of hanging around Sally all day, trying to impress her.

'That's the ticket,' said Colonel Fairfax. 'Before the weather turns.'

Wilmot had spent the last few years valeting Lord Bramhall, and Briggs was a groom. So it was just as well that the crop of hay was not likely to be of much use anyway, because the three of them started off making about as bad a job of it as any three men could. It was not until Colonel Fairfax came by to check on their progress, and gave them a few tips, which not only prevented them from burying the tips of their scythes in the earth, but also from endangering each other, that they began to make any real progress.

Of course, that wasn't the last of it. Over the next few days they had to get out with pitchforks to turn the windrows to stop the hay fermenting where it lay. And later, when locals warned them that the weather was going to turn, they had to pile the hay into mounds to protect at least some of it from the rain.

Which meant that at least, with all the hard physical work James was doing, he would fall asleep almost as soon as he went to bed each night. Which was preferable to lying there thinking about a certain young lady, who was either in love with another man, or so determined to marry well that she'd try to compromise the only lord she could get her hands on.

But one night, he awoke, in the dead of night, feeling unusually hot and uncomfortable. In the distance, he heard a rumble of thunder and then another, much closer. That was probably what had woken him.

As he turned over and punched his pillow into a slightly less uncomfortable configuration of lumps, he suddenly remembered that the reason he hadn't ever told Miss Fairfax that he had a title was because she'd warned him that her mother was one of those matchmaking mothers he disliked so much.

She'd warned him.

He sat up, his mind racing. Not only had she said that, but she'd also said something to the effect of having done something she regretted, to avoid the fate of being sent to Tunbridge Wells. He rubbed at his forehead, trying to make the memory of that day come clearer. She'd been crying, when he first saw her, because she felt so guilty about something she wished she hadn't done, he recalled that much.

Perhaps she wasn't as ruthless as all that. Perhaps she was just afraid of being sent away from her home. Perhaps...

Perhaps he was clutching at straws. He flung himself back on to his stubbornly lumpy pillow. He was searching for excuses for her behaviour, that was what he was doing. Because in spite of knowing what she'd done, he couldn't stop thinking about her. Bad or good, she was at the forefront of his mind from the moment he floundered out of bed in the mornings until the moment he flopped back into it at the end of the day. She even put in appearances in his dreams. That was what had woken him up. Not the rumbles of thunder and flashes of lightning, but the dream he'd had that was so explicit, in which Miss Fairfax was so naked, and so eager for his embrace that he'd taken her in his arms and...

Woken up. Hot and sweaty and angry and frustrated.

This wouldn't do. How could he go on thinking about her, wanting her, when she was, well, impure? Who was exactly the kind of woman his father had been warning him about all his life?

Or was she? To be honest, Father had tried to give him a deep distrust of all women. Before he even knew their names, he tended to wonder if they might be predatory, if not downright dangerous to his health and well-being. Especially pretty ones. Father was always urging James to marry a plain, homely girl, rather than allow a pretty one to muddle his thinking. But could all women really be as wicked as Father made out? Daisy, his sister, definitely wasn't, was she? And she'd been just about the prettiest girl in London when she'd had her comeout. And had she ever flirted, or tried to trap some man into marriage? No. Because all she wanted to do was get home to her books. Because she loved reading and had little ambition to make a figure in society. So if Daisy didn't fit in with Father's view of what women wanted, and how they behaved, perhaps others didn't, either. Perhaps Miss Fairfax didn't.

But on the other hand, perhaps she did.

He gave up trying to sleep. Got out of bed, went down to the stable yard and sluiced his hot, aching body under the pump. Saddled his horse and finally gave in to the urge to ride up to the hill where he'd first seen her, sitting under the oak tree. From there he watched the sun rise, defiantly pushing the last of the thunder clouds away, gilding their lower edges purple and orange.

And wished she was there to see it, with him.

It was no use, was it? The wanting wasn't going to go away. So perhaps *he* should. Leave the area. Get as far away from her as he could. And try to forget her.

The possibility of doing this made his ride back to the house a dreary experience. He no longer saw the spectacular display in the sky, but only the mud smearing Socks's white socks into a shade of mucky brown that exactly matched his notion of what his future would be like. Drab. Dismal. Lonely.

The very last person he wished to see, on reaching Bramley Park, was Colonel Fairfax. But there he was, beaming from ear to ear and striding across to meet him as he rode into the yard.

'Great news,' he said. 'Got it last night, so rode over here first thing to tell you. Wellington has trounced Bonaparte. The French army is on the run.'

A shaft of guilt pierced James as he swung himself out of his saddle. For here was he, feeling sorry for himself over a girl who was probably completely worthless, while on the other side of the English Channel Ben himself had taken part in a momentous battle.

'Any news,' he asked as he handed the reins to Briggs, who had for once come running the moment he'd ridden into the yard, 'of casualties?'

'Too soon,' said the Colonel brusquely. 'But I shall ride into Crickheath from here, to see if I can get hold of a London newspaper.'

James couldn't very well pack and leave after that. Daisy was bound to write to him, here, with news about Ben, if he'd been injured, or, God forbid, killed. He'd have to go over to Brussels if that were the case. And escort her home. Which was here now.

Perhaps he would pack, just in case the news was bad. He'd have to vacate his room, if Daisy was going to need it. Unless she wanted to go back to Wattle-sham Priory. She might need Mother, if she'd lost Ben.

Dammit, but why did the day have to drag by so slowly?

It was after the evening meal before Colonel Fair-fax returned. 'I have bought all the papers they'd let me buy,' he said as he popped his head in the kitchen door, which was open, it being such a sultry evening. 'Here's one for you, my boy,' he said, toss-ing one from his bundle of papers on to the kitchen table. 'Nothing definite about casualties yet, it's all rhetoric so far. However, there is one bit of news that will affect us all.'

'Yes?'

James kept his eyes firmly fixed on the Colonel as Wilmot pounced on the paper and scanned the columns with a deep frown.

'They are going to hold a celebration ball in the assembly room at the back of the Bull's Head. You will come with us, in our carriage, of course.'

Would he? 'I...'

'No, don't argue. I know you could get there on horseback, but you won't want to spoil your evening clothes doing that, will you? And there has been little enough in the way of entertainment for you young folk since you've been in these parts. Besides which, there will be some people there it would be useful for you to meet and you won't want to do that all muddy and smelling of horse, what?'

Never mind the useful people. A ball was not the

place to hold a sensible conversation with anyone much, with all the bustling of bodies and the screeching of violins, and the many other distractions and annoyances. He took a break to make a polite but firm refusal, just as he would have done had anyone else invited him to a ball, face to face. He never accepted invitations made in person, on principal. Unless, that was, the invitation came from a very close friend, or for a very good reason.

But then he pictured Miss Fairfax, dancing the night away with a succession of nameless men. Laughing and enjoying herself while he stayed at home nursing his grudges and, probably, a decanter of something potent.

And every feeling revolted.

He jolly well would go to the ball! And damn well dance with her himself. And be the one to take her into supper, while he was at it. Just to prove that he could converse with her like a sensible, rational person.

Why shouldn't he? There would be no harm in any of that, would there? It wasn't as if he was going to propose marriage to her, was it?

'Thank you,' he therefore said. 'I would be very grateful for the lift.'

Chapter Eleven

Mother, for once, had no fault to find with something Papa had done.

'You never know who might be at such an event, even if it is in such an unfashionable spot,' she'd said when he told them he'd purchased tickets for the Waterloo ball to be held in Crickheath. 'Anyone might be staying with an aged relative, or an old school friend, and although they wouldn't normally frequent such a place as the back room of the Bull's Head, this victory over Bonaparte is bound to make *anyone* unbend a little.'

Betsy had her suspicions that Mother was so bored that going to a ball, anywhere, would come as a welcome diversion, no matter the reason it was being held, or who might be there. Although her mood underwent a shift back to the more normal one of disapproval when Papa told her they would be collecting Mr Dundas on their way and taking him up with them.

As for Betsy, the news that she was going to be squashed in Papa's carriage with Mr Dundas, all the way to Crickheath, then all the way back again, did very strange things to her insides.

'I hope I need not remind you of all the reasons why he is unsuitable,' Mama had said to her earlier that day as they'd begun preparations for going out. 'Nor to warn you not to waste your time attempting to attract his interest.'

No. There was absolutely no need to give Betsy any such warnings. She'd learned what kind of man Mr Dundas was. He was the kind who expected extremely high standards from women, and had let her know that she fell very far short of them. Oh, not with words, but by his actions. He hadn't sought her out, since the moment she'd told him she'd kissed Ben. And when he'd seen her, at church on Sunday, his expression had been so flinty, so condemning, that she hadn't been able to face trying to make small talk with him. She'd simply fled.

However, she'd had time to recover from the initial blow he'd dealt her. And had given herself several stern lectures about the folly of hankering after a man who had such a judgemental, unforgiving attitude. It wasn't as if he was even eligible, was it? Even if he had started to court her, in earnest, Mother would never have permitted it to get very far.

Even so, she took great pains with her appearance. She bathed, using the expensive rose-scented soap, and washed and curled her hair. She wore her best ball gown, which hadn't been out of its silver paper since she'd returned from London. It might no longer be the height of fashion, but it suited her, which was far more important.

Besides, what would a man like Mr Dundas know of female fashion? All he would see would be a gown that fit her perfectly, flattering her curves, and her colouring, and which, when she twirled round in any of the figures of a dance, flared out, showing a lot more of her lower legs than was probably acceptable in a little rural town like Crickheath. Not that she was dressing to please or interest him. No! But, by golly, she was going to show him that even if he didn't want her, there were plenty of men who did! Hopefully, men with money, and connections, even if they didn't have titles. Not that she cared for such things, but the wealthier any man who showed an interest in her was, the more she hoped it would sting Mr Dundas.

Her heart was pounding so hard as the coach lurched to a halt by the front gates of Bramley Park she felt as if everyone must be able to hear it. Though she was determined not to let him, or anyone, know that his presence affected her one bit. She adopted the same disdainful expression as Mother wore as he clambered inside and took the seat next to Papa and opposite hers. She even managed to dredge up some real irritation when his knee brushed against hers, even though he couldn't help it, really, since the coach was so small.

She was gratified when he coloured up and apologised, before twisting ever so slightly to one side.

But since nobody had all that much room, both she and he were going to have to keep every muscle in their bodies braced, all the way to Crickheath, to prevent them from bumping into each other whenever they bounced over a pothole, or into a rut. She would be exhausted well before they even got there. And with every mile, she would wager, it would become harder and harder to resist the effect he had on her, simply by sitting there, looking so rugged, and indifferent, with his face newly shaven, and smelling of bergamot.

But then, it was the first time she'd been so close to him since she'd lost her temper with him and flung the bald truth about her behaviour at him. It was a hurdle she'd have to get over, one day. And when better than with Mother and Papa sitting there, too, which would prevent him from saying anything obnoxious? Or her, come to that. Yes, for if they were alone in this carriage, she'd tell him exactly how little his opinion meant to her. And how glad she was she'd discovered how fickle he was, before she'd done anything as foolish as to start to develop a tendre for him.

And she was *not* going to reach for a handkerchief to dab at her eyes, or sniff, or anything of the sort. She would deal with all these raging emotions by thinking of something else. And hum a jolly tune under her breath. And not look at him again, under *any* circumstances.

'Heard anything,' said Papa to Mr Dundas, as she loftily turned her face to gaze out of the window, 'about Lord Bramhall's injury? Saw his name on the list of casualties, but not how serious it is.'

What? Ben was wounded? Her stomach lurched. How badly had he been wounded? In spite of the vow she'd only just made, she couldn't help turning to Mr Dundas, to hear what he might know. But before he could reply, Mother put paid to that topic of conversation.

'I do hope you are not going to spend the entire trip to Crickheath talking about battles,' she snapped. 'It is not a suitable topic for Betsy's ears.'

'The whole evening,' Papa replied coldly, 'is on account of that battle.'

'Yes, but there is no need to go into the gruesome details,' Mother snapped back. 'I, for one, have no taste for such talk. If you really must dwell on woundings and maimings, I hope you will have the decency to restrain yourselves until you can do so out of my hearing.'

Oh, Mother! What a time to pick to insist on sticking to the kinds of things men and women could talk about over the dinner table. She turned to stare out of the window again, her determination to stay aloof from Mr Dundas disintegrating under the more pressing need to find out what he knew. Because he did know something. Before Mother had forbidden any more talk about the battle, he'd taken a breath, his face looking as though he was ready to impart something.

Why couldn't Mother have just let him say whatever it was he'd been about to say? And why did it

have to be Mr Dundas who had some news? Why
couldn't it have been someone else? *Anyone* else?
Because now she was going to have to unbend and
speak to him, perhaps even *beg* him to tell her what
he knew, if he wasn't inclined to speak to her. Because she had to know whether Ben had been injured. She just had to.

By the time they reached Crickheath, Betsy felt
as if she was going to explode with a mixture of
frustration and curiosity and chagrin at what she'd
decided she'd have to do. It was all she could do to
walk sedately to the ladies' changing room, and de-
posit her cloak and change into her dancing shoes,
when she would much rather have just grabbed Mr
Dundas by the arm, taken him somewhere private
and demanded he tell her what he knew of Ben's injuries, no matter what Mother might think.

But in the end, she had no need to do anything so
drastic. Mr Dundas was waiting for her as she came
out of the changing room. And the moment he saw
her, he bowed and asked her, in a stilted voice, if he
might have the honour of being her partner for the
first dance.

And then, perversely, she wanted to kick him.
He could have asked her on the way here. Then she
would have known she would have the opportunity
to talk to him and then she wouldn't have ended up
in this state.

She blew out a long, slow breath through her nostrils. Forced both her feet to stay firmly planted on the ground, then pasted on her best society smile.

'Thank you, Mr Dundas,' she said through gritted teeth. 'I should be delighted.'

She wouldn't be delighted. She wasn't in the slightest bit delighted. But it was what she had to say, or she'd draw attention to her turmoil. Which was a thing no lady should ever do, especially not in a ballroom. Not according to Mother.

The trouble was, she soon discovered, that it was impossible to start any kind of meaningful conversation during the performance of a cotillion. Not just because of having to concentrate on the complicated figures, or the fact that everyone changed partners so often, but because she feared that if he told her that Ben had taken a serious injury, or was even worse... no, she shook her head, she couldn't even give the word space in her head. She would start crying, she just knew she would.

She'd have to get Mr Dundas alone somewhere, that was all. As soon as this wretched dance finally ended. Not that it would be an easy matter to get him alone. He wouldn't want to go anywhere private with her, would he, not now she'd confessed she'd kissed a married man? And Mother would put a stop to it if she could. She'd have to sneak past Mother, then, somehow.

She glanced over to where Mother was standing with the most well-to-do matrons present, their heads together, all looking askance at some other ladies, who, by their dress, appeared to be married to tradesmen, and felt a flash of annoyance. Mother was always judging by appearances and condemning people for being of lower class, or having less money. But she wagered there was nobody in the room with less money than they had, right now, in spite of appearances. They might still live in a big house and keep a pack of hounds, and have influence in their village. But it was all hollow. Like a blown eggshell. One slight tap and it would all crumple away to nothing.

What was more, it was Mother's fault they'd come to this pass. It was all very well her going on about Papa's shortcomings, but it wasn't Papa who'd gambled all the money away, was it?

It was Mother's fault she'd kissed Ben, too. The idea would never have occurred to her if Mother hadn't insisted that if a woman wished to marry well, then sometimes she had to act decisively. Take risks.

In fact, it was starting to feel as if every time Betsy followed Mother's advice she ended up, for want of a better phrase, in a pickle. Perhaps it was time she did just what she wanted, for a change. Being a dutiful daughter certainly hadn't achieved anything. She'd come home from her Season without a husband, or a dowry, and had become so worried about facing a future as a paid companion to an elderly, cantankerous relative, that she'd forced her way into Ben's house and disgusted him, and herself, by kissing him.

When, oh, when would this dratted cotillion come to an end? Normally, she would have enjoyed the admiring glances the other men in the set gave her when they took her hands and twirled her round. And she would have admired how nimble Mr Dundas was on his feet, for a man of his build. Instead, it was starting to feel very like a form of ordeal by violin and etiquette by the time the master of ceremonies finally gave the signal to cease.

And, to her chagrin, when Mr Dundas bowed to her and offered his arm, she felt tears spring to her eyes.

'Please, please, don't return me to Mother, just yet,' she begged him, in spite of vowing that she'd behave in a dignified manner. That she'd demand, haughtily, that he tell her what he knew. That she would only beg as an absolute last resort. 'I need to know what you know about Ben's injuries, or I shall go mad.'

He looked at her steadily, as though turning something over in his mind, then his face softened.

'Very well,' he said, with a decisive nod. 'We will go outside and walk about in the courtyard I spied on the way in. The air is mild, so you won't need to waste time fetching a shawl. And by the time your mother notices you've gone, we should be able to say all we need to say to each other.'

Chapter Twelve

He was glad he'd asked her to dance. She'd looked adorable while she'd been dancing, that little frown on her brow showing how hard she was concentrating on the steps. So unlike the accomplished debutantes who tried to impress everyone by making out the cotillion was so easy they could perform it in their sleep.

He also liked the way she couldn't conceal her concern about Ben. She didn't have it in her to dissemble. Or not for long. It was, in fact, he supposed, to her credit that she'd admitted she'd kissed Ben. In a way. At least it showed she wouldn't be any good at conducting illicit affairs, if she was ever tempted into one. She'd feel too guilty. And with that expressive little face of hers, she'd give herself away.

Still, there was no denying the fact that she was entirely too wrapped up in another man. A married man. And while he sympathised with her concern, he could never get more involved with her than he already was.

The open space he'd spied, on the way in, was not really a courtyard, as such. But it was certainly convenient for taking the air, in between energetic bouts of dancing, especially on such a warm night as this. The cobbled area was divided up by gravelled pathways, with a few benches dotted here and there. Someone had put potted plants next to all the benches, in an attempt, he supposed, to try to make it look like the garden of somebody's home, but the attempt had failed dismally. Nobody would ever think that this was anything but a stable yard with delusions of grandeur. Still, the light from the windows, high up on the wall of the assembly room, meant that it was not completely dark. So it had all the necessary ingredients for couples to further an acquaintance begun in the ballroom.

'So,' said Miss Fairfax, with a quiver in her voice, the moment they were out of earshot of anyone else, 'you do know something about Ben, don't you? Has he been injured?'

'Yes, but—'

'Oh! It is as I feared,' she said, turning and gripping his arm with both her hands. 'Tell me the worst.'

'I will if you give me half a chance,' he said a bit irritably. 'And it isn't that bad. Cuts and bruises, only.'

'Cuts?' Her eyes widened in alarm.

'Minor cuts,' he reassured her. 'Grazes, really.' If it had been anything worse, his sister would have spent a lot more time writing about it, rather than merely mentioning it in a couple of lines before going on to other topics.

Miss Fairfax sagged against him, leaning her head against his chest. It was all he could do not to put his arms round her to comfort her. But he couldn't. Because if he held her in his arms, his body would react to her nearness. He was sure of it. And, yes, there it went, and all she'd done was lean her fore-head against his chest.

He swallowed. Counted to three.

'It is hopeless, you know,' he said, trying to sound stern. 'He is married. Happily married. He adores his wife...'

She lifted her head. Gazed at him in surprise. 'What? What do you mean?'

'He has been, apparently, in love with her for years. He will never look at another woman.'

Her eyes narrowed. 'Are you implying that I am pining for *Ben*?'

'Well...' he rapidly reviewed everything she'd said about Ben, since they'd met, and how she'd behaved whenever his name cropped up in conversation '...if you are not in love with him, then...'

'In love with him!' She took a step back, remov-ing her hands from where they'd been clutching at his arm. 'But he's married. How could you possibly think I'm in love with him? Why, I hardly know him.'

'But...you told me you kissed him. And when I first met you, you were sitting there, crying over him. What was I supposed to think?'

She pursed her lips, the way one of his sister's

governesses used to do, whenever she saw him, even when she hadn't caught him out in some boyish prank. But then, instead of planting her hands on her hips and delivering a lecture, the way the governess would most definitely have done, her face took on a perplexed expression.

'But I *told* you it was Tunbridge Wells,' she said. Which didn't help explain things at all.

'Tunbridge Wells,' he echoed, feeling excessively stupid.

She sighed. 'I lost my temper the day I came over to explain my odd behaviour in the study, didn't I? And made it all sound a lot worse than it really was when I did tell you the bald facts. And for two pins I'd walk away now and leave you in the dark. How could you,' she said, finally planting her hands on her hips, 'believe me capable of hankering after a married man?'

'I beg your pardon,' he said meekly, having learned from all those governesses that it was never of any use explaining why he was doing whatever it was he'd been caught out doing once it had got to the hands-on-hips stance. The best thing to do was to let them get the lecture over with, with as few interruptions as possible, so that he could go right back to doing whatever he'd been doing before they caught him.

Besides which, he wanted to hear what Miss Fairfax had to say. She wasn't in love with Ben, she'd just said. So what excuse could there be for having kissed him?

'It's…it's a bit complicated,' she said, with a frown.

'Why don't we go and sit on one of these benches, then?' he suggested. 'While you work out how to say whatever it is you want to say to me.' When she nodded, he led her to one which wasn't immediately visible from the door to the assembly room. There were other couples outside, taking a stroll round the area, so it wouldn't be improper. He wouldn't be alone with her. He would just be ensuring they had a modicum of privacy.

They sat down and she clasped her hands on her knees, gazing down at them with a rather tortured expression on her face. 'It was Mother who sent me to Bramley Park, the day I kissed Ben.'

'Hang on. She knew you were going there, but she didn't go with you?'

Miss Fairfax shook her head. He rapidly reviewed what she'd just said.

'Your own mother…*urged* you to go to speak to Lord Bramhall, alone?' What kind of woman did that?

The kind of mother with whom he was all too familiar. The kind who would stoop to any depths to get their daughter tied to a wealthy, or titled, man.

'She was desperate to see me married well.'

Yes! That was what they all wanted. And not one of them cared a rap for what their prey might happen to think about it!

'And for reasons of…well, reasons,' Miss Fairfax continued, shifting a bit uncomfortably, 'we'd had to cut my Season short, which I suppose she felt partly responsible for...' She gave herself a little shake. 'Well, be that as it may, she made me believe that Ben would welcome some female attention. I believed her all too easily, because I'd always felt a bit sorry for him. His father and older brothers were always so beastly to him that I thought that all I'd have to do was give him a bit of encouragement and I'd have him eating out of my hands. That I could marry him and I could be his Countess, and that would solve all our problems. And that Papa wouldn't have to sell the house, and I wouldn't have to go to Tunbridge Wells. You can understand exactly why I threw myself at him, can't you?'

Funnily enough, he could. He'd never looked at things from a woman's point of view before. But now she'd explained just what had driven her to do what she'd done, it made him wonder how many of the other females he'd despised and repulsed in his past for being designing hussies had been victims of their parents' ambitions. Or suffering from severe need in one form or another. It was hard for a girl, particularly, to stand against a parent who was pushing them into a course of action, because she'd have been trained up in habits of obedience and loyalty.

Had he been too quick to condemn them all? Without even trying to understand what might have driven them? Because he was predisposed to distrust women, thanks to his father's teachings?

'I suppose,' he said, hesitantly.

'Yes, you don't need to tell me *now*. But at the time nobody knew he was married, did they? And it was bad enough, after screwing my courage up all the way there and then leaping on him and kissing him when it was clearly the last thing he wanted, but then his wife came in and found me hanging round his neck like some clinging…monkey…' She gave a little shudder of disgust.

For some reason, James found himself wanting to laugh. It wasn't just that he could picture the exact expression Daisy would have had on her face when she'd walked in on such a scene, it was the way Miss Fairfax had just described herself. The relief that she didn't love Ben. And, more than that, the courage it must have taken her to confess all this and the trust she was placing in him by doing so.

And, most of all, the knowledge that if she wanted him to understand, then he must matter to her.

He reached over and patted her hand. 'And you have been consumed with guilt ever since.' She *was* a good, decent girl, at heart. 'But…'

'No. Don't start being all understanding with me yet,' she said, snatching her hand out from under his. 'I haven't finished. There is worse. Much worse.' She twisted her hands together in her lap as though she was wringing out a wet dishcloth. 'You see, Lady Bramhall was so…' She screwed up her face. 'Oh, I cannot describe it. Something just came over me… But…' she half turned her upper body, so that she was looking him directly in the face '…have you never looked at someone and felt that she had everything you wanted, and didn't even appreciate how lucky she was and was taking it all for granted, while looking down her smug, condescending nose at you, and just wanted to…smash it all to pieces?'

'Well, no, I haven't…' But he'd noticed that a lot of girls reacted badly to his sister. It was partly due to her own attitude, he couldn't deny it. She was actually rather shy and withdrawn, but because of her height, she couldn't help literally looking down her nose at everyone. Which made people think she was haughty and aloof.

'You probably don't suffer from having a temper like mine, then.' She sighed. 'But anyway, I behaved in such a spiteful manner and said something so awful that, as soon as they left, I started wondering if it had been my fault. Poor Ben had never looked very happy when he lived here, as a boy, and the moment he came back, to take up his position, I behaved so badly… Well, pretty soon I was sure that I'd driven them from the area with my shameful, awful behaviour and not just away from here, but into a battle. And if Ben had been hurt, or killed, it would have been all my fault!'

Tears formed in her eyes. Pooled on her lashes. But before they could go anywhere, she dashed them angrily away with the tips of her gloved fingers. 'My temper. My awful temper. I say such things…'

And his heart just turned to mush. He felt it go.

'Look, Miss Fairfax, I don't deny that what you did

sounds pretty bad, but Ben—that is, Lord Bramhall—
has been a serving soldier most of his adult life, hasn't
he? And I happen to know lots of chaps who went
haring off to join whatever regiment they could when
they heard Bonaparte had escaped from Elba and was
gathering his own troops. And none of them appeared
to think of it as some sort of sacrifice, even if they did
go about boasting of wanting to do their patriotic duty.
Men like that, military types, they crave adventure,
you know.' He couldn't help sighing. 'I envy them, in
a way. What must it be like to be able to just drop everything and go? Leave all the mundane, everyday responsibilities behind and, instead of being condemned
for being frivolous, get hailed as heroes?'

'So you don't think it was my fault they went
away? You think he'd have gone even if I'd been a
perfect paragon of propriety?'

He stifled a slight flicker of annoyance that she'd
ignored his own, first tentative attempt to let anyone
else know how he felt about the restricted life he had
to lead, as the oldest son and heir to his father's estates, and with his father's particular form of parent-
ing shackling him still further, because it was better
that nobody knew. Better that she was so wrapped
up in herself that she didn't look too deeply at him.
Or she might wonder who he really was and where
he came from, and he would never be able to enjoy
moments like this again. Even if she didn't start looking at him differently, that mother of hers certainly
would. She'd have them down the aisle before you
could say Jack Robinson.

'Miss Fairfax,' he said, taking advantage of her distracted state of mind to take possession of one of her hands. 'I shouldn't think that, having the background he did, anyone could sway him from any course of action he wished to take, or push him into doing something he did not want.'

She gave a juddering little sigh and just sat there, gazing at him for some time, although he couldn't be sure she was really seeing him. Her mind seemed very far away. Still, it gave him the chance to just sit looking right back at her, enjoying the view and pondering the fact that not only was she not in love with Ben, but she wasn't the kind of girl who'd stoop to trying to compromise a man into marriage, just because he had a title. She was just an impulsive, hot-headed girl who was trying to do her best by her family, by the sound of it, and falling into scrapes instead. And she really was the loveliest creature to look at. The light from the ballroom was bathing her skin with a soft, mellow warmth. He was just starting to think he could happily sit like this, just looking at her, holding her little hand, for ever, when she gave a little start.

'Mr Dundas, thank you for your understanding. You really are the most…sympathetic person.' She looked away from him, briefly, then lifted her chin and squared her shoulders. 'And now I find myself having to make a direct apology to you.'

'To me? What for?'

'For losing my temper with you when I came to visit you and found those two grooms fighting in the yard. My only excuse is that I had worked myself up to quite a state before I even got there, knowing what I had to confess.'

'Not at all,' he said, recognising an olive branch when it was being held out to him. 'It was just a great pity that I hadn't thought of applying a bucket of water to the situation myself. And I was most impressed by your stern lecture about a woman not being a prize to be won by strength of arms, like a pig at a fair.'

'Thank you,' she said, looking a bit startled, then licked her lips. 'For myself, it occurred to me, later on, when I'd calmed down and began to think the incident over rationally, that it couldn't have been easy for you to exert any authority over them, when you are just a fellow servant yourself. That perhaps it *was* better to let them settle their differences their own way, rather than act as though you were their employer...'

'Rationally,' he echoed, his eyes riveted by the sight of that little pink tongue, swiping over those plump, slightly damp lips, yet again. And although there was something she'd just said that unsettled him, something about not having the authority to discipline another man's servants, he couldn't focus on that, not while he was holding that hand, about which he'd had so many fantasies. Not when her lips looked so shiny and luscious. And then, to his horror, the most irrational sentence he'd ever uttered sprang from his own lips.

'Did you enjoy kissing Ben?'

'I beg your pardon?' She sat up straighter, looking offended. 'Didn't I just tell you it was the most mortifying, humiliating experience of my life? So bad that merely walking into that room again, that day when you were there, made me feel physically ill?'

'That wasn't what I meant. I know you suffered pangs of guilt upon discovering that you'd kissed a married man. But if he hadn't been married, would you have remembered it differently?'

'No,' she said, without even having to pause to think about it. 'The moment I planted my lips on his I knew it was wrong.' She made a little moue of distaste. Puckering up those lips in a way that made his own tingle. 'It was like kissing…I don't know…a statue. And a statue that I'd just had to climb, what was more. He's so *tall*,' she said, shaking her head.

'I'm not,' he heard himself saying. 'You wouldn't have to climb at all if you wanted to kiss me.' Had he really just said that? Out loud? His cheeks suddenly became rather hot. This wasn't the way to talk to a young lady who trusted him enough to share the motivation behind what had been an excruciatingly painful episode. He ought to be soothing her. Saying it didn't matter.

No wonder her eyebrows rose in surprise.

But not with annoyance. In fact, if anything, he would say she looked intrigued. And then something began to pulse, between them. Although it was a silent something. Like a sort of expectant hush.

'N-no,' she said, finally. 'It would not be anywhere near as uncomfortable trying to kiss you.' She looked at his mouth. His heart began to beat faster.

'I wouldn't push you away, either,' he said, which was a bit of a surprise, on the whole. He'd pushed plenty of women away, before, when they'd tried to plant their lascivious mouths on his. But he'd never felt the slightest interest in kissing them, before they'd leaped on him. Which was not the way it was with Miss Fairfax. He could hardly take his eyes off her mouth. Or stop wondering what it would be like to press his own against hers.

'In fact,' he said, inching closer, 'if you don't kiss me, I might just have to kiss you, instead.'

'You...you want to kiss me?'

Yes, he did. And, for the first time in his life, he took the initiative with a woman. While she was still gazing at him, in wonder and indecision, he closed the gap between them and brushed his lips against hers.

She gasped, but didn't slap his face, or move away.

And so he leaned in and did it again. With a bit more confidence. Their noses bumped. So he turned his head to one side a bit and slid his hands round her waist. He felt her hands creep up his chest, as she returned the pressure of his mouth.

He drew back. 'Was that all right? I've never,' he confessed, 'kissed a woman before. But with you...' His heart was pounding now. His whole body felt alive. Invigorated. Not the slightest feeling of wariness. No visions of deadly disease, or wondering if he was letting his family down. Just a steady, strong surge of ardour.

'May I,' he said, 'do it again?'

When she nodded, shyly, he almost gave a yell of exultation. Instead, he hauled her closer and this time stopped thinking and just revelled in sensation. In feeling.

'Miss Fairfax,' he panted, when he had to finally come up for air, or drown in her, 'you are amazing. No woman has ever made me feel like this before. I...' he declared, tugging her closer, almost on to his lap, 'I cannot get enough of you.'

'Mr Dundas,' she panted back, 'while this is most flattering, and enjoyable, we have to stop. We shouldn't be doing this. We shouldn't be out here alone.'

Her words might have had a dampening effect on his ardour if she hadn't been running her hands all over his chest while she was saying them. Playing with the ends of his hair and looking so tortured.

Nevertheless, she was right. They ought not to be alone, when their effect on each other was so potent. And how marvellous it was of her to point out that the sensible thing, the safe thing to do, would be to go back to the ballroom before someone discovered them. What integrity. What a girl!

'You are right,' he said. 'And I'm grateful to you for pointing it out.' Another woman might have tried to keep him out here, in order to compromise him. But not Miss Fairfax. She might tumble into scrapes because of her impulsive nature, but there wasn't a sly, manipulative bone in her lush little body. 'Let us return to the ballroom,' he said, getting to his feet stiffly. In all senses of the word.

Chapter Thirteen

She waited for him to apologise. That was what men did, in these circumstances, wasn't it? But he didn't. He just held out his arm and gazed at her in a way that made her feel rather wonderful. As though he'd never seen anything or anyone so lovely.

She laid her hand on his sleeve, deciding she liked him the better for not making an apology in form, when he clearly wouldn't have meant it. He'd enjoyed kissing her. And, well, she'd enjoyed kissing him, too, so trying to act as if either of them should feel sorry, or guilty, would be a bit hypocritical, wouldn't it?

Actually, she was half-tempted to *thank* him for kissing her so enthusiastically. Her self-esteem had taken a knock when Ben had thrust her off him with disgust. She'd felt guilty and slightly soiled ever since. As though no man in his right mind would ever look at her with admiration again. Mr Dundas had swept all that away. Not only with the kiss, but through listening to her confession and appearing sympathetic.

She wondered, as they strolled back in the direction of the open doors to the assembly room, if that was what people of the Roman Catholic faith felt, when they went to confession. This same sort of lightness as the guilt and shame lifted away.

'I won't ask you to dance a second time,' said Mr Dundas, as they reached the doorway. 'I do not want my attraction for you to be too obvious, or to damage your reputation in any way. Because, if anyone noticed our long absence outside, and then sees me gazing at you like someone infatuated as we go down the set together…'

She glanced up at him. His jaw was working in a way that made him look anything but infatuated.

'You need not worry,' she told him, wanting to giggle. 'Because far from looking enamoured, you look rather as though you are in pain.'

'I am,' he said.

'Oh, dear.' Whatever could be the matter with him? 'Is there anything I can do?'

'You have done enough,' he said through gritted teeth.

What had she done? She hadn't struck him, she didn't think. Although her mind had gone a bit blank while they'd been kissing. And she had lost control of her hands, which had gone wandering all over his chest and shoulders. But surely she hadn't accidentally scratched him, or pinched him, had she?

'But do not look so worried,' he said. 'The pain

you have roused is an exquisitely enjoyable sort of pain. And it will subside, as long as you don't smile at me too often, or look at me as though you wish to kiss me again, or dance with me, or…hang it. I shall have to leave you here and go for a walk.'

So saying, he bowed, with rather less grace than usual, turned on his heel and strode back out into the darkness.

Feeling slightly puzzled, she drifted back into the ballroom, where she was quickly solicited for a dance by the foreman of the local quarry. Since Mother was not nearby, to forbid her to have anything to do with such a man, she gladly accepted and spent the rest of the evening dancing with all sorts of ineligible and charming partners, of varying degrees of proficiency. Not one of them matched up to Mr Dundas, either in personality or accomplishment, in her opinion. Not that she watched him avidly for the rest of the evening, or anything like that. Mother would have been certain to notice if she had and would have had something to say.

Nevertheless, Betsy couldn't help seeing that he danced with several other ladies, or, at least, females, during the course of the evening. Naturally, he could do nothing else. If he'd only danced with her, it would have looked most peculiar. So she didn't mind that he danced with several other of the younger ladies present. Especially since he only danced with anyone just once and she didn't sit out a single dance herself.

He went into supper with them, since he was one

of their party, and gallantly carried the plates for both her and Mother, secured them chairs at a table which was not too full of people Mother would have thought beneath them and then fetched them both glasses of lemonade.

He spent the supper hour chatting with Father, which meant that Mother could not accuse him of flirting with her.

Later, when it was time to leave, he helped to escort Papa back to their carriage without making it too obvious that the older man was rather the worse for drink.

'Enjoyed the evening,' said Papa, waggling his eyebrows at Mr Dundas the moment the carriage jolted into motion. 'Did you, my boy? Like to see you youngsters enjoying yourselves. Liked to see you never having to sit out a single dance,' he said, turning abruptly to Betsy. 'Noticed,' he added, with a knowing nod. 'Might have spent the evening jawing with the worthies of Crickheath, but I have eyes in my head.'

'It is a great pity,' said Mother tartly, 'that you don't have a brain in there as well.'

'Whass that supposed to mean?' he said, glaring at Mother. 'I have a brain. A good brain. Everyone says so. Everyone comes to me for advice in these parts.'

'Which only goes to show the general level of ignorance prevalent hereabouts,' said Mother.

Betsy's heart sank. Mother usually refrained from

being so outspoken when others were present. But she didn't seem to think Mr Dundas counted.

'What's the matter with you now, woman?' said Papa irritably. 'Is it that we've all managed to enjoy ourselves without there being a single person of rank in the vish…viss…visnitity? Is that it?'

Was there anywhere worse for them to start bickering than in a coach which neither she, nor Mr Dundas, could get out of for the next few hours? She glanced across at him, to see how he was coping with the way Mother and Papa were going at it, now they'd fired their opening salvoes.

He was gazing down at the hands he had clasped in his lap, his brow puckered and his mouth drawn into a flat line, as though he felt just as uncomfortable as she did. Which was comforting, somehow. So that although the journey home felt as if it lasted at least three times as long as it had taken to go to the ball, at least she didn't feel as if she, alone, was ducking from the marital crossfire.

By the time they reached the gates of Bramley Park, there was hardly a single issue upon which her parents disagreed that hadn't been aired. When the coach stopped, she wouldn't have blamed Mr Dundas for leaping from the door as fast as he could. But he didn't. He paused, after opening it, with one foot still on the step.

'Thank you for taking me to the ball and for returning me home. I don't recall,' he said, glancing at Betsy, 'when I have enjoyed an evening more.'

Mother sniffed, but Papa waved his hand as though it was nothing. 'Glad you enjoyed yourself. Make the most of it while you can. While you're still single,' he concluded bitterly.

'How dare you say such a thing,' said Mother indignantly. 'You are always like this when you're in your cups. You say the most inappropriate things. In front of Betsy, too! Not to mention Mr Dundas!'

Betsy cringed, but Mr Dundas acted as though he hadn't heard. 'Miss Fairfax, I wish to thank you for granting me the honour of the first dance of the evening.' And then he smiled at her. Warmly. Just as though there was nobody there but the two of them. As though Mother and Papa had not just spent the entire journey quarrelling, and were only waiting for him to depart so that they could resume hostilities. 'I look forward to meeting you again, at church next week, or *wherever* our paths may cross.'

Her heart leaped. She darted a glance at Mother as Mr Dundas shut the door, just in case she'd picked up on his hint that he hoped they'd be able to meet somewhere, other than in the formal and restrictive setting of the churchyard. But Mother was too full of her own quarrel with Papa to notice anything. And Papa had consumed too much brandy to do much beside growl at Mother in response to her accusations and rub at his bleary eyes as though staying awake was a major effort.

For once, their bickering didn't have the power to lower her spirits. Her mind was too busy going over the way Mr Dundas had just smiled at her and what he'd said. And how she might contrive to meet him, over the next few days, without anyone else observing them. Not that she wished to do anything inappropriate. Like kissing him again. No, kissing him when there was nobody else around would be fatal. Kissing him was so thrilling, she might not have the ability to make him stop. And who knew where it would end? So, when they next met, they would have to keep their hands, and their lips, to themselves.

And so she would tell him.

Because she didn't want him to think she was the sort of girl who went round kissing just anyone. Oh, dear. Might he think she was, now he knew how she'd climbed up Ben and forced her lips against his? And how swiftly she'd agreed to kiss *him*, outside the ballroom? And how enthusiastically she'd responded?

Oh, dear, oh, dear. Perhaps she ought not to try to arrange an accidental meeting with him again. Perhaps she ought to just wait until they saw each other in church on Sunday. When lots of other people would be about, to make sure nobody did anything improper.

Yes, that would be for the best, she decided glumly, as the carriage swept into their own driveway. And it was a resolve she kept up all the while her maid was helping her prepare for bed. And prayed for strength to keep, along with her other nightly prayers.

When she awoke late the next morning, sunshine was pouring through the chinks in the curtains. She stretched, yawning and flexing her feet, which still ached pleasantly from all the dancing they'd done the night before. And her mind flew back to the way Mr Dundas had made her feel when he'd kissed her, the way he'd smiled at her as he'd got out of the coach, and his veiled hope that they might meet again.

She sighed as she remembered her decision not to go seeking him out. She really must not. She'd learned her lesson with Ben. Even if his wife hadn't caught them together, locked in that one-sided embrace, she'd have felt guilty and wretched after. And it would be the same if she went out hunting for Mr Dundas. Even if he was willing, or even keen, to steal clandestine kisses, she would not be able to go around with a clear conscience. She'd have trouble getting to sleep and she'd blush and fidget whenever Mother, or anyone, looked at her and asked her where she'd been and what she'd been doing.

She sighed again, half wishing she was the kind of girl who could carry on with a man without suffering agonies of guilt. But she wasn't. So she'd just have to...well, not avoid him. She wouldn't go that far. If she *happened* to see him, out and about, of course she would bid him good day and smile, rather than ducking down behind the nearest bush, which was what she'd done after that incident in the stable yard with the two grooms and the bucket of water.

But that was all.

It had to be.

Because nothing could come of it. They couldn't start up a real, earnest courtship. Mother would never permit her to marry a man who had to work for a living. She would *rather* Betsy went to work as a paid companion than see her only daughter marry beneath her. She'd said so when Papa had first mentioned the position at Tunbridge Wells.

Marry him? Was that what she wanted?

After considering the matter for all of five heartbeats, Betsy answered herself. Yes! She couldn't think of anything finer than to marry a man who made her feel so…beautiful. Irresistible. A man who listened to her and understood her, and wanted to look after her. She didn't care about his lack of money, or title. She'd met plenty of men in London who had both and they couldn't hold a candle to Mr Dundas.

He probably wouldn't want to marry her, though. Not after that awful coach ride home. He probably thought she'd end up as argumentative and peevish as Mother, especially now she'd given him a couple of examples of how easily she could lose her temper.

But, oh, wouldn't it be wonderful if he did?

Chapter Fourteen

She was avoiding him, blast it!

He'd thought they'd worked through their differences and he could start, well, courting her, properly. Or trying to fix his interest with her. That was what it was called, wasn't it, when a man began to pursue a woman in earnest? But even though he went up to the oak tree, every day, which was obviously the most convenient place for them to meet, being right on the boundaries of their estates, she never showed up. Once he saw her walking along the village street with her mother and she smiled at him politely, bidding him good morning. Once he saw her riding off into the distance, with her father, but either she didn't see him, or she pretended not to.

And he couldn't stand it. Now that he'd kissed her, and had experienced the explosive effect she'd had on him, he wanted to do it again. No, no, it wasn't just kisses he wanted, although he did want them. He wanted to get to know her. Find out what she believed. What she thought about…oh, everything.

And he wanted to confess the truth about himself, while he was at it. Tell her who and what he really was. He didn't want there to be any more secrets between them.

But if he couldn't find any time to be alone with her, how on earth was he to make a clean breast of, well, *any* of it?

And then, finally, one day, from the vantage point he'd taken up beneath their oak tree, he saw her venture out of her house alone. Straight away he could tell she wasn't just going out for a walk on her father's estates. For one thing, after coming out of the back door, she went round to the drive and along it to the lane that led into the village. For another, she was carrying a bulky parcel under one arm.

He mounted Socks, clapped his heels into her flanks and made his way as fast as he could straight down the hill and into the village. He arrived just in time to see Miss Fairfax slip inside the church.

By the time he'd tethered Socks up to a tree which he hoped would be out of sight from anyone who happened to be walking past the church, and gone inside, there was no sign of her. But he could hear some strange thumping noises coming from the direction of the vestry.

Pausing only to remove his hat, run his fingers through his hair and tug his jacket straight, James made for the vestry, where he was sure he'd find her.

She glanced up in surprise when he walked in. She was kneeling on the floor, several disintegrating hassocks spread in a semicircle in front of her, with sunlight pouring through the little, plain-glassed window and making her hair gleam like polished jet.

'Oh, you startled me,' she said, though she said it with a smile. 'I am just trying to decide which of the hassocks to repair next.'

He tore his eyes from her to examine the tattered kneelers spread out on the floor.

'You have plenty to choose from.'

You have plenty to choose from? What on earth had made him say that? He hadn't come in here to talk about hassocks!

'Yes,' she said, and then pursed her lips. 'And plenty of hours to spend in embroidering them, when I do make my decision. This,' she said, getting up and brushing down her skirts, 'is what females of gentle birth do with their lives. Sit about mending mouldy, mice-nibbled hassocks. Here,' she said, picking one up, and holding it out to him. 'You may as well make yourself useful now you are here.' She placed that hassock in his outstretched arms and then bent to pick up another one.

And still he couldn't frame the words that had been going over and over in his head since the moment he'd kissed her. And she'd kissed him back. His tongue felt too big for his mouth. His teeth were dry. And his neckcloth had suddenly grown too tight.

'Although,' she added with a little hint of a laugh, 'you are always being useful, aren't you? Riding about Ben's estates, meeting with his tenants, smoothing down ruffled feathers, promising them all sorts of things they've been demanding for years until they are all hailing you as a kind of latter-day Robin Hood.'

She didn't like the work he was doing? 'Don't you think I should right the wrongs that have been done to the locals?'

She pursed her lips again as she added a third hassock to the pile in his arms. 'Yes, of course I do. I am sorry. I am not in a good mood today. I spoke from a sort of jealousy, I suppose. I feel so…useless, whiling away my time with embroidery while you have the chance to actually *do* something about the conditions hereabouts. It makes me wish, sometimes, that I were a man.' She sighed.

'I for one am jolly glad you're not,' he said from the bottom of his heart. Although at the same time her attitude helped to explain why he liked her so much. She, too, chafed under the restrictions that society placed on her. She, too, suffered from the feeling that she was frittering her life away. And she, too, had spent her whole life trying to live up to the standards set by a parent who was impossible to please. It made him feel as if they were in tune with each other, on so many levels.

She paused in the act of picking up two more hassocks, shot him a look and blushed. 'You ought not to say such things, Mr Dundas,' she said, then went to the vestry door with her own pile of hassocks.

'Why not,' he said, following her closely behind, 'if it is the truth?'

She placed her hassocks under one of the pews, about a third of the way down the aisle, before an-

swering him. 'Because nothing can come of it,' she
said, looking despondent.

'Why not?'

'Put those hassocks down there,' she said, pointing to a pew on the opposite side of the aisle from
where she'd put hers, rather than answering him. 'I
am sorry, Mr Dundas. I have spent a lot of time thinking about…us, ever since the dance. And although…'

'No,' he said, striding to her and catching at her
hand. 'Don't say another word. I have something
to tell you. Something that will change everything.
You see…'

But before he could launch into his big confession, Miss Fairfax flinched. 'Someone's coming,' she
cried. And indeed, he could hear footsteps crunching
up the gravelled church path. 'They mustn't catch us
alone. Heaven only knows what they'll make of it!'

Before he could protest that he didn't care who
found them, or what they made of it, since he was
thinking very seriously about marrying her anyway,
she'd gripped his hand tightly and begun tugging
him back down the aisle in the direction of the vestry. Darting inside, she shoved him behind her and
pushed the door almost shut, but left enough space
to peep out.

'It's Mrs Knowles,' she hissed. 'It couldn't be
worse!' Wild-eyed, she glanced round the vestry,
before kicking the one remaining hassock into a corner, snatching something from the little table in the
centre of the room, which was piled high with all
the paraphernalia one would expect to find in a ves-

try, and then thrusting him in the direction of the cupboard in which the choir's robes, along with the vicar's vestments, were hanging.

As she pulled the door closed on them, he learned that the item she'd snatched from the table was the key to the cupboard, that it fit in the lock from the inside and could lock the door from that side as easily as it could from the outside.

He also discovered that the cupboard was nowhere near big enough to conceal two fully grown people, even if neither of them had grown as tall as they might have wished. Although it wasn't a question of the height of the cupboard, anyway, but its width. There was only room for them both to fit inside if they nestled together like spoons in a drawer, her back plastered against his chest. Her hair tickling his nose. Her bottom right against the top of his thighs. He had to put his arms round her waist. There was nowhere else to put them. Or that was what he told himself.

She didn't object, though. Well, she couldn't very well do so, could she? If she said anything, or made any kind of noise, Mrs Knowles might discover them. She could have tugged his hands away, though, if she'd minded him putting them where they were, rather than simply lifting her own hands to rest on the top of his. And curling her fingers over them.

From the other side of the cupboard door, he heard the vestry door open, and footsteps, and muttering, and objects being moved about.

All the while the inside of the cupboard was filling up with the scent of Miss Fairfax. Every breath he took it was as if he was inhaling her. And every breath he took grew shorter as his heart began to beat harder, because from the moment she'd pushed her bottom against him, he'd become aroused.

After a while longer, he was sure she must have been able to feel what was going on inside his breeches, because it was pushing against her back. But she didn't let go of his hands, or show any sign of disgust or displeasure. On the contrary, her own breathing became a bit ragged until it was matching his own. And after a bit longer, he was surprised that the woman pottering about in the vestry, doing heaven knew what, couldn't hear the ragged gasps and sighs that the pair of them were making inside the cupboard. Or see that it was vibrating under the influence of their trembling limbs.

He pulled Miss Fairfax closer. Nuzzled the top of her head with his nose.

She leaned back into him, her hips twisting a bit so that they were rubbing against his erection.

It was a good job she was holding on to his hands so tightly, because if not for those slender little fingers, his hands would be sliding up her front, so that he could shape her breasts. Or sliding down, to pull up her skirts and explore the basic differences between a man and a woman. Oh, God, he wanted to feel bare skin under his hands. Against his thighs. He wanted to explore and plunge, and thrust and explode into her.

But suddenly, she let go of his hands and began

fumbling at the door. And he realised, in some dim corner of his mind that wasn't completely taken up with carnal thoughts about Miss Fairfax, that the vestry door had slammed and Mrs Knowles had gone striding down the aisle and out of the church.

He groaned as Miss Fairfax opened the cupboard door and made to move out. He couldn't let go of her. But he didn't need to. Instead of pulling away from him, she twisted round in his arms, lifting her face to his for a kiss.

And then they were kissing, frantically, and pulling at each other's clothes and tumbling to the floor. And for the first time in his life, James was completely gripped by overwhelming desire. He didn't care about anything but her. He couldn't think about anything but her, under him, around him...

'Oh, no,' she suddenly cried. 'We cannot do this. Not here. We're in church!'

'And we're not married,' he said, coming to his senses as suddenly as though she'd thrown a bucket of water over him this time.

'It's no use talking of marriage,' she whimpered, plunging her fingers into his hair when he made as if to pull away from her. 'That was what I was trying to tell you before. Mother will never permit it.'

'I'll speak to your father,' he said, trying to re-assure her. 'Once he knows...'

'No. You cannot do that! I mean, I'm sure Papa wouldn't want to stand in the way of my happiness, but I couldn't ask him to give us his blessing, not when it would set him and Mother at odds even worse than they already are.'

Oh, what a darling she was. Not wanting to cause a rift in her parents' marriage. It was stormy enough as it was, he could see. But once her mother knew he had a title, she'd be so thrilled it might deal with the other problem they had. Which, he'd started to suspect, was to do with money. And he had enough to deal with whatever debts they'd run up. Probably. Anyway, he'd find out all about that when the lawyers discussed the settlements.

'No, no, they won't be at odds, not once they know...'

'There's only one thing for it,' said Miss Fairfax, pushing him off her so that she could sit up. 'We'll have to elope.'

'Elope?' She really cared for him so much that she would willingly give up everything for him, to run away with him?

He didn't think he'd ever heard anything so wonderful, yet so foolish, in his life. There was no need to elope. Absolutely no need. But to know that she would consider it made him feel like the luckiest chap in England.

'No, you are right,' she said, her face falling. 'It wouldn't do, would it? It would ruin your prospects. I mean, who would want to employ a man who'd caused a scandal by eloping with a penniless female?'

If he hadn't been certain of his feelings before, he was now. He was utterly, hopelessly in love with her. Because, torn between duty and desire, she was determined to put him first. To sacrifice her own happiness for his future welfare.

'You won't ruin my prospects, my darling,' he said, crawling over to where she was sitting, hunched over, and putting one arm round her shoulder. 'Because, you see, I am not merely a steward who needs to work for his living. I am actually the oldest son of the Earl of Darwen. And I am not plain Mr Dundas, but Lord Dundas, a viscount in my own right.'

There, that should turn her tears to joy, if anything could. He was everything her mother had ever wanted for her. And he already knew that she cared for him. Deeply. Or she wouldn't have first suggested eloping, then vowed she couldn't do it to him.

And now she knew that there was nothing standing in the way of her happiness.

No wonder she looked stunned.

Chapter Fifteen

Betsy couldn't believe her ears. He wasn't plain Mr Dundas at all. He was a viscount.

And he'd deliberately kept that fact from her.

'You have been lying to me from the very first moment we met,' she gasped, appalled.

'No,' he said, a frown flitting across his brow, 'not exactly…'

'Yes, exactly! And to think I trusted you. I told you everything.' She'd thought they were in tune. That he was understanding. 'I confided in you about how I came to kiss Ben and how his wife… Oh!' She flinched as another, even worse aspect of things occurred to her. 'If you are the son of the Earl of Darwen, that means Ben's wife is…your sister?'

'Well, yes, but…'

She couldn't bear to feel his arm about her shoulder a moment longer. She flung it off and scrambled away so that she crouched on hands and knees, staring at him in horror.

'And you let me say all those things about her.'
And he hadn't stopped her from being extremely
indiscreet about how Lady Bramhall had made her
feel, with her poise and her manners, and her condescending smiles. 'You positively encouraged me
to totally humiliate myself!'

'No, at least, I didn't mean to…'

He might not have meant to, but he jolly well had
humiliated her. Oh, and to think she had begun to
think of him as a friend. A confidant. But it had all
been very one-sided, hadn't it? While she'd bared her
very soul to him, he'd never confided in her. 'I bared
my heart to you while you kept all your secrets. You
gave me nothing. Nothing at all. You kept your very
identity from me.'

'Well, yes, but that was the only thing I did. And
I had good reason…'

What? He was admitting it? How dare he? And
as for the reason, she could see exactly what it must
have been. She got to her feet and backed away from
him on legs that were shaking, though she kept her
eyes fixed on his treacherous face.

'Do you think I am a complete idiot? When I think
of all that nonsense you spouted about never having
kissed a woman before. That was what this was all
about, wasn't it? You are the type of man who goes
round making poor, gullible country misses feel special so that you can seduce them!'

'Now, hold on,' he said, rising to his knees, 'that's
not fair!'

'No, I will tell you what isn't fair. Toying with me.

Mocking me. Leading me on. Almost…having me on the church floor!' She pointed to the spot where they'd been writhing about, less than a minute earlier. 'Oh, if I hadn't stopped when I did…' She shuddered. Backed away even further. She didn't think she'd ever be able to come into the vestry again. If she'd felt physically ill when she'd just stood on the threshold of the study where she'd kissed, and been rejected by, Ben, how much worse would she react to standing on the spot where he'd all but ruined her? With her complete, nay, enthusiastic co-operation?

'But, Miss Fairfax,' he said, holding out his hands in the kind of gesture that he probably thought made him look like an ardent, genuine suitor. He'd probably seen some actor on a stage doing it and had practised until he looked genuine. 'I asked you to marry me.'

'Did you?' She shook her head. 'No. I did hear some words come from the lips of a man I thought was plain, hardworking, hard-up Mr Dundas. But he, apparently, doesn't exist. And I have no idea who you are. For I have only just met you. And I have no intention of falling into the arms of a lying, cheating… stranger!'

She stormed over to the door, furious as much for falling for him as for muddling her argument to the point where even she could see that she couldn't very well claim to know he'd lied and cheated if he was a total stranger. But who could possibly keep an argument straight when they'd been duped and deceived, then yanked out of a wonderful dream into a cold, harsh reality that bore no resemblance to anything she'd believed to be true? She tugged open the vestry door and ran down the aisle. As she reached the church door, she thought she heard him saying, 'But, Miss Fairfax, I love you!'

She clapped her hands over her ears so she wouldn't hear any more of his lies, seductive, tempting lies that had the power to make her weaken, and broke into a run. Straight home. Without the hassock she'd intended to start repairing. Without one remaining shred of dignity. Tears began streaming down her face. Again. He'd made her cry again.

How dare he claim to love her? A man in love didn't lie, or cheat, or steal into a girl's heart without giving her anything in return. And anyway, no matter what *he* claimed to feel, she…she *hated* him. And what was more, she never wanted to see his deceitful, licentious face again.

Sobbing, she ran straight to Papa's study and barged in without knocking. 'I have changed my mind,' she said, when he looked up from his desk with a mixture of mingled surprise and wariness on his face. 'I am ready to go to Tunbridge Wells the minute you can arrange for me to leave.'

'Ah, Betsy,' he said, laying down his pen. 'There is really no need for you to go to Tunbridge Wells. There never was.'

'There…never…was? What can you mean?'

He sighed. 'I painted a picture of the worst possible future you might suffer if your mother wouldn't mend her ways. I thought the prospect of seeing you reduced to having to work for a living, rather than making what she sees as a brilliant match, might...'

'You lied to me!' Were all men so...sneaky? 'I trusted you!' Just as she'd trusted *him*. And opened her heart to *him*.

'Don't look at me like that, Betsy,' said Papa, getting to his feet.

'What, as though you have betrayed me?' She turned and rushed to the door. Then paused as she realised something else. 'You...you are as much to blame for what I did as Mother.'

'What did you do? Betsy, what have you done?'

'I don't wish to discuss it! Just...make it possible for me to leave here as soon as possible. Because if you don't, I'm leaving anyway!'

James groaned. How had it all gone so spectacularly wrong, so suddenly? One minute they'd been on the verge of consummating their lust on the floor and the next she was shouting at him and accusing him of humiliating her, then storming off.

He drew his knees up to his chest and bowed his head over them. If anyone was humiliated, it was him. He would wager no man alive had had his marriage proposal turned down in such an unflattering manner. Nor been so disabled by what felt like a walking stick between his legs, that he was unable to run after his beloved and beg her to calm down and reconsider. There was no way he could leave this room until it had subsided. He'd be a laughingstock. Stick. He groaned again.

He didn't understand women. He would have thought she'd be thrilled to discover he was a viscount and heir to an earldom. He'd been hunted through the drawing rooms and ballrooms of London because of those very facts, ever since he'd had his court presentation. It was what women wanted, wasn't it? A title and wealth? Her mother certainly wanted those things for her daughter. He would have sworn Miss Fairfax wanted those things for herself as well. Or she would never have gone to Ben's study and tried to compromise him.

All of a sudden a swell of resentment surged up inside him. Because he'd just remembered that she would have gladly married Ben, who was tall, handsome and penniless, if he hadn't been married already. But she'd turned up her nose at *him*.

He lurched to his feet and stood for a few moments with his hands on his knees, blowing hard through his open mouth. He'd never felt so short and ugly, and awkward and useless, in his life.

How he wished he'd never come to Bramley Park. How he wished he'd never met Miss Fairfax.

And how he wished he'd never discovered she was the only woman who could not only arouse him, but keep him in a state of painfully uncomfortable arousal long after she'd left the room. Left *him*.

His only hope would be if she reconsidered that rejection, after a few days, when her temper had cooled. Because she did have the deuce of a temper, there was no denying it. Why, only look at the way she'd flown up into the boughs when she'd caught

Briggs and Wilmot fighting over Sally. But she'd apologised after a few days and explained exactly why she'd been so angry.

And there was the fact that she did feel something for him, after all, or she couldn't have reacted the way she did after they'd squeezed into that tiny cupboard together. She couldn't have first suggested they elope, then thought better of it because of the risk to his reputation. She did care for him, really. It was the shock of hearing about his title, that was all. And the way he'd told her, probably. He hadn't been all that tactful, or led up to it in a logical sequence so she could understand the steps that had led him to let her think he was Mr Dundas, instead of Lord Dundas. Once she thought it over, she'd realise that he would never have deliberately deceived her. And she'd start to think about what it would be like to marry a viscount. About how much better it would be than being the wife of a mere steward.

It was all he had to cling to, because the prospect of losing her completely was too dreadful to contemplate.

But Miss Fairfax didn't calm down and come crawling back to him full of apologies and understanding, as he'd hoped. Instead, a couple of days later, he heard from her father that she'd left the area completely.

'Taken it into her head to go to, ah, visit an elderly relative in Tunbridge Wells,' said Colonel Fairfax, looking rather glum.

'Tunbridge Wells?' James was appalled. Because he knew what lengths she'd gone to in order to avoid being sent there in the first place. So the fact she'd now gone there of her own free will told him in no uncertain terms that she'd rather do anything than risk seeing him again. Leaving him in no doubt that she was never going to forgive him.

It felt as if the bottom had dropped out of his world.

He couldn't believe he was never going to see her again. And yet, at the same time, he knew that if she had her way, he wouldn't.

He turned his horse away and spent the rest of that day going about the routine he'd established, in a kind of daze. Everywhere he went echoed with memories of their few meetings, so that he kept on getting the feeling he might catch sight of her round any corner, at any moment.

And then fresh pain would assault him when he remembered it was not so. Because she'd gone. And he couldn't believe he had the ability to stay in the saddle, rather than drop to the ground and fling back his head and howl in pain.

After a few days that followed the same pattern of disbelief and unsettling hope, and painful despair, he began to suspect he'd never get over her if he stayed in the vicinity of Bramley Bythorne, where he was constantly reminded of every single encounter they'd shared. The only way he would even begin to recover would be to leave and go back to his own estates.

Except that would feel like giving up completely. And part of him retained enough sense to know that if he just slunk away with his tail between his legs he'd feel like a failure for the rest of his life.

What the hell was he to do?

Chapter Sixteen

For the next few days, while his brain was still too numb to make any kind of decision, he just stayed at Bramley Park, going through the motions. He'd promised Daisy, after all, that he'd do what he could on her husband's estates. And he reckoned he might as well be miserable here as anywhere. But at least he wouldn't be going back on his word.

It was getting on for a week after he'd told Miss Fairfax who he really was, and she'd told him she wanted none of him, when he returned to the stables after a long and dreary day to find an unfamiliar horse munching hay in the stall next to the one where he was taking Socks.

That was all he needed. Some tenant with a litany of complaints, or worse, helpful suggestions, when he could hardly cope with his own company. He almost mounted up and galloped away again, except that would not be fair to Socks, who was just as tired as him and didn't deserve to pay the price for her master's ill humour.

The one positive thing about his bad mood, he decided as he trudged across the stable yard, would be that it would discourage whoever had come to see him from staying very long. Because he was in no mood to make any effort whatever to even be polite. *Serve 'em right*, he thought vengefully as he thrust open the kitchen door and stepped inside. Only to come to a dead halt when he saw not a tenant, but one of his own brothers sitting at the kitchen table getting on the outside of a tankard of ale.

'Gem?' His brother's name was actually Jasper, but everybody nowadays addressed him by the nickname he'd acquired at school. 'What the devil are you doing here?' Although Gem was the closest in age to James of his four younger brothers, they were not close in any other way. It wasn't that either of them actively disliked the other. They just had very different lifestyles, as well as moving in distinctly different social circles. Over the last few years, the only times they'd been likely to see each other, socially, was if they were both staying at Wattlesham Priory.

'What the devil,' replied Gem, totally unabashed, 'do you think?'

'That you must be in the devil of a fix,' said James wearily. That could be the only thing that would bring Gem for a visit, since they weren't in the habit of just dropping in on each other.

'No matter what anyone else says about you,' replied Gem, with a grin, 'I've never doubted you was a downy one.'

'You must be in real trouble if you're trying to soft-soap me.'

Gem's grin slipped a notch and, beneath the cocksure attitude, James thought he could detect a glimmer of real desperation.

'Look,' James remarked to the room at large, because this being the kitchen, and supper due shortly, not only were the cook and scullery maid bustling about, but through the window he could see Briggs and Wilmot sauntering across from the stables, and he guessed Gem might value some privacy, 'I've been out all day and I'm sharp-set. You'd better come up to my room while I wash and change for supper.'

Gem nodded, downed his ale, then paused with his tankard in mid-air, his eyes widening as James picked up the can of hot water and the clean towel Sally had prepared the moment he'd come in. He could see his brother struggling with the longing to poke fun at him for acting as his own footman. It spoke volumes about the depth of his plight that he held his tongue, for Gem was the ringleader of most of the antics in which the younger cohort of his brothers indulged and loved nothing better than making James the butt of their jokes and pranks.

He still said nothing when they reached James's room to find no valet in attendance even though he was clearly bursting with curiosity.

Yes, his younger brother *must* be in the suds if he

couldn't even make one wisecrack about the state of affairs at Bramley Park.

James wondered, as he set the jug of water on the washstand and draped the towel over the nearby rail, how much Gem had already learned about the situation here while he'd been sitting in the kitchen drinking that ale. Decided to cross that bridge when he came to it.

'Out with it,' he said as he stripped off his shirt.

Gem strolled to the window and glanced out. Cleared his throat. 'Fact of the matter is,' he said as James started lathering up his hands, 'Father has disinherited me.'

'Oh?' James rubbed his soaped hands over his face and neck. 'What for this time? Money? Or women?'

Gem never seemed to have enough money, in spite of receiving a generous quarterly allowance, and often got into the kind of debt he couldn't admit to their rather puritanical parents. James had bailed him out a couple of times, particularly when the monetary difficulties stemmed from an entanglement with a woman. Because unlike James, Gem seemed to have taken Father's warnings about the perils of pretty women as a challenge, if not an outright dare.

'Both, of course,' said Gem bleakly. 'And, look here,' he continued as James started rinsing off the suds, 'I didn't come here expecting you to bail me out. Or not exactly.' He paced over to the bed and sat on the edge. 'It's just that I need a bolthole for a while. Just until I can come up with a plan. Or…

hang it,' he said, running his fingers through his hair. 'You know I'm not trained for anything, so it isn't as if I can just get work, is it? Not that I blame Father for *that*. I mean, I haven't got the brains to become a lawyer, or the temperament to become a clergyman, so there was no point in sending me to university, was there?'

James grimaced through the effort of holding his own tongue now, because he'd noticed how little Father seemed to value his younger sons and their own unique abilities. Gem had fared particularly badly in that regard. Whenever he'd 'disappointed' Father, for instance, he'd told the poor lad that it was just as well he had another three sons in reserve, should anything happen to his heir, claiming he was just about useless.

How could the man make his own offspring feel so…inadequate? Shouldn't a father encourage his children to reach their full potential, rather than constantly belittling and thwarting their ambitions?

'Hoped you'd put me up for a bit,' Gem said. 'Thought I'd remind you that the owner of this place is *my* friend, not yours,' he added, with a touch of defiance, 'so in a way I have more right to be here than you do.'

James flung the damp towel at his brother in irritation.

'What the devil makes you think you need to remind me of that? Did you think I wouldn't stand buff?'

Gem, who'd fielded the towel deftly before it got

anywhere near slapping his face, gave him a straight look. 'Couldn't be absolutely sure. Not with you turning into about as much of a Puritan as Father, lately.'

He wouldn't be saying that if he could have seen him crushing Miss Fairfax into his loins in that cupboard, or wrestling her all over the vestry floor the moment she'd unlocked the door.

'If you weren't sitting on my bed, where I've got to sleep later on, I'd toss the whole wash bowl at you,' he snarled, planting his hands on his hips.

Gem grinned. 'Why do you think I chose to sit here?'

With a growl, James went to the cupboard and took a fresh shirt from the pile left there by the laundry woman he'd recently hired, who lived in the village and was some sort of relative of Sally's.

'Has Father,' he asked as he thrust his arms through the shirt sleeves, 'really disinherited you this time, Gem? Or is this just another of his fits of bluster?'

'Well, he was pretty serious when he gave me this,' said Gem, reaching into his pocket and drawing out a black silk bag, then tossing it to James, who instinctively caught it.

'What's this?'

'The only thing,' Gem said rather grimly as James tugged at the drawstring, 'he said I deserved to inherit.'

At first James couldn't make out what the triangular, silver object, nestled in a tangled loop of black ribbon could be. But then Gem helpfully explained.

'It's our syphilitic grandfather's fake nose.'

For a moment James felt so nauseous he almost dropped the vile object. Oh, not because of what it was—all the boys knew the history of the silver nose their grandfather had had to wear to cover up the fact that the pox had eaten away most of his face. In the days when he still went out occasionally, that was, and didn't want to frighten everyone. No, it was because of what it might mean, for Gem. Now. He felt as if the outer edges of the room were growing dark.

'Gem,' he said hoarsely. 'Are you telling me you have contracted…?'

'Good God, no! I'm far too careful to do anything so bacon-brained. It's just that after my latest little, er, amorous adventure, somebody must have tattled. Because one day Father hauled me into his study, told me that because of my, er, proclivities, it would only be a matter of time before I needed this,' he said as he retrieved the disgusting family heirloom from James, who was still standing stock still, staring at it in sick fascination, 'before adding that it was the only thing I would ever inherit from him because he was washing his hands of me.'

'That sounds a bit extreme, even for Father, but no doubt when he's cooled off…'

'Ah, well, after he said that, I sort of lost my own temper,' Gem said ruefully as he stowed his inheritance in an inner pocket of his jacket. 'Said that Grandfather must have been all about in his head not to have used condoms, if he did have to have an affair while Grandmother was carrying her first child. I mean, they knew all about them even in those days. Did a bit of reading about them, after you told me about them.'

James had taken Gem aside not long after he'd had his educational visit to the hospital full of syphilitic patients, noticing how miserable he'd looked. He'd explained about the protective measures he could take, if he really, really needed to bed a woman. He was going to make jolly sure that all his brothers knew enough to make safe choices, when they grew old enough to start taking notice of women, so that none of them would go through all the agonising soul-searching he'd suffered after his own educational visit.

He was lucky enough to have a couple of good friends who didn't think less of a man for being cautious. Or, as one of them, Cherry, put it, for not wanting to sample what a woman had to offer without his emotions, and hers, playing a part. People sneered at Cherry for being a hopeless romantic, because he'd kept the one mistress for just about as long as he could remember. Claimed that if only his family would accept her, he would have married her to start with. But since they wouldn't, he treated her just as though she was his wife, staying completely faithful to her. Just wasn't interested in any other woman because he loved Gertie.

Most men of his rank, though, just seemed to look on bedding a woman the way they would about having a meal. They saw one they wanted, they felt hunger and devoured them, without engaging either their conscience or their emotions.

He supposed, if not for Father's horror stories, he might have...dabbled, occasionally, out of curiosity, or in an experimental way. But he would never have been much in the petticoat line. Unlike his less complicated brother, who liked women, all women, and saw no reason why he should not enjoy them if they were willing.

But that was, of course, why his body reacted so urgently to Miss Fairfax. It was because he'd fallen in love with her.

'I envy you, sometimes, Gem,' he said, turning away to select some fresh breeches.

'What, for opening my big mouth when it would have been better to have kept it shut?'

'Partly.' He chuckled. 'Only you would have the nerve to respond to one of Father's lectures about loose behaviour by trying to educate him in the use of condoms!'

'If it wasn't for the fact I'd been angry with him ever since Daisy's come-out,' Gem continued, 'I might have been able to keep my opinions to myself. But, I mean to say, it's one injustice after another with him, isn't it? Bringing Daisy's Season to an end just because she wouldn't marry the first chap to come up to scratch, just because he wanted to get back to the Priory. And telling her she'd let the family down, when all she was doing was being careful. I mean, what did we really know, any of us, about Lord Martlesham? And once Daisy had married him, if she'd said yes, she'd have been totally in his power. He would have had all the legal rights over her and none of us would have been able to do a thing to help should he have turned out to be a bounder. No, it was no surprise she hesitated, given the way we've seen Father treat poor Mother over the years. The only power a woman has is the right to choose whom she hands the power over to. And Father should have supported her, protected her, not tried to palm her off on to the first man to pop the question.'

James froze in the act of stepping out of one pair of breeches and into the clean ones. Because something that had been a bit of a puzzle to him before suddenly made sense. He'd never fully understood why Miss Fairfax had made such a huge fuss about the way the grooms had been fighting over Sally, claiming that it was for the woman to choose, not for the men to decide whom she should have.

Now he saw why it was so important. Once a woman handed over her life to a man, she was completely in his power, legally speaking.

'What's the matter? What have I said?' Gem was looking at him warily.

James wondered whether to confide in his younger brother. In one sense, it would be risky, given Gem's love of poking fun at him. On the other hand, Gem had experience with women. A lot of experience. In that respect there was nobody better qualified to advise him how to proceed.

'I have my own troubles,' he confessed. 'With a woman.'

Gem leaned back on his elbows. 'What's the trouble with her, exactly?'

'Well, Father would say she's totally unsuitable. To start with, she's pretty, stunningly pretty. She isn't meek and mild, like Mother, but has a temper that explodes at the slightest provocation. She doesn't have much of a pedigree, either. And worst of all, she doesn't have a penny to her name as far as I can discover. But to me...' he sighed as he finally got his legs into his clean breeches '...that isn't the worst of it. The worst of it is that she won't have me.'

'What?' Gem sat up straight. 'She won't have you? You mean, you, er...tried to bed her?'

'No,' James groaned, sinking down on to the bed next to his brother. 'I asked her to marry me.'

'Crikey.' Gem stared at him for a bit, then asked, 'Did she say why, exactly, she didn't want to marry you?'

James ran his fingers through his hair, before telling Gem pretty much everything that had happened since he'd come to Bramley Park.

'I suppose,' he said when he came to the end of it, 'that you think it's no more than I deserve. You can say that, if you like, as long as you don't tell me I've had a lucky escape because the chances are we'd spend the rest of our lives bickering, the way her parents do, if she had agreed to marry me. And I'll darken your daylights,' he said, making a slashing motion through the air, 'if you dare say anything at all derogatory about her.'

'First off, I would never speak ill of a lady,' said Gem, looking affronted. 'And as to the bickering, well, married people only fight with each other when they still care enough to do so. You've seen those fashionable couples who share nothing but a name, haven't you? Who don't care what the other one gets up to as long as they don't put a stop to their own pleasure?'

That was true. Which meant that Colonel and Mrs Fairfax still had strong feelings for each other.

'So,' continued Gem, 'if you really love her you'd obviously prefer to spend the rest of your life fighting with her, than not being able to have her in your life at all.'

'That's it. That's exactly it!'

'What's more, any woman who was docile would bore you silly.'

James thought back to that first day they'd met and the way she'd flounced off, her skirts swishing, her hair flying out behind her like a banner. And how he'd thought she was like a breath of fresh air.

And how insipid all those eligible females he'd had thrust under his nose in London had seemed in comparison. No wonder they hadn't roused anything in him more than boredom. He didn't want a wife who always agreed with him and treated him as if he was a god. That sort of woman was no match for him.

All of a sudden, the harmony he'd always assumed existed between his parents shifted and took on a darker, less rosy form. Gem was right. Mother never opposed Father, not even by the slightest hint. She lived to please him and make him happy. She had no thought for her own happiness at all.

And neither did Father.

And nor, during his time with Miss Fairfax, had he had any thought for what she wanted. He'd assumed that she would be thrilled to discover he had a title. When he ought to have known, from the way she acted, and spoke, that the most important thing to her was honesty. Integrity.

'I say,' said Gem, looking concerned, 'is something the matter? You look as if someone has just hit you with a cricket bat.'

'Somebody should have done,' he said grimly, 'then perhaps I wouldn't have made such a mull of things. Of course a woman has the right to her own opinions and to express them, and to be in full possession of all the facts when she makes her choice about whom to marry.' Miss Fairfax must have felt as if he'd robbed her of that choice, by hiding from her who he really was.

'Ye...ees...'

'I hadn't seen it before. But now I have, the answer is clear. I have to *show* her, Gem.' And then, once he'd shown her why he'd hidden part of himself from her, perhaps she might find it in her heart to forgive him.

'Ri...ight...'

'So,' he said, clapping his brother on the shoulder,

'you couldn't have come at a better time. I'm going to leave you in charge and go after her.'

'Me? In charge?'

'Yes. You might think you have no training, but you've lived all your life on an estate like this and seen how it's run. What's more, as you pointed out, Ben is *your* friend, so who better to look after his interests? You could even write and ask him to formalise the position and draw a wage for doing it.'

'But…I have no training in land management, not the way you have…'

'It won't matter much. For one thing, this place is in such a shambles you would have to be a complete idiot to make matters worse. And you are no idiot.'

'Thank you. I think.'

'For another, there are plenty of local men who can advise you—Colonel Fairfax in particular. And I've already started up a few schemes, which you can just oversee, until you find your feet. But don't look so worried, I won't abandon you right away.'

He couldn't. To start with, he'd have to contact his valet and get him to fetch some decent sets of clothes, and return his curricle, before heading to Tunbridge Wells.

'Let's go down to supper,' he said, clapping his brother on the shoulder. And feeling the urge to whistle as the gloom that had been hanging over him since Miss Fairfax had turned him down finally began to dissipate.

Chapter Seventeen

Almost from the first moment Betsy arrived in Tunbridge Wells she realised she'd made a mistake. Well, several mistakes to be honest. For one thing, Tunbridge Wells was not at all what she'd expected. From the way people had spoken about it going downhill since the days when Beau Nash had presided over a glittering social scene, and how, nowadays, the truly fashionable people went to watering holes like Brighton, she'd imagined it would be downright seedy. Yet, compared to Bramley Bythorne, the town positively bustled with activity.

To start with, instead of only having a couple of shops which sold the bare essentials, there was a whole parade with windows showcasing all sorts of toys, silver, china, the most fabulous millinery and beautifully crafted wooden ware. Once she'd finished browsing along the parade, or choosing a book from a library, she could take tea and cake in one of the coffee shops. And those were just the kinds of activities she could do during the daytime. In the evenings, there were concerts, or sometimes even dances.

It was the kind of place where she might have been able to enjoy herself, if it wasn't for the fact that her self-esteem was in tatters and it felt as if she was never going to be able to smile again.

Which brought her to what she thought might have been another mistake. Even during the coach drive there she'd begun to feel as if she understood that expression about burning her bridges. Or was it boats? Well, whichever it was, she knew there was no going back. In a fit of…well, there had been more than a touch of pique to it, if she was honest…she'd said unforgivable things to *him*. She still didn't know what name to think of him by. He was no longer her safe, comfortable Mr Dundas, that was all she knew. But anyway, she'd turned down his proposal in such unflattering terms that he would never, ever have repeated it, even if she'd stayed at home and calmed down, and begged his pardon.

Which she wouldn't have done. Would she? Well, she'd never know now. Because, hard on the heels of her discovery that *he'd* been lying to her, Papa had confessed that he'd been lying, too. It had felt as if she had nobody in the world she could trust. As if everyone had deceived and used her. She'd informed her parents that she was done trying to be a dutiful daughter. That she was not going to marry *any*one in order for *them* to benefit. That in fact she'd rather go and work for a crabby old spinster than have to spend one more moment under their roof.

And that had been that. Bridges burned. Boats scuppered. She was just going to have to get used to Tunbridge Wells.

Where at least there was shopping to take her mind off *him*.

However, the biggest mistake she'd made turned out to be in regard to Great-Aunt Cornelia, who she'd decided was a dragon without even meeting her. Oh, she didn't change that opinion straight away. On the contrary, at their first meeting Betsy thought her great-aunt had to be the most prickly, unkind woman she'd ever met. For when Betsy staggered from the coach, worn out with the effects of travel and misery, and calling herself all kinds of a fool, and hoping for sympathy in the form of an offer of tea and the chance to go straight to bed, Great-Aunt Cornelia's footman, Gregory, showed her into a parlour where she wasn't even allowed to sit down. Instead, the woman who looked as if she was not all that much older than Mother bid her take off her bonnet and turn all the way round. Then she'd sniffed, pursed her lips, and said, 'Have you any brains in that pretty head of yours, that's what I want to know? Any opinions beyond the trite?'

Betsy had been too shocked and tired from the journey, and perplexed by having actually come to Tunbridge Wells, after resisting that fate for so long, that she hadn't known what to say.

Great-Aunt Cornelia had. After sighing heavily,

she'd said a great many things. None of them complimentary. And Betsy was already in such low spirits that for the first few days, it looked as though Tunbridge Wells was going to be every bit as unpleasant as she'd always dreaded. In spite of the shops.

But after two days of moping about, wishing she'd never met Mr…that was, Lord…that was, *him*, and cringing whenever she thought about the way she'd responded to him in the vestment cupboard, and being hardly able to face her food because of the way he'd humiliated her from the start to the finish of their relationship, and worrying that, somehow, Mother would find out that he had a title, and that he'd made an offer, and would come after her with all guns blazing and drag her back and oblige her to do something dreadful like beg him to forgive her when the faults were all his, Great-Aunt Cornelia had given her an ultimatum.

'Either you buck up, or take yourself off,' she'd snapped. 'I can't stand girls who droop about the place, especially if they have no conversation to make up for it. Which, let me tell you, you don't. I want entertainment from my paid companion. Not sulks.'

'Do you think,' Betsy had snapped back, having reached the end of her tether, what with one thing and another, 'I would even have come here if I had any alternative? Is it surprising that I don't seem happy when you do nothing, whatsoever, to try to make me comfortable? Why, from the moment I walked in your door, you made me feel as if I was a burden you were taking in rather than someone who was doing *you* a favour, by agreeing to come here, when everyone knows what an ogre you are! Oooh, to think that I actually *asked* Papa to send me here, after all the time he'd been holding this position over me as a threat.'

'Hah,' cried Great-Aunt Cornelia when Betsy paused to take a breath. 'That's more like it. Now you're showing the sort of pluck I'd expect from a girl descended from the house of Mainwaring.'

'Really?' Betsy had been hardly able to believe her ears. 'You *like* me being rude?'

'I'd rather have someone who answered me back and stuck up for herself, than have one of those milky misses who flinch or dissolve into tears whenever I give 'em a piece of my mind drifting about the place. If there's one thing I cannot abide it's a watering pot.'

'Oh,' said Betsy, who had, until then, been guilty of doing rather a lot of weeping. Although only in the privacy of her own room.

'So. I'm your last resort, am I?' Great-Aunt Cornelia had looked her up and down with interest. 'Trying to escape some scandal, are you? What did you do? Have a baby out of wedlock?'

Betsy had gasped. 'Nothing of the sort!'

'Ah, well, probably for the best,' said Aunt Cornelia pragmatically. 'If you're the kind of girl with a weakness for the bucks... Although at least I wouldn't have been bored while you were staying with me. So, what was it, then? Why did they pack you off to evil old Aunt Cornelia?'

'They didn't. As I said, Papa kept on *threatening* to send me to you, because of a, er, financial difficulty. He *said*,' she said bitterly, 'if things didn't turn around, far from making a brilliant match, which is what Mother has been hoping for me, I'd have to work for a living.'

'Trying to put your mother in her place, I dare say, by frightening her with threats of retrenchment.'

'Yes,' said Betsy. 'Well, I discovered that eventually, but for ages I thought it was true. So…how on earth did you know it was all a hum?'

'Oh, but everyone…well, everyone in the family… knows about her losses at the gaming table, when you were in London. Shouldn't think anyone will have noised it abroad, though. We are not the type to air our dirty linen in public. Not surprising he would attempt something to try to rein her in. He's that type of man.'

'What type of man?'

'The kind that needs to feel he has the upper hand,' said Great-Aunt Cornelia with a curl to her upper lip. 'So, what happened to make you call your father's bluff?'

Betsy gasped. 'What makes you think I…?'

'Because you're here,' she said, 'when it was supposed to be the last resort. I'm guessing,' she said, leaning back and narrowing her eyes, 'now that I've seen you do it here, that you lost your temper with him and told him to do his worst.'

'Well, no, I mean, I did lose my temper with Papa, when I found out he'd been lying, but by then…'

'By then? Out with it! Don't leave me in suspense, girl.'

That was the moment when Betsy first began to suspect that Great-Aunt Cornelia shared her own mother's love of gossip. And decided she'd already said too much. Besides, she didn't know her well enough to confide in her. Who knew what she'd do with the information? She daren't risk anyone finding out about the vestment cupboard, or the vestry floor, let alone the matter of the proposal.

'I would rather not say,' she'd said.

Great-Aunt Cornelia shook her head. 'You'd just love to tell me to mind my own business, wouldn't you? I can see it in the defiant set of your jaw. You're a Mainwaring through and through. Well, there. I'm beginning to think we might rub along fairly well, once we get used to each other.'

Great-Aunt Cornelia liked her being rude and defiant? Well, that was certainly different. Very different from how Mother was always trying to mould her into what she claimed was the perfect young lady. But Mother, Betsy had recently begun to see, was not infallible. Mother, in fact, had acted so rashly that they'd had to cut Betsy's Season short and had then pushed her into trying to get Ben into a compromising position. In fact, it was a jolly good job she couldn't go back to Bramley Bythorne. Because if Mother ever discovered that Mr Dundas was in fact Lord Dundas, she'd be bound to want to stage yet another compromising situation, which Betsy simply could not take part in and which would lead to yet another argument with her parents, before the heat had even cooled on the current one.

So from that moment on, Betsy decided to just be herself, and say what she thought. It turned out to be extremely liberating not to have to guard her tongue all the time. Great-Aunt Cornelia never minded if Betsy didn't agree meekly with everything she said. She positively enjoyed it if she argued with her. In fact, the longer the pair of them managed to defend totally opposite opinions, the more the older lady seemed to enjoy it.

She certainly had a group of cronies with similarly waspish tongues. Betsy could see, after sitting through a couple of afternoons when Great-Aunt Cornelia's three closest friends gathered to discuss everything from European politics to the latest novel, just how a girl with a sensitive nature might have found their forthright manners rather intimidating.

But Betsy pretty soon discovered that she wasn't easily intimidated. For one thing she'd grown up in a household where frank speech flew about like missiles. She'd probably grown some sort of armour to deflect it. And recently she'd become a girl who no longer believed in her parents, or trusted them so implicitly she obeyed them without question. She'd started to think for herself before even reaching Tunbridge Wells.

Or perhaps it was because she'd already sunk as low as she'd ever feared she could. She'd lost her self-respect over the affair with Ben. She'd lost her hope of ever finding anyone she could love, after *he* had played her false. Mother had gambled away her dowry. What else did she have to lose?

Betsy had been in Tunbridge Wells for three weeks and the wounds *he* had inflicted were beginning to feel more like bruises than lacerating open sores. One day, she mused, when they'd developed into crusty scabs, she could even imagine she might start to settle into the kind of lifestyle Great-Aunt Cornelia had chosen. She was beginning to see the benefits of cultivating the persona of a crabby, impossible old spinster. She, too, would relish speaking her mind so freely, and so pungently, that everyone dreaded her. Or perhaps not everyone. Even Great-Aunt Cornelia had those three friends, who seemed not only to find her pithy comments amusing, but to pay attention to her opinions.

'Have you heard,' said Mrs Petersham, the moment she bustled into the room that day, which was the day of Great-Aunt Cornelia's regular at-home, 'the latest?'

'Probably,' said Great-Aunt Cornelia drily. 'You always do think you hear everything before everyone else and you are seldom right.'

'Well, I should think I am this time,' said Mrs Petersham, dropping into what Betsy had noticed was her favourite chair, 'since I saw him driving into the yard of the Angel with my own eyes from my bedroom window this morning.' She then made great play with removing her gloves, one finger at a time, clearly hoping someone was going to say *saw who*?

It was Mrs Bradbury, predictably, who weakened first. 'Saw who, Lydia, dear?'

'Lord Dundas,' said Mrs Petersham, making Betsy feel as if all the air had suddenly been sucked right out of her chest. *He* was in Tunbridge Wells? Why? What for? 'Heir to the Earl of Darwen,' Mrs Petersham continued.

'Very interesting, I'm sure,' said Great-Aunt Cornelia, in a tone of voice that implied it was anything but.

'Are you,' said Mrs Corcoran, who was always the first to arrive, as she was, according to Great-Aunt Cornelia, determined not to miss a single morsel of gossip, 'quite sure?'

'Oh, yes,' said Mrs Petersham airily. 'His mother made her come-out the same year I did. Still see her, occasionally, if she and I are in town at the same time. So I have seen and spoken to him on several occasions. Besides,' she added with a titter, 'there's no mistaking the family resemblance.'

He couldn't have come after her, could he? No. At least, if he had, why wait for three weeks? If she meant anything to him, surely he would have come hot-foot, the moment he knew she'd left Bramley Bythorne.

'I fail to see why the arrival in town of the son of a friend of yours should make you quite so excited,' said Great-Aunt Cornelia.

'Well, my dear, because he is single,' said Mrs Bradbury before Mrs Petersham could even draw breath. 'And fabulously wealthy in his own right.'

Was he? Betsy's heart sank. If Mother ever found out that she'd spurned a titled man, it was going to be bad enough. But a fabulously wealthy one? It was a good job she'd escaped from Bramley Bythorne, or Mother would probably have strangled her after denouncing her as her life's bitterest disappointment, throwing her down the stairs and pulling out all her hair.

'And you may not have any unmarried daughters,' said Mrs Petersham, archly, 'but I have a brace of 'em.'

'And I have a goddaughter,' said Mrs Corcoran. 'The most darling girl. I shall have to write and invite her to stay with me.'

Nobody asked why. It was too obvious. If a single, titled, wealthy young man was in Tunbridge Wells, it was an opportunity. A much better opportunity than a girl would get during a London Season, if she didn't have the right connections. There might not be as much going on in comparison to London, or Brighton, or half a dozen other more fashionable places, but the advantage for girls on the lookout for a husband was the fact that here, anyone could buy a ticket to any of the subscription assemblies. Anyone could get into one of the places where men and women alike went to play at lottery, or Hazard.

'I wonder,' said Great-Aunt Cornelia, 'what he's doing here? A man of his age isn't likely to need to take the waters. Is he? Do you think he has some unfortunate complaint?'

Oh, how Betsy wished he had. In fact, she'd *give*

him an unfortunate complaint if only she could get her hands on him. Because, just when she was starting to feel as if she might, one day, start to get over him, he'd turned up, pulling the rug from under her feet and setting her thoughts and feelings tumbling all over the place.

'He didn't look the slightest bit unwell to me,' said Mrs Petersham.

'Perhaps his mother is unwell,' suggested Mrs Bradbury. 'After all those children she's presented to the Earl,' she put in as if to show everyone that Mrs Petersham was not the only one who knew something about his background, 'it wouldn't be a bit surprising, would it? Perhaps he's come to arrange rooms for her and so forth. Spy out the land. See if there is anything suitable.'

'Why on earth,' said Great-Aunt Cornelia in a withering tone, 'would he do that? His father would have come if it were a case of arranging things.'

'Pooh, not he,' replied Mrs Petersham. 'He is the most selfish beast in nature, by all accounts. Never takes a thought for poor dear Mary. But her sons are all devoted to her.' She spread her hands wide, as though she'd proved her point to her own satisfaction, while showing Betsy that *everyone* seemed to know more about the man she'd thought she wanted to marry than she did. So far today, in rapid succession, she'd discovered that his father was a selfish earl, that he adored his mother and that he had more than one brother.

Great-Aunt Cornelia pursed her lips. As did Betsy.

It was too much of a coincidence for him to turn up here, even though it was after a gap of three weeks, when she'd told him, over and over again, how much she hadn't wanted to come here. And then *had* come here in spite of everything.

Could he have come to gloat? Was he that kind of man? She wouldn't have believed it of him.

But then, she wouldn't have believed he'd make her fall in love with him, under false pretences, either, would she?

What, wait—*fall in love* with him? Was that what she'd done? She almost shook her head and would have done had she not suddenly remembered she was in company with four of the most avid gossips in the county.

'Anyway,' Mrs Petersham was continuing, with a sort of gloating air, 'I shall ask him myself, when he calls to pay his respects.'

'You think he will do that,' said Mrs Bradbury, 'do you?'

'Oh, yes. The moment I saw him drive in I sent Paul—' who was, Betsy recalled, her manservant, something between a butler and footman, since she couldn't afford both on her widow's jointure '—straight over with a little note, reminding him of the friendship between me and his mother and telling him that he would be welcome to call any time.'

'I'm surprised to see you here, then,' said Great-Aunt Cornelia waspishly, 'if you are expecting such an eligible *parti* to visit.

'Oh, the girls will entertain him perfectly well

without me, should he call today,' she said, with a titter. 'After all, the whole point is to get him to take notice of *them*, isn't it? I'm sure they will all get on far
better without me hovering over them. Young people
don't want chaperons spoiling their fun, do they?'

No. No, they didn't. In her experience with him
thus far, she was all too aware that the last thing *he*
wanted was to have a chaperon interfering with his
plans. He was good at arranging things so that he
could be alone with a female, when the mood took
him. He'd even ambushed her in a church! And, yes,
it was true that *she'd* been the one to drag *him* into
that cupboard, but he must have known she'd do that
when they heard Mrs Knowles approaching.

'Ah, here is the tea,' said Great-Aunt Cornelia.
'You will pour for us, won't you, Betsy?'

'Of course, Great-Aunt,' she said demurely, rising from her chair to go to the tea table.

As she picked up the pot, she pictured the scene
which was probably taking place, this very moment,
in the drawing room across from the Angel. The two
pretty Petersham girls would be doing their utmost
to entertain *him*. The wealthy, single Lord Dundas.
There, she'd finally thought of him by his title.

'Betsy! What are you about? I don't pay you to
stand about wool-gathering,' snapped Great-Aunt
Cornelia, making Betsy realise she'd frozen with
the teapot in mid-air. 'Pour the tea. And hand round
the cakes.'

She knew where she'd like to pour the tea. And it
wasn't into the cups on this table.

She knew where she'd like to fling the cakes as well, even though they'd just bounce off his thick hide like the insubstantial morsels of sponge that they were. She swept the fantasy ruthlessly aside. Said 'Yes, Great-Aunt Cornelia' mechanically. And poured the tea into cups for the four ladies and handed round the cakes, while the others discussed the chances that *he* would attend the concert that evening.

She sincerely hoped he wouldn't.

But if he did, at least she was forewarned. She wouldn't come across him suddenly and betray the way she felt by blushing, or bursting into tears, or fainting or anything stupid like that. She'd be able to be calm and polite, and behave as if he were merely a casual acquaintance.

Rather than the man who'd so comprehensively, and carelessly, crushed her.

Chapter Eighteen

Betsy hadn't calmed down all that much by the time they went out that evening, to attend a performance of *The Four Seasons*. In fact, she was fairly simmering with resentment as they entered the rooms. Because, before she'd learned that *he* had come to Tunbridge Wells, she'd been really looking forward to coming to this concert. But now she wasn't going to be able to settle until she knew whether *he* was likely to be there as well.

And nor, by the looks of it, would Mrs Petersham, who was loitering just inside the door, fluttering about in a way that put Betsy in mind of a hawk, hovering in hopes of swooping down and seizing some poor unsuspecting mouse in its talons.

The mouse in question walked into her trap not five minutes after Betsy and her great-aunt had taken their seats. Betsy didn't see it happen, but hearing a commotion at the door, she half turned in her seat to see if her worst fears could be confirmed.

They were.

Mrs Petersham had him by the arm and was towing him to the row of chairs where she'd already installed her daughters. Just a couple of rows behind Betsy.

He saw her looking at him. He must have done, for she'd looked right into his eyes. But he made no sign that he'd recognised her. And a hot pang of...*something* twisted through her as he allowed the Petersham women to flutter him into a seat in a flurry of flattery and flummery.

Betsy whipped her head round to face the front, where the orchestra was making a series of discordant sounds which totally matched her own mood. So, he was going to pretend he didn't know her, was he? Going to *cut* her, in fact? Fine. She wouldn't admit she knew him, either, then. Well, she didn't, did she? She'd *begun* to get to know a man she thought was a steward. A rugged, hardworking man who had gained the respect of Lord Bramhall's tenants and her father alike. But this, this *viscount*? She knew nothing about him at all.

The discord from the front of the room ceased and the musicians all began to exert themselves to entertain the audience. Betsy kept her face forward, her eyes on the orchestra, hoping she looked as though she was rapt with the performance. Although she might as well have had cotton wool stuffed in her ears. Every nerve in her body was attuned to the man who was sitting two rows behind her. What was he doing? Was he watching the violinists as they tossed the tune from one to the other, in an almost playful manner, or was he looking at the back of her neck? At the way she'd allowed a few curls to escape the rather severe hairstyle she'd adopted since coming to live in Tunbridge Wells, as befitted a paid companion.

Oh, she did feel peculiar, knowing he was in the same room as her. The places on her body which his hands had touched, caressed, began to burn. And her lips tingled. And her heart beat fast. And after a bit every muscle in her body was aching with the effort of not turning round to look at him.

And then the Petersham girls both let out a chorus of giggles. And her fingers clenched on her fan so tightly she was in real danger of snapping one of the struts. But she wouldn't turn round, as though she was curious as to what he'd said, or done, to create such a gust of hilarity. She would not! Instead she flicked open her poor abused fan and began to waft it in front of her heated cheeks, with an air, she hoped, of complete insouciance. Because she was blowed if she was going to allow anyone to notice the state she was in. She would *not* make a spectacle of herself.

She was concentrating so hard on looking as though she was enjoying herself that it came as a bit of a surprise when a smattering of polite applause marked the end of the performance.

'Well, I must say,' Great-Aunt Cornelia remarked, 'that performance has almost reconciled me to Vivaldi. That was nowhere near as dreary as most of his works.'

'Wasn't it?'

Great-Aunt Cornelia sighed. 'Don't tell me that you have no opinions about music, either?'

'Not about Vivaldi,' said Betsy, rather grateful to have her aunt goading her into conversation. At least if she appeared to be talking about music, it wouldn't look as if she was straining to hear what the Petersham party were talking about. With such animation. And what *he* was replying that was making them behave as if they'd never had so much fun in their lives. 'I have not had the opportunity to attend many concerts, so I don't really know what I like, or don't like.'

'Hmmph. We'll have to remedy that,' said Great-Aunt Cornelia, while, in spite of all her intentions, Betsy noticed *him* getting to his feet.

'I must say,' Great-Aunt Cornelia continued, while Betsy perceived, through means of a series of brief, darting glances, that *he* was extricating himself from the Petershams, and beginning to amble in her direction, 'that although this isn't exactly a fashionable place any longer—' yes, he was definitely coming closer, she hadn't been imagining it '—there is still a varied programme of musical events to which... Yes? What do you want, young man?'

The reason Great-Aunt Cornelia had snapped that final question was because *he* had come to a halt right in front of them. And was standing there, staring at them, intently.

'I thought I was not mistaken,' he said. 'Miss Fairfax, is it not?'

She wanted to reply that he knew very well who

she was. You couldn't spend ten minutes squashed together in a cupboard, so tightly that you knew every contour of the other person's body, and then another few minutes rolling around on the floor learning those contours with your hands, without having that person etched, deeply etched, into your memory. Although he didn't look all that much like the man she'd seriously considered eloping with.

To start with, he was wearing clothes that were clearly expensive and expertly tailored, rather than work-worn riding gear. And she'd never seen his jaw so closely shaved. But mostly it was his expression that made him look so very different from the man she'd thought she knew. This man had hard eyes and a haughty, forbidding expression, which made him look every inch the son of an earl.

'*You* know Lord Dundas?' Great-Aunt Cornelia turned to look at her sharply.

'N-no,' she said, remembering the way he'd deceived her into thinking he was one thing, when really he was nothing of the sort. But then, because this was a public area, with all sorts of people watching the exchange, with great interest, she added, feebly, 'That is, not really.'

He regarded her stonily for a moment, then turned to address Great-Aunt Cornelia.

'I had the pleasure of making the acquaintance of Miss Fairfax shortly after my sister married Lord Bramhall, a neighbour of hers. While I was staying in the area, her father, Colonel Fairfax, was kind enough to invite me to dine.'

Well, that was true enough, as far as it went. And it chimed with her own, stammered version of not really knowing him, she supposed.

'Is that so?' Great-Aunt Cornelia gave her yet another sharp look. 'Well, aren't you going to introduce me, girl?'

Betsy had no option but to do so. *He* granted Great-Aunt Cornelia the briefest of bows, as though he'd done her a great favour, before turning his attention back to Betsy.

Betsy wanted to ask him what he was doing here. Why he'd lied to her. If he'd ever had any fondness for her at all, or if she'd just been a huge joke to him. But this wasn't the time, or the place, to ask any of those things. Perhaps there never would come a time when she could ask them. Because then he'd know how badly he'd hurt her. And she had no intention of letting him, or anyone, suspect she was one of those females who broke their hearts over unworthy men, went into a decline, and, in short, made complete fools of themselves. And, oh, how glad she was that she'd told him so, the very first time they'd met! Although then she'd been referring to millponds, not… not…

Oh, but she couldn't just stand here, looking as though the fact that he'd deigned to notice her had robbed her of the power of speech. Particularly since it happened to be true.

'Do you,' she found herself saying, since it was the first polite thing to enter her head and what everyone asked visitors to the town, 'make a long stay in Tunbridge Wells?'

'That depends,' he replied.

'Upon,' she snapped, 'what?'

'Upon how long it takes to remedy what ails me,' he said, giving her what felt like a very meaningful look. 'Or if,' he continued, 'the waters here prove beneficial at all. May I call upon you, while I am staying here?'

'The impertinence!' Great-Aunt Cornelia poked him in the waistcoat with her fan. 'If you are to ask anyone, it should be me. And I am not in the habit of encouraging my companions to have gentlemen callers. Most improper!'

'Gentleman callers?' He gave Great-Aunt Cornelia a look that could have frozen the blood in her veins, had she been a more sensitive sort of person. 'I would hardly categorise a visit to a family friend, to assure myself that she is settling in, that I might inform her parents how she fares, in that light. They are both very conscious that she has never had to work for her living before, and would, I feel certain, like to hear the impressions of a disinterested party.'

So. He was determined not to be mistaken for a gentleman caller, was he? His only reason for singling her out was to be able to relate to her parents how she was settling in? In a *disinterested* way?

'Are there,' he continued, turning to Betsy, 'any messages that you would like me to convey to your parents?' Plenty. She'd like to know if either of them ever planned to write back to her, since so far they'd ignored her short missive letting them know she'd arrived safely.

'We have a perfectly good postal service if she wants to send any messages,' said Great-Aunt Cornelia. 'Every morning bar Monday and every evening bar Saturday. And of course she's happy. Why wouldn't she be happy?'

He gave Betsy a searching look. 'No reason at all, of course.'

At this point, Mrs Petersham, who'd been edging steadily closer, now made her presence felt. 'Oh, you mustn't take any notice of Mrs Warboys's crotchets,' she said with a playful titter. 'Even if she doesn't think it is quite the thing to go calling on her companion, I am sure there could be no objection to your attending one of her at-homes when you would be able to see for yourself how wonderfully Miss Fairfax is fulfilling her duties as her companion.'

Betsy tried not to flinch. But, oh, how humiliating it would be if he did come to one of those gossipy gatherings, to watch her pouring tea and serving cakes, and fetching shawls and plumping cushions while being almost totally unable to contribute a single intelligent comment to the conversations raging around her. It was almost enough to drive her to picking up a book and reading it.

'I am sure,' Mrs Petersham continued, 'you would be a most welcome addition to any gathering, my lord, and are bound to have a great deal to contribute to our discussions. We gather together on Wednesday afternoons at three to discuss the news. We have a lively, intellectual social circle in Tunbridge, you know...'

'Just one moment,' said Great-Aunt Cornelia, getting to her feet, so that she could look Mrs Petersham in the eye. 'Just what makes you think you have the right to go inviting people to attend my salon? In my house?'

'Oh, but, Cornelia, dear,' Mrs Petersham twittered, 'we have always been free to bring along friends of ours, haven't we?'

'And what,' Great-Aunt Cornelia plunged on, ignoring that rather pertinent fact, 'makes you think that His Lordship would wish to spend his afternoon drinking tea and gossiping with a parcel of withered old crones? He must have far better things to do with his time.'

Mrs Petersham gasped and drew herself up a fraction taller. 'I, for one, can scarcely be described as *withered*...'

At which point, Betsy glanced up at him, wondering what on earth he must be thinking of the two ladies, quarrelling over him like two dogs over a juicy bone, rather than simply asking him what he wanted. But he was wearing the hard, flinty expression that made it impossible to tell what he was thinking. Except, perhaps, that he was not a man to trifle with.

So it came as a surprise to hear him interject, before the argument between the two ladies could progress any further, 'On the contrary, I *have* nothing better to do with my time while I am in Tunbridge Wells. I shall therefore see you all tomorrow, at three.' And then, with a brief, rather dismissive bow, he turned and stalked away.

Mrs Petersham went scurrying off back to her daughters, full of the news that she'd managed to find out where Lord Dundas would be the next afternoon, at three, to judge by the triumphant expression on her face.

'Hah,' said Great-Aunt Cornelia crossly. 'I suppose *that*,' she said, indicating the squeals of excitement emanating from all three Petersham females, 'means we will have her vapid daughters coming round tomorrow as well.'

'You could always have Gregory deny them admittance,' suggested Betsy, tentatively.

'No,' said Great-Aunt Cornelia, pensively. 'Their antics may well serve to amuse me.'

They were unlikely to amuse Betsy. Particularly not if he responded favourably to them...

'And as for you...' Great-Aunt Cornelia poked her in the ribs with her fan '...you sly creature. Fancy not telling us you knew him, the moment we began to discuss him.'

'Well, it isn't exactly my place, is it?'

'Poppycock! You know that if there is a morsel of gossip to unearth, we all want to hear it. No matter where it comes from. And you have *dined* with him.' She gave Betsy a hard look. 'I am beginning to wonder if you know something about him you are deliberately trying to hide.'

'No! Nothing of the sort,' she said, or rather squeaked, her face flushing hotly.

'Well, that settles it,' said Great-Aunt Cornelia, looking at Betsy's heated cheeks. 'You are hopeless at telling lies, young lady. If I don't detect a whiff of romance and scandal, I am a Dutchman. And I shall have the truth out of you. But,' she added, glancing round the room, 'this is hardly the place for sharing confidences. It will have to wait until we get home.'

Far from being a Dutchman, Great-Aunt Cornelia was more like some grand Spanish inquisitor. For in spite of Betsy's determination to admit to nothing, they hadn't been in the front parlour for more than half an hour before she'd told Great-Aunt Cornelia pretty much everything. Everything that related to *him*, anyway. Great-Aunt Cornelia had no interest in learning anything that had happened before *he*'d arrived in Bramley Bythorne, so she was able to keep the fact that she'd climbed up Lord Bramhall and kissed him to herself.

'So,' she said, sitting back and eyeing Betsy with a sort of fascination, 'he told you he was a steward and led you to believe he was an ordinary man, a working man, made you the object of his attentions, caused you to act indiscreetly and all but seduced you in the vestry.'

Betsy nodded, wringing her hands as she braced herself to receive a blistering scold, followed by an ignominious sacking. And it was strange, that, having regarded working for this woman in the light of a form of purgatory before coming here, the prospect of being turned off now felt as though it would be a punishment, rather than a release.

'And now he's pursued you here,' Great-Aunt Cornelia said thoughtfully.

'I...I don't think so. I mean, he barely spoke to me. And when he did, it was with such coldness, such indifference.'

'Hmmph. What I think is—' She broke off, lowered her head and shifted in her seat. 'Well, we shall see, shall we not?'

'You—you aren't going to dismiss me?'

'You haven't committed any indiscretions while you've been with me, so I have no grounds, have I? Besides, I know what it is to be pursued by mountebanks,' she said, screwing up her face with disgust. 'Even at my age, they still come round from time to time, thinking they can get me to fall for them, when I know that all they have ever wanted is to get their grubby hands on my fortune.' She rapped on the floor with the ebony cane which she flourished to great effect from time to time, though very rarely actually leaned on when walking about.

'And you have shown the sense to turn down his dubious offer of marriage and chosen to remain single. Which shows, to my way of thinking, that you have more sense than many girls, whose heads would be turned by the attentions of a man with a title. And a good deal of the Mainwaring pride. Nobody who watched the way you and he spoke after the concert would have guessed that he had almost ruined you.' She drew herself up to her full height. 'I am not going to turn you out and possibly render you prey to a villain of that sort. You have a safe haven, here, with me.'

'Oh. Well, thank you,' Betsy stammered. Although she didn't think she really needed a safe haven from *him*. She wasn't sure what *he* was doing here in Tunbridge Wells, but it didn't sound, so far, as if he was planning to, well, pay court to her, or anything of that sort.

'In fact, I shall look forward to sending him about his business if he becomes a nuisance. He won't find *me* toad-eating him the way Lydia,' she said with a curl to her lip, 'has been doing. I wonder what sort of cakes he likes the least. Do you know? If so, you may order Cook to serve them up tomorrow, if he should deign to attend our gathering. A gathering that has been blessedly free of masculine interference, until now. Well, off to bed with you, girl,' she said, waving a gnarled hand in dismissal. 'And don't worry your head about his visit tomorrow. I know how to deal with villains of his stamp.'

He *wasn't* a villain, she wanted to protest. Not really. He could easily have seduced her. Nor need he have proposed marriage.

But even as the words formed on her lips, she swallowed them back. Because Great-Aunt Cornelia was so looking forward to going into battle on her behalf. She hadn't uttered a single word of rebuke, or told her she was foolish for having held him at bay. Mother would have done both. Even Papa would have been disappointed in her if he'd ever found out how she'd behaved. For the first time in her life, Betsy had found somebody who was eager to take up the cudgels on her behalf, rather than using her to further their own ends.

And so she just curtsied, meekly, before running up the stairs to bed.

Chapter Nineteen

Promptly at three o' clock, James knocked on the door of a comfortably-sized house in a street on Mount Sion, which was full of houses that all looked equally prosperous. A young man in plain livery answered the door and led him up an elegant staircase to a room that contained, at first glance, what looked like a couple of dozen women.

He tried hard not to search for Miss Fairfax among the throng, but it was as if some part of him just knew where she was anyway. She was standing by the tea table, presiding over the cups and plates. And studiously ignoring his arrival.

As though to emphasise the different way they felt about him, the Petersham women surged round him, cooing and fluttering, and urging him to what they said was the best seat in the room. He caught Miss Fairfax exchanging a wry look with her aunt. Or great-aunt, or whatever relation she was. And no wonder. He was not only the only male there, but

he would warrant no male had ever been invited
to this particular gathering before. And, to be honest, he hadn't been invited by the hostess, had he?
But by these ambitious, marriage-minded Petersham
women, who were so determined to get their hooks
into him that they would stoop to practically any
level to achieve their aim.

Just as he'd hoped. If he was ever going to get
Miss Fairfax to understand why he'd been reluctant
to admit exactly who he was, he needed to show
her how it was for him when people, specifically
marriage-minded women, *did* know.

As he allowed himself to be drawn across the
room to a set of chairs grouped round a low table,
before a bay window which gave an excellent view
down to the street below, he took a second look at
the other ladies present. There were only, in truth,
another couple of older ladies, one of whom was sitting with Miss Fairfax's elderly relative. The other
was occupying a sofa, next to a startlingly pretty girl
who had arranged herself in a languid pose designed,
if he was any judge, to draw his eyes to the curve of
her hip, the trimness of her waist and the fullness of
her bosom. She had also managed, somehow, to get
her skirts to ride up to a point where they revealed
rather more ankle than was strictly decorous for an
afternoon tea.

In short, the room was full of the kind of women
he would normally avoid like the plague. Ah, the
lengths he would go to, he reflected as he took the
seat Mrs Petersham had suggested, in order to gain

ground with Miss Fairfax. He hoped she appreciated
what he was deliberately enduring for her sake. He
hoped that she was perceptive enough to see what he
was doing, by coming here and permitting the Petersham women to monopolise him while that minx on
the sofa cast him sheep's eyes.

It was just a pity he hadn't thought of it sooner.
Although, to be honest, even if he had come up
with a plan, he couldn't very well have come after
her before fulfilling the responsibilities he had at
Bramley Park. He couldn't very well have dashed
off and left Gem in charge without first introducing
him about the neighbourhood as his replacement,
while showing him what work was in train and what
still needed setting in motion. To cap it all, not two
days after Gem had arrived, so had the first batch
of long-expected and oft-delayed ex-soldiers who
were going to start working on the rebuilding of
Lord Bramhall's derelict estate. And, even though
Wilmot had said that he was well up to dealing with
them, since he'd been in the army for many years
himself, James hadn't felt it would be right to just
abandon everyone. It would have been selfish of him
to leave Wilmot alone with the task of discovering
what the men were capable of doing, since they all
had injuries of one sort or another. Or leaving Gem
with the task of protecting Mrs Green and Sally,
should any of the newcomers prove to be unpleasant. In the event, most of the men who came had
wives and a couple had children, and were all ex-

tremely grateful to have work and housing, when so many of their fellows were reduced to begging on the street. The only one among them who'd looked as if he might become a troublemaker was a gangly youth, the son of a former quartermaster, who kept disappearing rather than performing whatever task Wilmot had given him. However, rather than just loitering somewhere, causing mischief, they kept on finding him at the village smithy, trying to get Humboldt, the blacksmith, to let him work the bellows. Humboldt said that far from being a nuisance, he'd be only too glad to take the lad on as an apprentice, so that was that problem solved.

And while all that was going on, he'd had to contact Bishop, and arrange for both him and the curricle to return, along with a selection of clothing more suited to going courting in a respectable, gentrified town.

'Tea?' Miss Fairfax was brandishing the pot in his direction, looking as if for two pins she'd march right across the room and pour the steaming liquid right into his lap. Thanking heaven that they were in company, and that she'd have to restrain her natural impulses, he gave her a curt nod.

It was deuced awkward, being in company and having to restrain oneself. Although what he'd like to do had nothing to do with the teapot and everything to do with slipping his arm about her waist and kissing her until she couldn't remember her own name, never mind why she was so angry with him.

But he knew that wouldn't work. Since having that

conversation about women and marriage with Gem, James had started to see that simply dropping the handkerchief was never going to work with a woman who was truly worth winning. And nor was kissing her into submission. A woman worth wooing, that is to say, Miss Fairfax, needed to understand him and all about him, so that she could choose him. *Him.* Not his title or his wealth or whatever that might represent for her.

He turned to the nearest Miss Petersham, the one with the freckles. If striking that sort of bargain was all that he wanted, he could have settled for a girl like this one, during one of his visits to London. But he didn't want a woman who would tamely agree with everything he said. A woman like his mother, who treated his father as though he was some sort of god. Marriage to a woman like that would be calm and settled, yes. But it would also be damnably dull. There was nothing dull about Miss Fairfax. Even the way she was pouring his tea was dramatic. She was bristling with hostility. Placing the spoon in the saucer with a deliberation that made him think she was imagining half a dozen ways she could employ it to cause him bodily injury.

She was walking across the room to him now, her eyes snapping, her whole body sort of pulsing with emotion.

She set the cup and saucer down before him. And turned away.

'Is there any cake?' he couldn't resist asking, so that she would have to turn round and look at him.

So that he could breathe in the scent of her, as well as feasting his eyes on the sight of her.

'Oh, yes, my lord,' cooed the freckled Miss Petersham. 'You must try some of the seed cake. It is absolutely delicious.'

'I dislike seed cake,' he informed her. 'I dislike the way the seeds stick in the teeth and how one is constantly finding them hours later.'

'Oh, yes, indeed,' said the freckled Miss Petersham, 'that is very uncomfortable to be sure. I only recommended the cake because…' and she lowered her voice and leaned in '…it is a speciality of Mrs Warboys's cook. She prides herself on it.'

He thought he heard Miss Fairfax give a slight snort as the freckled Miss Petersham performed such an abrupt about-face. Miss Fairfax would never deign to say she liked seed cake if she didn't. Not even to impress him. She'd always tell him the truth. And lose her temper with him when he did something stupid.

She wouldn't be a comfortable wife. At times he'd wondered why he'd ever proposed to her at all. Especially during those first few days after she'd turned him down. He'd brooded long and hard over all the characteristics he could regard as deficiencies. And still come to the conclusion that if he couldn't get her to marry him, he didn't think he could bear to ever marry anyone else.

'I rather like the lemon sponge,' the other Miss Petersham, the one with the snub nose, put in. 'It is lovely and moist.'

'What would you recommend, Miss Fairfax?' he said, ignoring both Petersham girls, who were annoying him by the way they were completely ignoring her, as though she was merely a servant.

'Me?' She considered for a moment, then gave him a challenging look. '*I* would recommend the seed cake.'

Yes, in the hope that the seeds would annoy him for hours.

'Then, since two of you have recommended it, I suppose I really ought to try it,' he said, causing the freckled Miss Petersham to smile and sigh, and blush. He could only hope that the way Miss Fairfax curled her upper lip before she went to fetch the cake was a sign that she despised Miss Petersham, rather than scorning his mute declaration of intent to face the torture of picking seeds from his teeth for hours, if she thought it a suitable penance for his sins.

Across the room, Mrs Warboys cleared her throat. 'Well, if you are all done discussing the merits of the cake, perhaps we can get down to the topic of discussion. Which is the latest excrescence produced by that charlatan Byron.'

'Oh, Cornelia, really,' protested Mrs Petersham. 'How can you judge his work so harshly? He is a great poet. Everyone says so.'

'Then everyone is an idiot,' snapped back Miss Fairfax's great-aunt. He was starting to like her. Mostly because the way she spoke her mind, no matter what, put him so forcibly in mind of Miss Fairfax.

'What do you think, my lord,' said the freckled Miss Petersham, 'of Lord Byron's poetry? For myself, I think it is sublime,' she ended on a sigh.

'I never read poetry,' he replied curtly.

'Oh, well, what,' asked the snub-nosed Miss Petersham, 'do you read?'

'Mostly books that can teach me something about land management.'

'Yes,' put in Miss Fairfax as she returned to the table with a plate bearing such a massive wedge of seed cake that he could feel his teeth shrinking in protest at the prospect of what lay before them. 'You are never happier than when discussing drainage and turnips, are you?'

'Untrue,' he replied, and looked her straight in the eye as he relived those glorious minutes they'd spent in the vestment cupboard. From the way she blushed he could tell she was thinking of it, too. And then, to judge from the fury that flashed from her eyes, she was remembering what had happened immediately after they'd tumbled out of the cupboard. Or, rather, the admission he'd made.

He cursed himself. Instead of reminding her what they'd been to each other, all he'd done was remind her of her main grudge against him.

'Oh?' The freckled Miss Petersham was looking from one to the other of them intently. 'What is it that you do enjoy, my lord?'

All the colour drained from Miss Fairfax's cheeks as though she feared he might reveal, over the teacups, the interlude which he held so dear, but of which she appeared to be so bitterly ashamed. How low an opinion of him did she have, to think that he could behave in such a fashion...could even *consider* doing anything so dastardly?

Pretty low. She'd already accused him of lying to her, deliberately, in order to trifle with her affections.

'I,' he said, turning to the Petersham girls with a feeling akin to despair, 'am not much of a one for sitting reading at all, to tell you the truth. I prefer being out of doors, preferably on horseback, riding the land and checking that it is in good heart.'

Even without looking at her, he could feel Miss Fairfax breathing a sigh of relief. She really had feared what he might say. Why on earth did she think he'd come here at all? Couldn't she see that he would do anything to make amends? To get her to forgive him his stupidity? Even to the point of eating the kind of cake that he disliked above just about anything else?

Clearly not.

'In fact, if you ladies will forgive me, I think I should take my leave now. Although this has been a delightful interlude, I am sure you will all enjoy discussing your poetry far more without me here to blight your conversation with my rustic, male opinions.'

There were cries of protest from the Petersham women, as well as the old lady on the sofa with the young beauty.

Miss Fairfax's elderly relative, however, Mrs Warboys, nodded her approval.

'That's the first sensible statement I've heard from anyone today,' she declared.

'Really, Cornelia,' he heard the beauty's relative protest as he stalked to the door, 'that was extremely rude of you.'

'You know I always speak my mind,' Mrs Warboys replied. 'And if you don't like to hear it, you shouldn't have come.'

No, *he* was the one who shouldn't have come. What had he been thinking? That Miss Fairfax would take one look at him in all his new clothing, with his face expertly shaved and his hands neatly manicured, and swoon at his feet in gratitude that he was offering her a second chance?

Obviously not. It was going to take time to win her round. Time and effort, and a good deal of suffering occasions like this afternoon.

But anything worth having was worth working for. Worth even suffering for. He had no right, as Gem had pointed out, to treat any woman as though she should be grateful that he'd noticed her.

'You need to make her look on you as a knight of old,' Gem had suggested, 'going on a quest to win her favour.'

'Knight of old,' he muttered to himself as he retrieved his hat and gloves from the footman. It was all very well for Gem to talk about behaving like a knight of old, but knights of old could slay dragons, or giants, to impress their women. There were no giants in Tunbridge Wells, even if some of those women in that room just now could be described as dragons.

Still, he couldn't give up. Not yet.

Because the thought that he might have lost Miss Fairfax irretrievably was unthinkable.

Chapter Twenty

Betsy watched him leave her great-aunt's house with mixed feelings. Although uppermost was anger.

Why had he come here? What did he want? To see her humiliated? Acting the part of a servant to girls who were virtually flinging themselves at him?

Or was he pointing out that any other girl would be flattered should he drop the handkerchief? That she had been foolish beyond measure to turn him down when he could have any woman he wanted for the crooking of his finger? Well, she already knew that!

'We didn't realise,' said Miss Petersham, jolting her back to the fact that there were still a good many people in the room, people with whom she needed to interact, 'that you knew His Lordship so well.'

'Yes,' said Great-Aunt Cornelia, 'tell them how you came to know him and what you know of him, swiftly if you please, and then we can get on with the real purpose of gathering here.'

The real purpose of gathering here? If Great-Aunt

Cornelia really believed that anyone, but her, had come to talk about poetry, she was deluding herself. They'd come to try to get to know *him*. And to see how they could best impress him.

'His sister, Lady Marguerite...' said Betsy, reflecting that this was the first time since she'd moved here that either of the Petersham sisters had shown the slightest bit of interest in her, or where she'd come from. And it hadn't escaped her notice that, even now, they were only asking her about the bits of her past that concerned *him*, '...married the man who owns the property which runs next to my father's. Lord Bramhall is his name. He is a military man, Lord Bramhall, that is, and rushed off to the Continent the moment he heard that Bonaparte was trying to win back his empire. Before he went, he invited...' She felt her tongue curl up in resistance. Her throat thickened. But she was going to have to force herself to say that title. She could not very well spit out the word *him*, with all the animosity she was feeling. It would give rise to speculation. She swallowed. Took a breath. Pulled her lips into the semblance of a smile. '...*Lord Dundas* to come and oversee some work he'd set in train.' She didn't need to go into the tale of how Ben's estates were encumbered because of his father's profligacy and downright meanness. Nor touch upon the fact that when she'd first met *him* she'd had no idea he had a title. Nobody did. Not even Father had suspected he was anything more than a steward. He'd kept his identity from everyone.

Not just her.

Oh. Perhaps it hadn't been as personal an insult as it had felt.

But she couldn't dwell on that now, because everyone was waiting to hear what she'd started to say. And if she didn't want to admit to more than was wise, she'd need to keep her wits about her and be careful what she said.

'My father knows everyone in the area, so naturally Lord Dundas sought his advice about, well, various things. Which was why he visited our house.' There, that was the gist of it. At least all she was ready to admit in this type of gathering.

'And he really enjoyed talking about turnips,' said Miss Petersham, wide-eyed, 'and drainage?'

Betsy had a startling vision of Miss Petersham sending for every book she could find on land management and conning it industriously so that she could impress *him* with how much she'd learned. And was seriously tempted to tell her that he loved nothing more than turnips…how to cultivate them, how to employ them to help overwinter cattle, how to make them palatable to humans…

'Never mind turnips,' snapped Great-Aunt Cornelia, before Betsy could succumb.

She turned to her great-aunt, deeply grateful that she was not going to permit the topic of *him* and his supposed interest in turnips to take over what was supposed to be a meeting to discuss literature.

'If you want to talk about turnips you can take yourself off to the nearest market stall and consult

with a farmer,' said Great-Aunt Cornelia frostily.
'We are here to discuss *The Corsair.*'

'We already know you dislike it,' put in Mrs
Corcoran mildly, as Betsy busied herself tidying the
plates from the table at which the Petersham women
were still sitting.

'Yes,' retorted Great-Aunt Cornelia, 'but nobody
else has ventured an opinion.'

Even though everyone else would far rather have
carried on discussing *him*, and how handsome he
was, and how manly he looked, and what fine clothes
he wore, and what a large ruby he had for a tiepin,
and what strong opinions he held, and how fascinating they were, and the likelihood of his staying
in Tunbridge Wells for the rest of the summer, and
if it was true that he had come because he was suffering from melancholia, Great-Aunt Cornelia val-
iantly kept on steering the conversation back to the
epic poem that Lord Byron had brought out the year
before.

It felt like an eternity before the battle to discuss
what was of most interest to most of the visitors came
to an abrupt halt when the mantel clock struck five.
Betsy could not have said which of the factions could
declare victory, because, although Great-Aunt Cornelia had obliged everyone to say at least one thing
about *The Corsair*, they'd all outmanoeuvred her,
time after time, by wheeling round to the more fascinating topic of *him*. It was hard to say who looked
the most disgruntled as they began getting to their
feet and gathering up gloves and bonnets. Apart from

Mrs Bradbury, who'd said very little, but watched the others sparring with very evident enjoyment. She'd reminded Betsy of someone who had a front-row seat at a particularly enthralling performance at the theatre.

During the bustle created by the departure of the Petersham party, Miss Beech, who'd so far had nothing whatever to say, apart from the fact that she hadn't had a chance to read the poem, sidled up to Betsy.

'I was wondering,' she said hesitantly, 'if, well, since I don't know anyone in Tunbridge Wells, if you would be willing to show me about. I believe there are lots of shops and things, as well as the wells, only…well…' she lowered her cornflower-blue eyes, before raising them again, with an expression of pleading '…I don't like to put myself forward and the Misses Petersham,' she said, darting a glance at the door through which they'd just gone, 'have not offered me the hand of friendship.'

Betsy immediately felt sorry for the girl. She knew what it was like to come to a new town, where she knew nobody apart from the elderly relative with whom she was staying. And Miss Beech hadn't vied for *his* attention, either, the way the pushy Petersham girls had done, even though she'd gazed at him the whole time he'd been there, as though he was some sort of marvel. And on the few occasions he had looked her way, she'd lowered her eyes demurely and blushed.

'I am sorry,' said Betsy, almost meaning it, 'but

I am not at liberty to just go gadding about as the whim takes me. I am here as paid companion to Mrs Warboys.'

'Oh, but you must have some days off, surely? Mrs Warboys,' she said, turning to Great-Aunt Cornelia, 'you wouldn't object to Miss Fairfax showing me about the town, one day, would you? I mean, there must be some errands she could run for you, while taking me round the shops?'

'I have Gregory to run my errands,' said Great-Aunt Cornelia witheringly.

'Oh, come now, Cornelia,' said Mrs Corcoran, 'I am sure you can spare Miss Fairfax for an hour or two. It's about time, isn't it? To my knowledge, you have not granted her one single hour of leisure since she's come to stay with you.'

Betsy thought Great-Aunt Cornelia was going to explode, so furious did she look at this criticism. And indeed, the two old ladies promptly launched into such a bitter exchange that Betsy wouldn't have been surprised if they'd come to actual pulling of caps.

However, Miss Beech put a stop to things, by the simple expedient of bursting into tears.

'I am so s-sorry,' she sobbed. 'I never meant to cause trouble. I just thought that Miss Fairfax perhaps wouldn't despise me and wouldn't mind s-spending a morning with me, but I s-see that it will not do.'

'Oh, for heaven's sake,' snapped Great-Aunt Cornelia, as Mrs Corcoran came over to her goddaughter and began applying handkerchiefs and hugs. 'Let the girls go off gallivanting about town in the morning, then. As long as it will put paid to this revolting display of waterworks.'

Betsy was a bit taken aback by how swiftly Miss Beech stopped crying the moment she'd achieved her goal. And by what a radiant smile she bestowed on Great-Aunt Cornelia.

'Oh, thank you so much, Mrs Warboys,' she cooed. 'You are so kind.'

'Hmmph,' declared Great-Aunt Cornelia. Then, as the last two of the guests turned to leave, muttered something that sounded remarkably like 'cutting a wheedle', but couldn't possibly have been, because a lady of her great-aunt's standing would surely never use cant terms such as that.

Betsy wasn't sure, the next morning, whether she was looking forward to escorting Miss Beech round the shops or not. Although in theory it should be more fun to have a companion of about her own age, rather than that of a rather cantankerous older lady, she had a sneaking suspicion that the real reason why Miss Beech wanted to get her alone was so that she could pump her for information about *him*. Information she was perhaps too shy to ask for in the presence of the rather more forceful Petersham sisters.

However, she determined to be friendly and cheerful, just in case Miss Beech really was as lonely as she claimed. And, after only a short while in her company, she began to relax. Miss Beech asked her nothing whatever about *him*, keeping her remarks to enquiries about the town, or exclamations of delight over all the variety that the shops in the parade had to offer.

They were just admiring the selection of bonnets on display in a milliner's, when a shadow dimmed one corner of the window. A shadow with a man's outline.

Both girls turned at the same time, to see *him* standing just behind them.

'Good morning, ladies,' he said, doffing his hat and executing the kind of bow she'd never before seen him employ. It made him look every inch the grand man condescending to the lower orders. It made her want to curl her upper lip in scorn.

'Oh,' sighed Miss Beech, dipping into an extremely graceful curtsy, 'my lord, how good of you to acknowledge us.'

Because we are so far beneath your notice, Betsy added mentally as she dipped her own, rather more restrained curtsy.

He, she noticed with annoyance, did not immediately say something gallant, such as, *nonsense, it was his pleasure to see them*, or anything that might have put them at their ease in the presence of such a great man. On the contrary, he sort of looked down his nose at them, then nodded curtly, as though agreeing that they were so far beneath his notice that, really, he ought to have either stepped on them, or kicked them aside.

'Isn't it,' cooed Miss Beech, undaunted by his lofty air and forbidding manner, 'a lovely day? So pleasant to be able to take the air along such an interesting street, don't you find?'

He raised one eyebrow as though astonished at her pretensions, making Betsy want to kick him. Why was he being so beastly? And why couldn't Miss Beech stop fluttering her eyelashes and smiling up at him when he was being so rude?

He pulled out his watch, and looked at it pointedly.

'I am sorry,' his action goaded Betsy into saying sarcastically. 'Is there somewhere more interesting you are supposed to be right now?'

Miss Beech gasped, then shot Betsy an appalled glance.

'No,' he replied, putting the watch back into his pocket. 'I was just wondering how long it would take you to say something outrageous.'

Miss Beech giggled. 'I declare, you are a wag,' she said.

That was not the word Betsy would have used to describe him.

'Perhaps,' suggested Miss Beech, employing her eyes-down-then-up-full-of-entreaty move, the one she'd used to get the old ladies to do her bidding the day before, 'you would like to escort us through the town? It is always such a pleasure to have a man's arm to hang on to, isn't it, Miss Fairfax?'

Or to have that man's arms round her and his mouth upon hers. To feel the roughness of his clothing rub against the finer cotton of her own. To breathe him in. To feel as if nothing else in the world had any substance…

'That depends very much on the man,' said Betsy, appalled at the sudden longing for him that swept over her, even though she was cross with him. Even when she should know better.

He bowed, curtly. 'A pleasure to see you, as ever, Miss Fairfax. Good day, Miss, er...'

'Beech,' said Miss Beech.

As he made to step round them and be on his way, both girls turned to watch him go. And then, all of a sudden, Miss Beech let out a sharp cry and clutched hold of Betsy's arm so hard that the force of it sent her cannoning into the corner of the bow window.

Lord Dundas whirled round. 'What is it? What has happened?'

'Oh, oh,' sobbed Miss Beech. 'I have turned my ankle on one of these stupid flagstones.' Betsy glanced down at the pavement, which was uniformly smooth, and wondered how on earth anyone could claim to have tripped because of them. 'However,' wailed Miss Beech, leaning even more heavily against Betsy's arm, 'shall I manage to walk home?'

He frowned. 'I shall go and fetch a chair,' he said with a touch of irritation. 'I believe I saw some for hire near the market. One of them can carry you home.'

That was not, to judge by the look on Miss Beech's face, the result she'd been hoping for.

'In the meantime,' he said to Betsy, 'you had better help her inside this shop, so she can rest until I return.' And with that, he sauntered off, without a backward glance, leaving Betsy to get the injured girl into the shop and organise a chair and a stool, and a glass of water for the now-weeping Miss Beech.

At least, she was making sobbing sounds and making a great play with a handkerchief, but she didn't seem to be producing any real tears. Even so, everyone in the shop made a great fuss of her, which made Betsy feel a bit ashamed of wanting to shake her and tell her to pull herself together. Or to stop play-acting, because she was almost sure that was what Miss Beech was doing. Goodness, was she turning into a copy of Great-Aunt Cornelia, after staying with her for such a short time?

It felt like an age before the shop door opened, to reveal a man who resembled Betsy's idea of an oak tree. At least, how an oak tree would look if it grew legs and started walking about rather than staying in one place. Big, and sort of gnarled and weathered.

'Is there a Miss Fairfax here,' he said, in a voice that contained a strong country accent, 'with an injured party needing a lift home?'

'Yes, I'm Miss Fairfax,' she said.

The oak man grunted in response, strode over to the chair where Miss Beech was sitting, leaving in his wake a strong smell of onions, and without preamble hefted her into his arms and carried her from the shop. Betsy was left to offer her thanks to the shopkeeper for her kindness, while Miss Beech, uttering a series of increasingly plaintive protests, was reverently ensconced in an extremely tattered-looking sedan chair.

The human oak tree doffed his hat as she approached. 'His Lordship said as how he'd like you to walk beside the chair to the injured party's house, to make sure there was someone there to receive her.'

Oh, he did, did he? So, Miss Beech was to be carried through the town like a queen while she would have to walk beside her, or behind her, she pretty soon discovered because the walking oak tree had a companion equally as large, so that what with them, and the chair, there wasn't always room for her on the pavement. The smooth pavement, she noted resentfully.

When they reached Mrs Corcoran's house the entire household flew into such a bustle upon seeing their young guest brought home in a sedan chair. Mrs Corcoran herself was so full of remorse that Miss Beech had been hurt while under her care, that Betsy might as well have become invisible.

The sedan chair men took off at a trot the moment they'd deposited their passenger, too, which meant that they couldn't have had instructions to carry her back to town. Which wouldn't have mattered to Betsy, who was used to walking for miles, for pleasure, except that a few moments after she set off back to town, it began to rain.

It felt like a metaphor for her life. While girls like Miss Beech got cossetted, and pampered, and treated like princesses, she was the kind who ended up having to trudge through mud, alone, in the rain to reach her own home. Not even Gregory the footman to escort her.

Oh, but *he* could be ruthless in his pursuit of revenge, if this was what it was. Ordering a chair for Miss Beech, but making no provision for her whatever, even though Mrs Corcoran lived so far up the Castle Road on the way to Mount Ephraim she might as well be on the Common. She was going to be soaked to the skin by the time she reached the town centre, never mind the walk across to the far side of Mount Sion, where Great-Aunt Cornelia lived.

If only she'd had the foresight to take an umbrella. Although she hadn't foreseen doing anything more than strolling along the covered arcade of shops in the parade when she'd set out, had she? Miss Beech hadn't struck her as the kind of girl who'd want to take a walk up to the Common, which was what Betsy would have done had she had the choice about what to do on a half-day off.

She wasn't even wearing a bonnet that might have withstood a soaking. Vanity, or something like it, had made her put on her prettiest, flimsiest, most flattering confection, just in case…

Well, didn't that just serve her right? For it was already starting to lose its shape. She could feel it sort of dissolving in the rain. Pretty soon it would be flopping into her face, so she'd look like that proverbial drowned rat that people spoke of so often.

But perhaps it was only what she deserved. Because she'd harboured several very mean thoughts about Miss Beech today, totally forgetting the vow she'd made to never think, or say, anything nasty about any other female, after the episode with Lady Bramhall.

And besides, who was she to judge Miss Beech? Or the Misses Petersham? All they were doing was what every genteel young lady was brought up to do, which was, to do their utmost to try to win the wealthiest, most eligible men they came across. What right had she to criticise the lengths any of them went to, to achieve their aims? She had no idea how much pressure their family might be bringing to bear, or for what reasons. Mrs Petersham seemed to live comfortably and Mrs Corcoran's house was impressively large, but she should know how deceptive appearances could be. How successfully people could cover up dire financial straits with a veneer of affluence.

And at least none of them had forced their way into a man's house, a *married* man's house, and tried to compromise him into anything, because they all knew that *he* was single and therefore fair game.

But even though she was halfway to considering a soaking in the rain a just punishment for her many misdeeds and uncharitable thoughts, she didn't, she suddenly realised when she heard footsteps approaching from the direction of town, want anyone to see her looking like a drowned rat.

She hoped it was nobody she knew. Although she didn't know anyone in town all that well, so with any luck anyone she had met might fail to recognise her with the hat flopping into her eyes, and with sopping clothes. Hopefully they would just walk past with their own heads down as they scurried to get out of the rain.

But her luck was out. For the person hurrying up the hill she was trudging down was none other than *him*. Even half-concealed as he was, beneath the shelter of the most enormous umbrella she'd ever seen, there was no mistaking him.

So, he was on his way to the house that held the pretty, blue-eyed, blonde Miss Beech, was he? Using the pretext of enquiring after her health, no doubt. A pain shot through her middle, making her want to bow over, clutch her arms about herself, before perhaps sitting down in the nearest puddle for good measure.

Instead, she lifted her chin and looked straight past him as she approached the point where they would pass each other.

Except that he did not let her pass. Instead, he stepped into the middle of the path, blocking her way.

Why he should do so she couldn't imagine. Unless it was to mock her. Laugh at how low she'd sunk since she'd turned him down. So she decided she'd better look him straight in the eye. Whatever he had to say for himself, she was not, not, *not* going to let him know that he had any more power to hurt her.

Chapter Twenty-One

She looked magnificent, standing there, eyes flashing fire, fists clenched at her sides, with the wind flattening her damp skirts against her legs, outlining her tantalisingly feminine shape. Words like *elemental*, *natural* and *goddess* flitted through his brain as he drew nearer, when he ought instead to have been marshalling his thoughts into some kind of order.

How he wished he'd had more experience with women. That he knew how to talk to them. But since he didn't and since the part of him that wanted to just kneel at her feet in the mud, while simultaneously pulling her into his arms and kissing her breathless, was growing more and more dominant the closer he drew to her, he abandoned any notion of trying to come up with a clever speech.

Actions spoke louder than words, didn't they? And so he stepped as close as he dared and lifted the umbrella over her head.

For a moment or two they just stood there, she

glaring up at him and he gazing down at her, as though they were both struggling to find the words suitable to the occasion.

How he wished she was the sort of woman who'd just fling herself into his arms and say she was sorry, she hadn't meant it, that seeing those other girls flirting with him had made her see that she couldn't bear to think of him marrying anyone else. That she'd been miserable anyway ever since they'd parted. But she was too proud. She'd warned him the very first time they'd met that she wasn't the kind of girl who'd go into a decline over some man.

Which, actually, now he came to think of it, was a hopeful sign. He could believe that the fact she looked perfectly content with her lot, and acted as though she hadn't a care in the world, was because she had too much pride to let anyone know she was, deep down, pining for him.

Seizing that hope in both hands, he cleared his throat.

'It's no use, Miss Fairfax,' he said. 'I cannot carry on with this charade any longer.'

'Charade?' If he'd thought she was cross before, the use of that word had made her even crosser.

'Yes. I was trying to show you what it is like for me. But then it started to rain and I couldn't bear to think of you getting wet on account of that scheming baggage who pretended she wanted to be friends with you, as well as pretending to fall and hurt herself outside the hat shop. So I came to meet you, with

an umbrella,' he said, twirling it a bit, making drops
fly off in all directions.

'You...you *knew* she'd only pretended to fall?'

He nodded. She tilted her head and looked at him
with, did he dare hope, a shade less anger?

'You...you didn't send me along with her, as an
escort, to remind me that I'm only a servant now. You
weren't showing me how little I mean to you now,
or...' her breath hitched '...trying to humiliate me?'

'No! That wasn't it at all. Thank God I decided to
put an end to this, then, if that was what it was making you think. And to explain about that...that minx,
well, I couldn't let her think I would ever offer her
any encouragement to pursue me, could I? Which she
would have assumed, had I behaved in the slightest
way like a gentleman.'

'Before you came to Tunbridge Wells,' she said—
looking, did he dare hope, a bit penitent?—'I would
have said you were arrogant, to say any such thing.
But having seen how the Petersham girls behaved...
And then Mrs Corcoran, who I thought was a perfectly sensible woman, sent for her goddaughter, who
put on that performance just now...' She shuddered.

'So, you can see, then, why I didn't reveal exactly
who I am, when we met in Bramley Bythorne?' If
she did, then there was hope that she'd forgive him.
'That is why,' he said eagerly, 'I came to Tunbridge
Wells, as myself, puffing off my title all over the
place like some kind of...coxcomb. I thought perhaps, once you saw how it is, how whenever I walk
into a room their eyes light up like stalkers sighting

a deer, how they pursue me, how they will employ any means at their disposal to force some kind of intimacy, and how they won't stop, no matter how rude I am to them…'

'You have been rude to rather a lot of people in Tunbridge Wells,' she said speculatively, 'haven't you?'

'So, you do understand how hard it is for me to find a woman who wants me, for myself, rather than the title?'

She lowered her head, then looked to one side for a moment before nodding.

Thank God!

'And, look here, Miss Fairfax, you must believe I never set out to deceive you. Not deliberately. You just assumed I was a mere steward and I didn't see the need to correct that assumption. To start with it was because, *mostly* because, I'm not in the habit of explaining myself to anyone. I assumed the confusion would just get cleared up, in due course. But then… well, I…you see…' He could feel his face heating and his collar growing tight. He would sound like a complete nincompoop if he told her about that moment in the churchyard, when he'd felt what people called a *coup de foudre*. 'The longer it went on, the harder it became to confess,' he finished, rather pathetically.

'Especially,' she pointed out with a touch of bitterness, 'when I said all those uncomplimentary things about your sister.'

'Yes, now, that is another thing we need to address. I cannot deny that some of the things you said to me did make me a bit wary of you. Because, you see,' he went on swiftly when she flinched, as though he'd wounded her, 'my father has always warned me to beware of women like you.'

'Women like me?' Now she looked really annoyed.

'Yes. Pretty women with no fortune of their own, let alone a title, and, worst of all, the kind of woman who will pursue a man for his title without feeling the slightest bit of affection for him.'

Her face went white. And then, without warning, she took off down the hill, obliging him to trot after her, extending his arm if he wanted to keep the umbrella over her head and shield her from the rain, which was coming down in earnest now.

'Miss Fairfax, Miss Fairfax,' he panted. 'Just stop and think for a minute, will you? Remember that even though all those things were going on in my head, I didn't stop pursuing you. Wanting you. Because I could see that you'd just gone astray and that you'd regretted it, and that you aren't a bad girl at all, just one who gave into temptation...'

'To *pressure*,' she spat, spinning round so that he almost barged right into her. 'I wasn't *tempted* to pursue Ben for his title, I was pressured into it by my mother! You are making me sound as if I am... as bad as Miss Beech! Whereas I was trying to save my family from ruin!'

'I know, I know,' he said placatingly. 'But you felt guilty for trying to trap Lord Bramhall, didn't you?'

'Don't make excuses for me,' she said, confusingly. 'I behaved very badly. As badly as...that Miss Beech,' she said with revulsion.

'No, you didn't. She wouldn't have stopped at anything to get her way. Whereas you turned down my proposal and left the area so that I had no chance to try to make you change your mind. Because you have integrity.'

'Integrity? Me?' She looked at him with incredulity.

'Yes. You always play fair.'

'Not always,' she countered. 'At least, I try to, now, but at one time...' She shook her head.

'I know,' he said gently. 'You have learned your lesson, haven't you?'

She darted him a suspicious look. 'Is that why you have come? After all this time? To tell me that I have passed some kind of test?'

'No. Absolutely not. I came here because *you* are here. And I miss you. If I said I cannot live without you, would you believe me? Would you take pity on me and marry me? Knowing the worst? You see, my brother Jasper came to stay not long after you left and he explained to me how important it is that a woman has a choice in whom she marries. I... My parents, you see, well, my mother is like a servant to my father. He rules our household like a benevolent despot and she upholds him in everything... At least, that was not what I meant to say.

'The thing is, Miss Fairfax, Jasper made me see that men have all the power in marriage. And the only power a woman has is the power to refuse. You are perfectly right to turn down a man who is unworthy of you, whom you can't trust. And let me tell you, it was pretty painful coming to the conclusion that I'd made you think you couldn't trust me, what with all that not telling you who I am.

'And I understand, now, why it made you so angry and why you felt you couldn't trust me, but can't you see, now, why I tried to make you like me, for myself? Why I wanted to find out how people, and particularly you, would treat me if they thought I was just…nobody? I didn't set out to deliberately deceive you. And I have never mocked you,' he said, recalling that accusation she'd levelled at him from the vestry floor. 'You just drew me, from the start, and I wanted to see if I could make you like me, for myself. And that when I revealed the truth, it would seem like…'

She'd been softening up to that point, he would have sworn it. But as soon as he referred to the moment he'd revealed his identity, she went rigid again.

'A treat? Like giving a present to a child who'd passed a test?'

'Why do you keep harping on about passing a test? There was no test!' It had stopped raining. But it didn't feel as if the sun would ever come out again. 'You are not going to forgive me, are you?' he said, putting the umbrella down. 'When I thought you'd understand… After all, it isn't as if you've never done something stupid, and a bit reprehensible, and told me, and I forgave you, and even offered you my sympathy,' he finished bitterly. 'I didn't blame you when you explained what drove you. So I thought perhaps you might not blame me for behaving the way I did, once you saw what I normally have to contend with.' He waved the furled umbrella up the hill to where he assumed Miss Beech was staying.

'That,' she said haughtily, 'was a low blow.'

'But I'm fighting for my life here,' he countered. 'For my happiness, anyway. Can you not even consider marrying me, now that you know all about me and what I usually have to contend with?'

'But you lied to me,' she whimpered.

'No. I only left out a few details...'

'You told me you'd never kissed a woman before!'

'But I hadn't. I haven't. You are the only woman I've ever wanted to kiss.'

She frowned, as if she couldn't believe it. 'But... I'm nothing special...'

'Miss Fairfax, you are absolutely unique. There is no woman in the world like you. No woman I can imagine being able to find fascinating for more than a week, never mind a lifetime.'

'I don't know, I don't know,' she said, raising her hands to her cheeks and looking thoroughly torn.

Well, that was better than a flat no, wasn't it?

'Miss Fairfax,' he said, pressing his advantage, 'I am the same man you considered eloping with. It doesn't matter whether I am a steward, or a lord, you felt so strongly for me that you would have faced ruin with me. So strongly that you would have even given me up entirely rather than blight my career.'

'You...you haven't got a career to blight,' she retorted.

'That is beside the point! I am still the man you

kissed in the vestry. The man you would have yielded your virtue to, if I hadn't put a stop to things.'

'Of all the ungallant, infuriating things to say...'

'Yes. I am ungallant. And infuriating. I dare say I will infuriate you ten times a week. Ten times a day. But will you marry me anyway?'

'You think that I will keep on losing my temper with you? That we will fight all the time? And you still persist with this proposal?'

'At least our life won't be dull. At least you won't trot around behind me agreeing with everything I say. At one time, I did think that was what I ought to look for in a woman. Meekness. And then I met this firebrand of a woman, who accused me of trespassing and warned me not to let anyone know we'd met in private if I didn't want to end up getting dragged down the aisle. And I learned you are everything my father warned me to beware of in a woman and I still wanted you. You should be the last woman I ever proposed to.

'Instead, I feel as if it's all I can do to keep my hands off you. I can't resist you. I really have never felt like this about any other woman. And I know I've gone about it all wrong and I've inadvertently insulted you. In fact, every time I open my mouth I say the wrong thing. Or put what I mean in the wrong way. But please believe that the very last thing I ever wanted was to insult or mock you. And, Miss Fairfax, please, please put me out of my misery and say you will at least *think* about it. About us.'

She gave a little sob. 'I have hated seeing all those

women fluttering round you. I suppose I knew you were showing me why you'd kept your identity a secret. But can't you see how much that hurt? Thinking that you thought I was as bad as all of them?'

'You were worse,' he said rashly. 'Because I have no trouble keeping the likes of the Petersham girls at bay. But I was afraid, so afraid, that if you knew I had a title and you tried your wiles on me, I wouldn't be able to resist. *Knew* I wouldn't be able to resist. And then I'd never know if you wanted me for the title, or for me. It wasn't until the vestry and you turned me down once you knew, that I saw that you really cared for me.' He struck his chest with the flat of his hand. 'And then it was too late. I'd ruined everything. In a flash, all your regard for me turned to hatred.'

'Not hatred. Oh, never that. You know what a hot temper I have. How quickly I lose it. And how quickly I regret it.'

'Do you regret it?' His heart began thumping. 'Do you regret turning me down? And coming to Tunbridge Wells?'

'I think,' she said, tilting her head to one side as though she was thinking really hard about something, 'that I *had* to come here and find out just how much I missed you.'

'You missed me?' His heart soared.

She nodded. 'And I bitterly regretted storming off the way I did. But how could I go back? I couldn't very well write to you and say, oh, by the way, I've changed my mind. Because I hadn't, about some things. But then when you came here… Oh, I have been so confused! You seemed so different to the man I thought I knew. So cold...'

'I wanted to make you understand why I'd kept my identity a secret, that is all. So that you'd forgive me...'

'I understood. I understand, now,' she said, rather meekly, for her. 'The way you extricated yourself from Miss Beech's attempt to compromise you...' She shook her head. 'That alone was enough to show me you'd had to do similar things before.'

'Then I am grateful to her. And the Petersham girls,' he added, rather generously he felt.

'And...' she looked at him warily '...you still maintain you want to marry me, do you? Even though you've seen the worst of me?'

'I have seen the best of you, too,' he vowed. 'How selflessly you gave up the love of your life because it might blight his career.'

'I never said you were the love of my life! And your career was fictitious.'

'You *showed* me I was the love of your life,' he reproved her gently, 'by offering to elope with me in the first place when you feared your parents would oppose the match.'

'And what of your parents?' she asked, looking worried. 'Won't they object as strongly to me, as I feared my mother would to you when I thought you were just a working man? After all, you've said your father warned you against *women like me*.'

'I don't care,' he said recklessly. 'And anyway, when I tell him that you agreed to marry me when you thought I was nobody, then turned me down when you learned of my title, and even went as far as to flee to Tunbridge Wells...'

'You wouldn't tell him that,' she cried, looking appalled.

'Never mind my father and what he'll say, or what I'll say to him,' said James, a bit impatiently. 'What is more important is to hear you say you will marry me, no matter what anyone else says, or thinks.'

'Well, of course I will,' she said, looking at him as though he was an idiot.

With a whoop, he tossed aside the umbrella, took Miss Fairfax in his arms and kissed her, long and hard.

She kissed him back.

Which was all that mattered. He didn't care what kind of scene her great-aunt would create when he told her she was going to have to look for a new paid companion. He didn't care what his father would say or do when he took Miss Fairfax home and introduced her as his betrothed. He could cut him off without a penny, as he'd done to Gem, if he liked, and he'd still feel like the richest man in England.

As long as she stood with him, he could face anything that life might throw at him.

With a smile on his face.

* * * * *

If you enjoyed this story,
be sure to read the other book in
The Patterdale Siblings miniseries

A Scandal at Midnight

And while you're waiting for the next book,
why not check out her other great reads?

His Accidental Countess
From Cinderella to Countess
The Scandal of the Season
A Marquess, a Miss and a Mystery